MW01092964

RED TIDE

THE CHINESE INVASION OF SEATTLE
(SECOND EDITION)

Chris Kennedy

Theogony Books
Coinjock, NC

Copyright © 2015 by Chris Kennedy.

All rights reserved. No part of this publication may be reproduced, distributed or transmitted in any form or by any means, including photocopying, recording, or other electronic or mechanical methods, without the prior written permission of the publisher, except in the case of brief quotations embodied in critical reviews and certain other noncommercial uses permitted by copyright law. For permission requests, write to the publisher, addressed "Attention: Permissions Coordinator," at the address below.

Chris Kennedy/Chris Kennedy Publishing
1097 Waterlily Rd.
Coinjock, NC 27923
http://chriskennedypublishing.com/

Publisher's Note: This is a work of fiction. Names, characters, places, and incidents are a product of the author's imagination. Locales and public names are sometimes used for atmospheric purposes. Any resemblance to actual people, living or dead, or to businesses, companies, events, institutions, or locales is completely coincidental.

Cover art and design by Brenda Mihalko.

Ordering Information:
Quantity sales. Special discounts are available on quantity purchases by corporations, associations, and others. For details, contact the "Special Sales Department" at the address above.

Red Tide/ Chris Kennedy. – 2nd ed.
ISBN 978-1942936107

As always, this book is for my wife and children. I would like to thank my mother, without whose steadfast belief in me, I would not be where I am today. Thank you.

Author's Note

All times in *Red Tide* are given in military time, using the 24-hour clock. To find a time that occurs after noon (12:00 p.m.), simply subtract 12 from the first two digits of the number. For example, 1400 becomes 2:00 p.m. Of note, most countries use this as their standard method for keeping time, with the notable exceptions of the United States and Canada.

"Taiwan is part of the sacred territory of the People's Republic of China."

— *Constitution of the People's Republic of China*

Interlude One

"Can Chinese Automakers Penetrate the U.S. Market?"

China is by far the largest producer of automobiles in the world, and the United States has one of the world's most open and welcoming marketplaces. From the outside, this would seem to be an ideal match.

While China built almost 30 million vehicles last year, though, the truth is those vehicles have failed to make it into U.S. showrooms. Many Chinese companies have stated intentions for selling their autos in the U.S., but none of them have been able to make it work. Undaunted by these failures, they keep trying.

Guangzhou Automobile Group, China's sixth-largest automaker by sales volume, stated earlier this week its intentions to expand into the U.S. market as global growth accelerated. Industry analysts noted that this could come about within the next two years, if everything went according to plan.

- World News Online. Posted January 15 by Sam Simmons

Four Years Ago

Beijing, China

"It is the opinion of the committee that the only way forward is war."

The President of the People's Republic of China, Jiang Jiabao, looked around the room as the premier sat back down. Jiang was new to the presidency, having recently been selected when his predecessor died suddenly of a heart attack in his first term. A vibrant man who radiated an aura of confidence, Jiang had never once failed to accomplish anything with which he had been tasked. China was at a crossroads, and he had been selected for one reason.

It was time to reintegrate Taiwan.

As the president's gaze swept across the room, he could feel everyone's eyes upon him, awaiting his decision. In addition to the premier, State Council meetings normally included the four vice premiers, the five state councilors, and the 29 ministers. The chamber seemed cavernous today without the 29 ministers and all the staff who normally filled it. Due to the topic of this meeting, the ministers and staffers had all been excluded, and guards had been posted outside the doors to ensure their privacy.

Jiang was first among equals on the State Council; he held the three most important offices in China. Not only did he serve as the President of the People's Republic of China, but also as the General Secretary of the Communist Party and the Chairman of the Central Military Commission. He knew it was his decision to make, and history would either applaud or condemn him for his next words. He also knew there was only one way he could proceed.

"It will be war," he said.

He looked across the table and met the premier's eyes. "Where do we stand diplomatically?"

The premier, Rong Xiannian, stood back up. Rong and Jiang were 'fast-movers' within the party. Sons of influence, they had come up through the ranks far faster than their contemporaries who lacked such patronage. It surprised no one when Jiang had nominated Rong for the position; they were also long-time best friends. Rong was slightly shorter than Jiang, but exuded the same spirit and self-confidence from their long association.

"We have waited patiently for the other nations to return Taiwan and the rest of our lost territories to us," the premier said. "We were rewarded for our patience when the United Kingdom restored Hong Kong to us in July, 1997, but the nations have been slower to return Taiwan. The United States, in particular, has actively opposed us with laws like their Taiwan Relations Act, which instructs their military to defend Taiwan if we try to take it back by force. We have waited, hoping for a peaceful reintegration, but no further progress has been made. We have been ignored, and a separate Taiwan remains a slap in our faces. With the last election in Taiwan, it is obvious that peaceful reunification will not be considered by Taiwan. We have no choice, therefore, but to go to war to recover it."

The premier turned to his right, where his Executive Vice Premier sat. "I asked Vice Premier Li Min to brief the Council on the current status of the United States' treaties to defend Taiwan," the premier said. "Vice Premier Li?"

Vice Premier Li stood and addressed the Council. A thin, waspish man, he looked far more intellectual than either the president or premier with his horn-rimmed glasses. "The Americans have prepositioned enough forces to mount a credible defense of the island if given enough warning," the vice premier said. "The United States' Seventh Fleet has a number of units forward-deployed to bases in Japan, led by the aircraft carrier USS *George Washington*. Although the United States has never stated the reason for the carrier's forward-deployed status, it is obvious the carrier is there to either deter us from attacking Taiwan or, failing that, to aid in Taiwan's defense. It is an additional slap in the face by foreign powers thousands of miles away, forcing us to kowtow to their perceived preeminence. It is like the upstart nation has placed a guard dog just outside our property to make sure we do not leave it."

A low growl permeated the council chambers at the affront.

"Unfortunately, the United States is not alone," Vice Premier Li continued. "They have concluded treaties with both Japan and South Korea to aid in Taiwan's defense. Japan is the bigger threat of the two, having embarked on a rearmament program in 2000 that continues to this day. They obviously believe we will eventually invade Taiwan, and they are looking to bolster their forces, just as they did prior to the first Sino-Japanese war. Their planners probably expect us to launch preemptive strikes on their bases, and they are worried about keeping the shipping routes open. This makes sense; if we take Taiwan, we would be able to shut off a large portion of their trade. Taiwan's capture makes our traditional enemy much more vulnerable. South Korea, while not as capable as Japan, also has some naval forces that would be able to participate in a conflict." He stopped and sat down, although he looked like he had something more to say.

"Was there something else?" the president encouraged.

Vice Premier Li stood back up. "Yes, sir, I am not sure if it is my place to say so or not, but our analysts note that these nations, whether together or on their own, would not be able to stop us without the participation of the United States." Vice Premier Li sat down.

The president nodded and looked back to the premier. "Do you have a status report on the United States?" Having previously coordinated with the premier, he knew the premier had additional information.

The premier looked down at his notes. "Yes," he said. "I have asked Vice Premier Sun Juan to discuss the current state of affairs in the United States."

Sun Juan, the only female vice premier, stood up. She was small of stature, but highly intelligent. The president knew she normally saw her position as a balance on the excessive testosterone of the war council; today, however, he saw that she was in full agreement. "It is a very favorable time to proceed!" she exclaimed. "The Americans' economy is in shambles, and it is their own fault! Not only have they not passed a budget in two years, they implemented a mandatory budget cutting process two years ago that is crippling their military. With mandatory cuts in effect, they have postponed deployments, canceled required equipment repairs and reduced training and operations. They have even wrapped their airplanes in plastic so they do not have to maintain them. How can they expect their pilots to remain proficient if they do not fly? Their readiness is the lowest it has been since the drawdown after the end of World War II. Now is the time to proceed, while their focus is on internal matters."

The president nodded his head. "Good," he said. "If they want to do our work for us, we shall let them." He looked back to the premier. "Do we have the right people in place?"

"Nearly so," the premier answered. "Vice Premier Zhu?"

Vice Premier Zhu Jie stood. Tall and heavy, the Vice Premier was the direct opposite of Sun Juan, large where she was small, loud and outgoing where she was quiet and reserved. President Jiang knew that Zhu had come up in the intelligence community; he was familiar with the PRC's efforts to place people into key areas of American society where they would be needed for an attack.

"We have the majority of the people needed for Operation Lightning in place now," Vice Premier Zhu stated, "with the last few positions soon to be filled. As far as hardware goes, the equipment required to carry out an attack is either already in place or expected to be there soon. We should be ready in no more than 2-3 years."

Premier Rong stood back up as Vice Premier Zhu sat back down. The president had placed him in charge of the planning for Operation Lightning, so it was his duty to give the final summation. "We recently became aware of a 2008 report by the RAND Corporation of the United States," he said, "which analyzed a theoretical attack by us on Taiwan in 2020. The report said the U.S. wouldn't be able to defend Taiwan because the new cruise missiles we are developing will enable us to destroy the United States' aircraft carriers and bases. The report found the United States' claims of being able to achieve air superiority were questionable and largely unproven."

He paused. "Since then, everything has continued in our favor. Our forces have continued to grow stronger, while theirs have grown weaker. With our new plans in place, we are more ready than we have ever been."

The president agreed. "It is time," he said. "Let the Lightning strike!"

Interlude Two

"From Concept to Production"

Chinese auto maker Guangzhou Automobile Group Co. (GAC), Ltd., announced today that it would be building its first American automobile assembly plant in Seattle, Washington, later this year. GAC will be the first of at least three Chinese firms to begin manufacturing cars in the United States in the near future. GAC will be building on the relationship with Chrysler that it developed building Jeeps in China, which it calls crucial in moving forward.

GAC made a name for itself three years ago when it showcased three vehicles at the Detroit Auto Show. The most exciting vehicle was its E-Jet, a derivative of which it intends to build at the new plant in Seattle. Not only is it stylish, it's also a range-extended electric vehicle along the lines of the Chevy Volt (although its appearance will probably be more appealing to the general public). The car has evolved somewhat from its initial exhibition, claiming a pure-electric range of about 100 miles, or roughly 160 kilometers. It has a top speed of about 100 miles per hour and uses a 1.0-liter gasoline engine as its range extender.

Although public opinion has been very favorable on the plan to build the facility here, there has been some dissent, as GAC purchased the Interbay Golf Course and will be building its facility on it. GAC justified the purchase because of the site's proximity to Seattle's north-ern port facilities and its access to the railroad lines there. In an ef-fort to improve its public relations, GAC purchased memberships at the Broadmoor Golf Club for all of the current Interbay members, which has gone a long way toward smoothing things over with them.

- *World News Online*. Posted February 27 by Sam Simmons

Two Years Ago

VFA-34 Ready Room, Naval Air Station Oceana, Virginia Beach, VA

Lieutenant Shawn 'Calvin' Hobbs stood outside his squadron's ready room, his head pounding, as he waited for Captain's Mast. Captain's Mast, a form of non-judicial punishment, was a proceeding where the commanding officer (CO) of a military unit could dispense justice to those under his or her command for a variety of relatively minor offenses from unauthorized absence to the illegal use of drugs. At a Mast, the CO listened to the facts of the case, gave the accused a hearing as to those offenses and then disposed of the charges by either dismissing them, imposing punishment under the provisions of military law or by referring the case to a court martial.

"What are you here for, Torch?" he asked Lieutenant Junior Grade Steve Berkman, who was standing nearby. He spoke softly so his voice didn't carry down the hall to where the accused sailors were waiting.

"You know I hate it when you call me that, right?" Torch asked, violating one of the cardinal rules of call signs. Aviators were usually given call signs based on either a play on their name (from which 'Calvin' got his) or by doing something stupid. Berkman's was earned the second way; he had landed his aircraft when it was too heavy, jumped on the brakes too hard and had caught them on fire, burning up the wheel assemblies and earning the call sign, 'Torch.' There were three rules regarding call signs: (1) if you don't have a call sign, it is the duty of your 'friends' to give you one; (2) you probably won't like it; and (3) if you complain about it too much, it will either become permanent or you'll get a new one you'll like even less. By continuing to gripe about 'Torch,' he only ensured it would continue to stick to him like glue.

"Of course I know that," Calvin said. "That's why I do it. It makes me smile." Calvin smiled to show he meant it. Calvin was six feet tall, blond and had a smile the ladies loved, although he knew he needed to spend more time at the gym than at the bars. He was starting to put on a few extra pounds and was worried that, if he didn't start exercising more, and soon, he would be over the maximum weight allowed for his height on the next physical fitness test.

"In any event," Torch said, answering the original question, "I'm here because Airman Jones was late for duty again last week." Torch was the Line Division Officer, responsible for the enlisted men and women who kept the planes serviced and ready to fly; Airman Jones was one of his assistant plane captains.

"Yeah, hard for plane captains to stay focused when there aren't any planes to work on," Calvin remarked. "I'm here because Airman Sanders was late for duty and showed up still under the influence. This is his second Captain's Mast and my *third* Captain's Mast in the last two weeks, which I'm sure the XO is going to let me know is *not* a great testimonial to my leadership." The squadron's second-in-command, or executive officer, was generally responsible for training and disciplining the officers. In the "good cop/bad cop" tandem of CO/XO, the XO was the bad cop. As the Ordnance Division Officer, Calvin had a similar responsibility for the members of his division, of which Airman Sanders was a part.

"I know," Torch said. "This is my second Mast this month, and the XO has already given me shit about it. I wish we'd get some money for fuel so we could fly again. If the squadron only had something else to do besides sit around and go to the bars, our guys might not get into so much trouble."

"Yeah, maybe we wouldn't, either," Calvin said. "It's hard to work on keeping your troops' morale up when your own is so completely in the toilet."

"What do you think he's going to get?" Torch asked, looking down the hallway at the accused.

"Well," said Calvin, "this is Airman Sanders' second Mast in 4 months, so I doubt the Skipper is going to be very lenient with him. Based on the outcomes of the last couple of Masts I've heard about, it looks like the Skipper is getting tired of all the problems the squadron's had and is starting to set some examples. I don't think this is going to go well for him."

The two officers stood thinking for a couple of moments, and then Calvin said, "At least we're not underway on the carrier; if we were, the CO could confine him for up to three days on bread and water." He paused and gave Torch a wry smile. "I know I need to lose a couple of pounds, but that wouldn't be the way I'd want to do it."

The Master-at-Arms called everyone into the ready room for Captain's Mast. As they began to take their places, the Executive Officer pulled Calvin aside. "Perhaps you need to be a little more involved with your people," he said. "Airman Sanders could use a bit more leadership, it appears."

"Yes, sir," Calvin said. "I'll make sure I provide it." As the XO left to take his place, Calvin continued under his breath to Torch,

"And why don't you do the same for us officers, XO? Our morale sucks, too."

The University of Washington, Seattle, WA

"The next four years are going to be the best years of our lives!" Sara Sommers said as she walked toward McMahon Hall.

"I've been waiting for this my whole life!" her roommate Erika Murphy agreed. Best friends from high school, they would be rooming together on the second floor of the 11-story dorm for the next year. "What are you looking forward to most?"

A freshman just starting her first year at the University of Washington, Sara was attractive with long dark hair. "I'm looking forward to the challenges of college courses, the freedom of being on my own and the boys." She paused. "Well, maybe not exactly in that order," she said with a giggle.

Erika, for her part, while also pretty, was a little shorter and as blond and light-skinned as Sara was dark-haired and tanned. "Definitely the boys," Erika opined.

Sara agreed. They had grown up 30 miles east of Seattle in the tiny town of North Bend, Washington. Located along I-90, North Bend and the towns near it served as bedroom communities for Seattle. Although the girls' school district was one of the largest geographic districts in the state at 400 square miles, it only had 6,000 students, largely because the area did not have a local industrial or economic base. The opportunities to meet suitable members of the opposite sex had been somewhat limited, as their graduating class from Mount Si High School in Snoqualmie had only totaled 303.

"I'm also looking forward to joining the Adventure and Wilderness Outdoor Leisure Club," Sara said. "I just found out that even though they haven't had one for ten years, some of the upperclassmen are going to restart it this year!" Civilization only extended for four or five miles on either side of I-90 in the Cascade Mountains where she had been raised, and Sara had grown up an avid hiker.

"Yeah, I heard that, too," Erika said. "I'll join it with you." Sara knew Erika liked to go hiking, although not as much as she did. As a young girl, Sara's dad had spent many weekends with her in the wilderness near North Bend. They had started out camping and hiking at the Middle Fork Campground 10 miles northeast of North Bend along the Middle Fork Snoqualmie River, but then had gone further afield as her skills and stamina improved. Erika had gone with her on many of these trips, as they shared the same love of the forest and nature. Erika also liked the boys, though, which was becoming a bigger part of her life and absorbing more of her time. Sara wasn't *quite* ready for that yet.

"Have you figured out where all of your classes are?" Sara asked.

"Yes," Erika answered; "I think I can find all of them now."

Although Erika was sometimes directionally challenged, Sara didn't have any problems finding her way around campus. She guessed that was due to all of the time she had spent navigating in the woods. "It's all about finding landmarks you can remember," Sara told her friend.

"I can't wait to get up to the room and relax," Erika said. "It's been a long day."

"It's going to get a little longer," Sara replied, opening the door to the dorm. "The elevators are out again." They had been out a lot during the first week of orientation.

Both girls sighed.

Snoqualmie National Forest, Washington State

"The hell with them," Ryan O'Leary grunted as he swung the axe, thinking about his dismissal from the United States Navy. A veteran with over 26 years of naval service, he was a victim of the latest round of Navy downsizing to meet its ever-shrinking budget. At six feet, two inches and 220 pounds, the former Senior Chief Petty Officer was a big man; however, with a body fat of only 8%, he was obviously someone that was used to physical exertion. He should be; O'Leary was a SEAL. Well, he used to be, until the Navy had told him six months earlier they no longer needed his services. "Damn it," he finished.

"I'm not sure I'm any better off," replied First Sergeant Aaron Smith, who had come up to the cabin Ryan was building to give him a hand putting on its roof. "I keep wondering why I didn't retire, rather than take this set of orders. I had enough years in the Army that I could have easily retired and taken half-pay for the rest of my life. Maybe I could find a little job on the side for some spending money, and then I could come up here and live the sweet life with you."

"What's so bad about your job?" asked Ryan, happy to have something to take his mind off his own problems. He had known Aaron Smith off and on for almost 20 years, ever since they collaborated on a mission in Kosovo to capture a Serbian war criminal behind enemy lines. Although they respected each other's skills, a friendly rivalry over whose unit was better existed between the two men. The same height as the SEAL, although a little slimmer, Aaron had just taken over as the senior non-commissioned officer for the Rifle Company, 2nd Battalion of the 75th Ranger Regiment.

"I checked into the command yesterday," First Sergeant Smith said, "and it is the most fucked up unit I've ever had the misfortune of being associated with. My commanding officer, an Army captain, has to be one of the most worthless officers I have ever met. Usually the Rangers are pretty good at weeding out idiot officers at Ranger School, but somehow this moron made it through. He must either know someone or be related to someone important," Smith guessed.

"So what?" Ryan asked. "You've trained a lot of officers over your many years in the Army. What's different about this one?"

"Well, it's not just that the CO sucks; the first sergeant I'm replacing was also terrible, so the company is all fucked up. In just one day with the company I can already tell they can't march, they can barely stand in formation and there's no *way* I'd trust them to even *hold* a rifle, much less point it at something and fire it," Aaron grumbled. "Now I understand what the 'Powers That Be' meant when they gave me my orders and told me I needed to clean up the unit. If I had known the company was this bad, I'd have retired rather than come here."

"So why don't you just quit?" Ryan asked. "You can come join me here in the forest."

"Well, first of all," Aaron replied, "I'm pretty sure it's illegal to build a house in a national forest. I really doubt you own this land or have permission to build on it. When last I looked, this was part of the Snoqualmie National Forest."

"That might be true," Ryan answered, looking at the one-room cabin he was building, "if I gave a shit. I've got an apartment in Seattle in case I need it, but I've always loved nature and needed a place to get away from it all and unwind before joining the rat race. I'm self-sufficient here. Besides, no one is ever going to find the cabin. It's unreachable except by hiking to it. I looked at the satellite imagery, and it's in the shadows of the mountain. I'm also going to camouflage it once I'm done which will make it pretty damn hard to find."

Aaron didn't doubt it; when they had driven in, Ryan had driven his jeep off state road NF-5640 and up a dry stream bed until it was out of sight of the road and then had hidden it in the shrubbery. Aaron knew he never would have seen it. And even if anyone *had* found the jeep, it was still extremely unlikely they'd find the cabin, as it was a several mile hike over some fairly steep terrain. Although Mt. Garfield had been climbed many times, it required someone with excellent skills to do so, limiting the traffic through the area.

"Also," Aaron continued, "it's not in my nature to pawn off my problems on someone else. Now that I've taken over as the company's first sergeant, the unit is my problem." He paused, watching Ryan swing the axe for a couple of strokes while he gathered his thoughts. "In the German Army," he continued, "a first sergeant is often referred to as the 'Mother of the Company,' because he is the peace-maker, the disciplinarian, the provider, the counselor, the trainer, the confidant…basically, everything that's important to the success of the unit. He is the leader that interacts with the troops every day, and the one who sets the standards they all live up to. Previously, those standards were set pretty damn low. It's my job to bring them back to where they should be."

"Fuck 'em," Ryan said. "That's what they did to me." He put another log on the chopping block and continued making firewood.

The winter was long and cold in the mountains of Washington, and he knew he needed a *lot* of firewood.

"Funny you should say that," Aaron said, "but that's just what I plan to do. I looked at the weather report, and it is supposed to be raining tomorrow morning. I thought a 0500 early morning run would be just the thing to let them know there's a new sheriff in town."

Ryan chuckled. That was just what he would have done. "I like it," he said. "Are you going to invite your company officers?"

The first sergeant sighed. "Yeah, I'm going to invite them, but I doubt the CO will come. Apparently, he barely talks to any of the enlisted soldiers in the unit and only when he has to."

Ryan grunted. "Stupid officers."

Aaron shrugged and gave Ryan a half grin, "I know you don't have much use for them, but officers are good for doing all of the unit's paperwork while we're getting the real work done." He shrugged again. "The one bright spot is that, even though the CO is an ass, the executive officer seems pretty cool, although he can't overrule the CO. The XO is young, but appears trainable; I just hope the CO doesn't ruin him or try to make the XO into a carbon copy of himself."

"Well, if it's going to rain tomorrow morning, we better get the rest of the roof on," Ryan said, looking at the sky. "I can do more firewood later."

Interlude Three

"Chinese Auto Invasion"

Today, Chinese auto maker Guangzhou Automobile Group Co. (GAC), Ltd., rolled out the first E-Jet automobile built at its American assembly plant in Seattle, Washington. GAC is the first Chinese auto maker to complete a car in an American plant. In addition to the E-Jet, GAC is also expected to begin producing a full-size van called the "J-Van" at its Seattle plant. This vehicle will have a new, modular seating system that will allow its owners to easily reconfigure the cargo compartment as needed. Two other Chinese firms, SAIC Group and Zhejiang Geely Automobile will also be rolling out their first vehicles later this year. In an effort to reduce costs, all three firms have built their American assembly facilities in the Seattle/Tacoma area so they can combine their parts shipments from China. Zhejiang Geely Automobile also has its plant in Seattle, while the SAIC Group facility is in nearby Tacoma, Washington.

It is unknown whether the American public will embrace the E-Jet. Although it is stylish, its safety ratings are suspect. The range-extended electric vehicle claims to have a pure-electric range of about 62 miles, or roughly 100 kilometers, and a top speed of about 100 miles per hour. Although this is comparable to its competitors, the Insurance Institute for Highway Safety, a nonprofit scientific and educational organization dedicated to reducing automobile losses, was unimpressed with its safety features, as the E-Jet received grades ranging from "Acceptable" to "Poor." In comparison, the Chevy Volt, its closest domestic competitor, received ratings of "Good" in all categories. Despite this disparity in ratings, GAC has decided to press on with its production, in a move that harkens back to the "Field of Dreams" movie line, "If you build it, they will come." The other two Chinese manufacturers have similar issues with safety concerns, but have also decided to remain in business for at least another two years, to see if the problems can be resolved.

This decision is in spite of some less-than-positive public relations news from all three plants that has come to light recently. When they were initially built, residents thought the plants would create a number of well-paying jobs for their local economies. In most cases, though, that hasn't happened, as the management of the plants has hired mostly Chinese immigrants to man their facilities. Citing language difficulties, as the managers of all three facilities do not speak English, very few non-Chinese language speakers have been hired, and nearly all of the second and third shift workers are of Chinese descent.

- *World News Online*. Posted March 18 by Sam Simmons

One Year Ago

Beijing, China

"The Americans are idiots!" the President of the People's Republic of China, Jiang Jiabao, said with a laugh. "They are so hungry for peace that they will believe anything if you just say the word 'peace' to them. I told their ambassador we were going to have several ships make an 'Around the World' tour to promote 'peace, openness and better diplomatic relations.'" Jiabao laughed again, his laugh loud in the large, empty room. "He became so excited that he offered several of their west coast ports, including Seattle, for our fleet to make port calls. They have agreed to all of our proposals, even this 'softball challenge.'"

Looking to Vice Premier Li Min, he said, "Please tell everyone where we stand with our preparations for the Dragon's Bite portion of Operation Lightning."

"We have received all of the diplomatic clearances we need for the operations in the United States," the Vice Premier replied in a firm voice. "I supervised them myself as they are crucial to Operation Lightning and will ultimately determine its success or failure. We have received port clearances for both Vancouver and Seattle, although we are still waiting on final authorization for the other ports. Those, however, are all misdirection. If we do not get them, we will change the story to accommodate the ports we get. We have also received permission for your state visit to Washington, D.C. It was not as hard as when President Hu Jintao made his visit in 2011; as expected, that visit helped open the door for this one. Diplomatically, everything is progressing on schedule."

"The Dragon's Bite naval forces are ready, with all of the ships fully armed," the Commander-in-Chief of the People's Liberation Army Navy (PLAN), the naval branch of the People's Liberation Army (PLA), noted. One of two newcomers to the meeting, he was the one with the least seniority. "The aircraft are tested and ready," he continued, "and we are continuing to train all of the personnel involved. We have gradually increased our operational tempo across the country so the Americans will not think our preparations are out of the ordinary."

Sun Juan stood up next. The president had tasked her with coordinating the automobile plant deception operations and knew she had made several trips to the United States to check on operations there. "We have two ocean-going car carriers ready for deploying our vehicles and two additional freighters for personnel. Over the last year we have successfully staged the additional equipment required at the factories in the United States. Additional assault personnel will begin deployment two months prior to Dragon's Bite so they are all in place on time."

Vice Premier Zhu Jie stood next. Well versed in intelligence and special operations, he had been directed to oversee the outlying operations of the Dragon's Bite campaign. "Our paratroops have stepped up their training and will be ready for the drops they need to make. We currently have ten Y-20 Kunpeng transport aircraft available. As we will only need six for the operation, we will have plenty of spares."

"What can you tell me about Seattle?" the president asked, looking back to Vice Premier Li Min. "What will our troops experience when they get there?"

"The city of Seattle has over 600,000 inhabitants," Vice Premier Li said, "and there are over 4 million people in the metropolitan area. It is the Americans' largest city in their northwest region and their major gateway for trade with Asia. The city of Seattle is located on an isthmus between the saltwater Puget Sound to the west and Lake Washington to the east. The city rests on a number of hills and there are fairly tall mountain chains to the east and west of the city. During the time we will be there, the climate is generally temperate, with temperatures between 56 and 76 degrees Fahrenheit, and there is about one inch of rain per month. Our troops will not need any special cold weather or rain gear."

"It sounds like the Dragon's Bite preparations are well in hand," the president noted. "Where do we stand with the preparations for the main invasion?"

"The main invasion preparations are continuing and are on schedule," briefed the Chief of the General Staff of the People's Liberation Army. The other newcomer to the executive war council, he looked more nervous than the head of the PLAN. Of course, thought the president, the man was responsible for all of the combat operations, so he was under a good deal more stress to ensure everything was properly prepared. "We have over 200 Yubei assault craft available, in addition to the naval forces detailed to support them. The Yubei landing craft carry six combat vehicles or 150 troops, so having 200 operational, in addition to all our amphibious assault ships, will give us the ability to move all the equipment and personnel required, even if some experience mechanical difficulties. We will be ready when it is time."

"Everything is proceeding in accordance with our plans," the president said, looking around the room. "We will continue with our original schedule. Keep me informed if anything changes. That concludes our meeting today."

As the leaders started to file out of the room, the president motioned to Vice Premier Han Yong to stay behind. Once everyone else had left, the president asked, "And how is your portion of the plan proceeding?"

Han smiled. Of all the council, he was the most nondescript, which had served him well in all of the espionage he had conducted over the years. An excellent spymaster, he was the perfect person to handle the things that the president didn't want known by the rest of the council. "It is done. Everything needed is prepared and in place."

"Good," said the president, "That is very good."

VFA-34 Ready Room, Virginia Beach, VA

"We've got gas money, Torch!" LT 'Calvin' Hobbs said to Lieutenant Junior Grade Steve Berkman, walking into the Maintenance Officers' office. Five of the junior officers from the Maintenance Department shared a room just marginally bigger than the five desks shoehorned into it. Department Heads received their own offices, but that was at least one promotion away for the lieutenants, and two more for the junior grade lieutenants. At the moment, the only desk occupied was Torch's; with nothing better to do, the rest of the officers were taking an extended lunch.

"Do you *always* have to call me that?" asked Berkman. At six-foot-one, he was an inch taller than Calvin and tried to use it, usually good naturedly, to intimidate Calvin.

"Pretty much," said Calvin, pushing him away. "Even you should be happy today, you big grouch. We finally got the word that we are going to deploy at the end of next year. We're getting gas money shortly to start flying so we will be ready to go!"

"When?" asked Torch. "Let me guess, we're going to deploy right before Christmas and miss spending it with our families, right?"

"Boy, you sure are a grouch," said Calvin. "Maybe we should have named you 'Oscar.'" He paused and considered, "It's not too late to change it, I guess."

"No! I like that even less!" said Torch.

"Some people never learn," said LT John 'Constant' Gardner, shaking his head as he walked up. "Hey, did I hear you say we had money to fly again?"

"Yes," said Calvin. "Our boat is going to deploy at the end of next year, so we're going to start working up for it soon. We'll continue working in the simulators while the maintenance folks get the jets ready to fly again; we'll probably start flying next month. We will most likely go out on the boat early next summer and then out to the air base at Fallon, Nevada, in late July or August." Although the USS *Ronald Reagan* was considered a "ship" by most people, to the aviators, it would always be known as, "the boat."

"Cool," said Constant. "I can't wait. I love Fallon!"

"What's so good about it?" asked Torch.

"Lots of things," said Calvin. "First, the flying is great. We get to fly a bunch at Fallon, including flights where we get to drop live bombs. We also get to do a bunch of dog fighting against the rest of the air wing, as well as the aggressor squadron there that simulates enemy aircraft. All of the squadrons in our air wing will be there, and we'll get to fly together as an air wing and practice the kind of strikes and missions we'll do on deployment." Constant was nodding his head. He'd been to Fallon once before and loved the flying there.

"In addition to the flying," Calvin continued, "the air base at Fallon is only about an hour from Reno, Nevada, and just over two hours from Lake Tahoe. If we're not flying on the weekends, we can go to the casinos and have a blast! Did you know that drinks are free in the casino?" He paused, thinking. "And, if memory serves, Caesar's Palace still owes me $200 from the last time I played Black Jack there."

"You're just unlucky," said Constant. "I think I won $100."

"I don't want to gamble," griped Torch. "I'd probably just lose my money."

Calvin looked at Constant, shaking his head. "He's definitely 'Oscar,'" Calvin said. Some people never learn.

Guangzhou Interbay Assembly Plant, Seattle, WA

"I can't wait to be done here," Colonel Zhang Wei said. "I am not sure if the Americans don't know Zhang is my family name, or if they're just too lazy to care." Colonel Zhang hated many things about being in America. He hated wearing glasses. He hated being called "Mister," instead of "Colonel," a title which he had spent 20 years earning. More than anything, though, he hated lazy people, regardless of their nationality, and there were plenty of them in the United States.

"I think they're just too lazy," Lieutenant Colonel Peng Yong, his executive officer, confirmed. The colonel had asked Peng and the rest of his regimental officers to meet him for a late night briefing in the meeting room of Guangzhou's Interbay Assembly Plant. They wouldn't look out of place there; all of his staff masqueraded during the day as assistant managers for the facility.

"Which is exactly as I thought," Colonel Zhang replied. As a special forces colonel, he was in excellent shape, another fact lost on the Americans. At five foot nine inches, he probably weighed half of what American automobile plant managers did. If any of them had ever noticed, none had ever commented in the two years he had been assigned as the manager of the Guangzhou Interbay Assembly Plant. Two *long* years.

Zhang had been picked to command the ground forces in the coming war, and he was also responsible for all the Chinese operations in the United States beforehand. "Where do we stand with getting the rest of our troops into the country?" he asked his XO.

"Our people will be entering the country on both business and tourist visas," Lieutenant Colonel Peng replied, displaying a slide on the meeting room's screen. "We will be getting 2,000 soldiers, or almost half of our regiment, into the country on business visas. I tasked our regimental officers to come up with innovative methods for using these visas, and they have been quite creative."

"One company of troops will be entering the country for 'consultations' at each of the three auto plants," he said as he brought up the first slide. He switched slides and continued, "In addition, over 600 troops will enter the country for the 'Import Automotive Manager's Association' convention that several of the officers from this plant will be hosting. Captain Liu Fang is spearheading this project.

Surprisingly, there has been a tremendous amount of interest in this convention among many of the American auto makers, and the officers involved in hosting this convention are actually going to put on the first couple of days of a real convention. I endorsed this project not only as a method of bringing a large number of troops into the country, but also as a project for helping develop their planning skills."

"I approve," Colonel Zhang said, nodding. "That will not only provide a cover for the troops, but also continue to develop them as military officers as well. Very good."

"Thank you sir," Lieutenant Colonel Peng said. "The conference has expanded to the point where they have had to enlist the services of quite a few of the staff here." He brought up the next slide. "Another company will enter the country to negotiate contracts for additional facilities for the three plants currently in operation, and a third company will enter to negotiate new facilities for three new firms that are interested in coming to the United States." He switched slides and topics.

"The other half of the regiment will be entering on tourist visas." He looked up and smiled. "Timing is everything, and the officers found several ways to use them to our advantage. For example, Captain Chou Min noticed the SAIC plant in Tacoma was due to roll out its first car in July. He thought it would be easy for the plant to have a small setback that postponed the rollout until August. If that happened, then it would be very appropriate for the Chinese plants in the area to have a big celebration for the rollout, especially with the fleet coming to town. This would be an excellent opportunity to bring additional company employees, well-wishers, and a variety of other staff members into the country for the festivities. Personally, I think this is a brilliant idea. Not only does it create a number of reasons to bring people into the country, it also provides a way to disguise a number of our activities that week."

Lieutenant Colonel Peng looked up to find Colonel Zhang nodding. "He is to be commended," Zhang said. "Has the facility had its unfortunate accident yet?"

"Yes, it has," Lieutenant Colonel Peng confirmed. "The SAIC facility experienced a mishap two days later on one of its assembly lines. Not only did that push back their first rollout so that it now occurs in August, it also gave us a justification for bringing the destroyer *Changsha* to Tacoma. We have developed a cover story for the assembly line piece that is needed, where it will have to be transported by ship, due to its sensitivity to pressure changes. As the destroyer is the fastest ship available to bring the part, we will request that it be given clearance to dock in Tacoma, so that we can bring it to the facility by helicopter." Peng grinned. "The piece is proprietary, of course, so we can't tell them what it is; we'll be happy to share the information with customs when it arrives."

The two men shared a knowing grin.

Peng continued, "With the schedule worked out, it was easy to arrange for a couple of companies of troops on tourist visas to come in for various vacations, tours and visits with their 'relatives' that work at the three plants in the area. Two additional companies will also be coming in as the "Guangzhou People's Symphony Orchestra," which will be performing at both the IAMA Convention and at the rollout ceremony."

"I grew up in Guangzhou," Zhang interjected, "and I wasn't aware such a symphony existed."

"It didn't," Peng agreed. "This idea required a bit more coordination, as our officers had to find people in the regiment who could play the instruments required. It also required a couple of transfers from two of the other special operations groups to fill out the strings section, but the officers were able to put it together. The orchestra is currently practicing back home, in addition to their regular training, and has scheduled several performances in China to establish themselves as a legitimate band." Peng chuckled. "I heard their first performance sounded somewhere between a train wreck and ten long-tailed cats in a room full of rocking chairs, but they are apparently starting to come together. I hope so, because I will have to be present for at least one of their performances when they arrive in the United States."

"That was very creative," Zhang commented. "I knew we were the first People's Republic special forces unit to be capable of sea, air and land operations, like the U.S. Navy's SEALs, but I did not realize we were musically capable, as well." He paused. "Is that it? Unless my math is wrong, we are still at least 1,000 troops short."

"No," Peng said. "There is one more item, and I think you might like this one the best. The final idea involved a little extra coordination, but provided an avenue to get the remainder of the regiment to the United States. Several years ago, the first luxury cruise liner of the People's Republic, the *M.S. Henna*, made her maiden voyage. The *Henna's* first season of cruising was very successful and was enjoyed by many, including Captain Guo Jing, who took her husband on one of its outings. When she approached me with the idea of using the *Henna* as a troop transport, I found the idea intriguing, as it opened up many possibilities. You will remember last year when I asked if I could coordinate a special project with the chain of command while I was back in China?" Zhang nodded. "This was it." The General Staff agreed and further forwarded the idea to the premier, who 'suggested' to the management of Star Cruise Lines that they implement a new cruise route from Guangzhou to Vancouver and Seattle, and then back to Guangzhou. Not surprisingly, Star Cruise Lines implemented the route this year, and will be using it next year, so the ship will be available for our use. With accommodations for 1,900 'tourists,' the rest of our transportation needs are not only taken care of, but taken care of in style." Peng grinned. "That gets everyone in the regiment into the country."

Zhang nodded. "Just so they do not get too soft riding across the ocean on a luxury liner," he warned.

"There are no worries about that. Sergeant Major Tso will be one of the ones riding the ship. He will ensure the troops are gainfully employed and spend their time in the exercise room and on other appropriate endeavors." There was a general chuckle from all assembled. Sergeant Major Tso was a harsh taskmaster who accepted only perfection. If he was on the *Henna*, there would be *no* slacking off.

"Those all sound like excellent ideas; continue with their implementation," Zhang ordered. "We have been given the "go" for the operation, with a target date of next year of August 19. I thought our biggest challenge would be getting our troops into the country, but it seems like things are proceeding as planned. There are many moving pieces to continue to track, but for now, we are a 'go.'"

Joint Base Lewis-McChord, Tacoma, WA,

"How's it going with your troops?" Ryan O'Leary asked. He had stopped by the base while he was in town to pay off the beer he owed his friend for his latest help at the cabin.

"It's going better," First Sergeant Aaron Smith answered. "I still wonder periodically why I didn't retire rather than take these orders, but I'm only wondering it every week or two now, not every day. The company is starting to shape up, and I've worked with the people that write our orders to get some new blood into the unit. I've played the "you owe me" card often enough that it's starting to wear pretty thin, but I've got a good number of noncommissioned officers in place who are starting to take some of the burden off my shoulders."

Aaron laughed. "I don't think I ever told you about the first 0500 company run we did. The run was everything I'd expected; we had our first person drop out within 100 yards of where we started, puking his guts up."

"Rangers are wussies," Ryan interjected. He laughed. "I've always known *that*!"

Aaron continued as if Ryan hadn't spoken. "It was a punishing run, but the way I saw it, I'm the oldest; if they couldn't keep up, it was their fault, not mine. In the end, less than half of the company finished the run—"

"Wussies," Ryan interrupted again.

"—although most stayed with it until the end, choosing to walk across the finish line rather than ride back on the bus I had follow us for any medical emergencies. I've kept my eye on the ones that quit and most of them are no longer with company. I've helped them along to positions where their presence wouldn't have such a negative effect on national defense."

Ryan laughed. "Rangers are our 'National Defense' now? Well, if that doesn't just scare the absolute shit out of me, nothing will. Frankly, now I'm *glad* I'm living in the woods. It'll take the bad guys longer to find me here."

"Yeah, you laugh," Aaron said, "but my company *is* in the business of national defense. At any given time, one of the Ranger battalions is designated as the Ranger Ready Force, a designation that lasts 13 weeks. During that time, we are *supposed* to be capable of deploying within 18 hours to anywhere in the world, to do any mission the nation requires. When I arrived at the unit, the company could probably have deployed within a week or so, to do about one third of the missions we're supposed to be able to do. Now, after a year of intense training, I think we might be able to deploy within two days and accomplish about 80% of the missions. Even though we're headed in the right direction, we're still not good enough. Maybe we aren't 'national defense' yet, but at least we aren't quite as dangerous to ourselves anymore."

"What was so fucked up?" Ryan asked, taking a sip of his beer. It was bad form to bring over beer and not stop to have one, after all.

"The worst part was our weapons training," Aaron answered, looking sheepish.

Ryan laughed, explosively spraying beer all over the room. When he was able to talk again, he said, "Well, at least it wasn't anything important!"

"No kidding," his friend replied. "That's been fixed; I doubt there is currently a Ranger in the company who can't completely disassemble and reassemble his weapon with his eyes shut. More importantly, their marksmanship, which was laughable when I first got to the unit, is now among the best in the battalion. As I continue to stress to them, marksmanship is something that *will* save your life, as well as the life of the Ranger next to you."

"Amen," Ryan agreed. "I like to reach out and touch the enemy before I'm in range of their weapons. It's a lot more survivable that way."

Aaron nodded. "Amen, my brother! My sniper teams, especially, are now consistently among the best in the battalion, led by my .50 caliber sniper team. You should see the shooter on that team," he said; "he's so big the .50 caliber rifle looks like a toy in his hands. He's pretty much acknowledged to be the battalion's best sniper. He's also been pretty good at teaching the other teams. Although they don't quite have his touch yet, they're getting to be pretty damn good in their own right."

"You know," Aaron continued, taking a pull from his beer, "for that matter, the weapons platoon, of which the snipers are a part, is without a doubt the best platoon in the company. I just got a set of identical twins in the company who operates one of the Ranger Anti-Tank Weapon Systems. You'd like them; they work hard when they are on duty and play even harder when they're not. They've also got a casual disrespect for anything that resembles authority."

"No doubt I'd like them," Ryan agreed. "Sounds like they're my kind of people."

"I was initially worried their off duty antics would impact their work during the day," Aaron commented, "but so far those fears haven't been justified. The twins are always the first ones there in the morning, the first ones to get to work and the first to lend a hand when needed." He shook his head. "If I could only figure out how to tell them apart, I'd be all set…and if I could get them to lose the surfer accent, too, that would be nice," he added as an afterthought.

"I don't know," Ryan said. "You almost sound like you're happy you stayed on active duty, after all…"

Terminal 30, Port of Seattle, WA

John Huang looked around nervously as he walked off the *M.V. Xin Ou Zhou*. Realizing he needed to act normally, he stopped glancing around and focused on his car. "If I can just make it to the car," he thought, "everything will be all right." When he reached his car, he jumped as he heard someone behind him clear his throat.

"Any problems?" the voice asked. He turned to find himself face-to-face with Colonel Zhang Wei.

"Umm…no…no problems, whatsoever, Mr. Zhang," he replied. "Should you…umm…be meeting me here?" John had spent *years* getting into position for this day; he was one of many people the People's Republic had pre-staged in a variety of occupations on the off chance they would one day be needed.

Zhang smiled. "Is there something wrong with a shipper asking the customs agent if there were any problems with his shipment?"

John's face, already pale, went another couple of shades paler. "Umm, no, I guess not," he said. John knew who Zhang was and, truth be told, Zhang scared him. A lot. John had seen many crime dramas and knew the 'loose ends' *always* got eliminated. He was worried that, with his mission completed, he had just become a loose end. "And, no, there weren't any problems; all five of the containers I was told to expect are through customs," he finished.

"That's good," Zhang replied in a voice guaranteed to add one more layer of fear to John's heart. Zhang understood the need to Americanize his name to fit in, but never would have done it himself. "I'm *so* glad our previous efforts paid off." Zhang had known about John for many years, although he had only met him recently. Zhang had been responsible for feeding the customs inspector several tips. Two of these had led to his biggest busts, a shipment of rhino horns valued at over $59,000 on the Black Market, and a load of 61 children bound for the slave trade. Even though it was because of a tip, John was extremely proud of the last bust and knowing he had made a difference in the lives of 61 children.

"Ye...yes, sir," John said. "Everything went exactly as you said it would."

"Of course it did," Zhang said leaning close as he spoke. "Did you expect otherwise?"

"No, sir, I...umm...thought it would go exactly as you said it would!" If John had been scared before, the menace in the Colonel's voice now had him completely petrified.

"Good," Zhang said, "then stop calling me "sir." You wouldn't want to blow my cover, would you?"

"No, s...I mean, no, Mr. Zhang." John said, shaking.

"Good," Zhang replied again. "I'm sure I am keeping you from something. Perhaps you should go see to it?" John, realizing that he had been dismissed, quickly took the opportunity to jump into his car and leave. Zhang smiled. "Civilians are so much fun to play with," he thought.

Zhang walked over to his car where Lieutenant Colonel Peng waited in the driver's seat. As Zhang got in, his executive officer asked, with perhaps a little too much enthusiasm, "So, is he a loose end yet?"

Zhang paused to consider. For many years, Zhang had helped build John's reputation as one of the toughest inspectors at the port, especially for ships coming in from China. The son of parents who had "narrowly escaped the wrath of the Communist Party" by fleeing to the United States, he told all his friends that being tough on Chinese vessels was his way of paying the People's Republic back for the suffering they caused his parents.

"No," Zhang finally decided. "We will let him live a little longer so he can inspect the *Changsha* when it arrives." He didn't need to say that after he had inspected the *Changsha*, though, John *would* be a loose end.

"It's a good thing he was selected to inspect the ship today," Lieutenant Colonel Peng said. "If anyone else had looked inside the containers, there would have been a lot of explaining to do." They watched as the ship started unloading.

"It would have been inconvenient for me to have to explain why there were containers of uniforms, weapons and ammunition going to the plant," Zhang said. "Not impossible, though, just inconvenient…"

Interlude Four

"China Announces Good Will Tour"

The Chinese president announced today that a flotilla of ships would make an 'Around the World' tour at the end of the summer to promote 'openness and better diplomatic relations' with a number of nations. The squadron of ships will be led by the brand new Type 081 amphibious assault ship PLAN *Long*, and will also include two Aegis-like destroyers, the PLAN *Kunming* and the PLAN *Changsha*. The group will be accompanied by a Chinese oiler, the PLAN *Qinghaihu*. The Chinese president noted that he would be making a state visit to the United States in conjunction with the ships' port call in Seattle to conduct what he called 'high-level negotiations to improve trade and diplomatic relations.'

The ships will make a port call in Vancouver, Canada, prior to stops in Seattle and Los Angeles in the United States. They will then transit to South America for stops in Manta, Ecuador and Lima, Peru. It is expected the Chinese will participate in a number of events while in the U.S. to promote improved ties between the two nations.

American President Bill Jacobs said, "We welcome this gesture and hope it will lead to progress on a number of long-term issues we have had with China. Plans are being developed for us to return the gesture." The president also confirmed off the record that there would be at least one conversation on human rights issues, a topic the Chinese had previously refused to discuss.

- *World News Online*. Posted March 4 by Susan Clements

This Year

Naval Base Kitsap, WA, March 20

"Tell me about the ships that are coming," Rear Admiral Dan Barnaby ordered the assembled members of his staff as he looked out the window at the Bremerton Navy base. Rear Admiral Barnaby was Commander, Navy Region Northwest, the officer in charge of all of the Navy activities in Washington, Oregon, Idaho, Montana, Wyoming and Alaska, and all of the associated commands and facilities therein. If it was Navy-related in the northwestern United States, he was responsible for it. With over $3 billion spent annually, the Puget Sound region was the U. S. Navy's third largest fleet concentration area. The admiral was a man of some importance, which he was happy to tell anyone who asked.

A tall man at six feet, three inches, he was not recruiting poster material. His uniform might have fit 20 pounds ago, but the buttons were now being perilously stress-tested by his ever-increasing girth. His dark hair was also on the outside edge of regulations; if he had been anyone else, he would have been ordered to visit the barber over two weeks prior. He already knew this was his last command; having received that message a couple of months ago, he no longer cared much about uniform regulations.

He did care about doing a good job so that he could get a suitable position in the defense industry upon his retirement, though, and had called his staff together in the conference room at the headquarters building to discuss the Chinese visit. This was his last "big thing" as the Navy Northwest Commander. It was going to be a high-visibility event, and one he intended to ensure *would* go well.

His operations officer, Captain John Galloway, replied, "The Chinese squadron has a Type 081 LHD, which is an amphibious assault ship with both helicopters and a dock for small landing craft, two Type 052D destroyers and an ocean-going oiler." As he mentioned each ship, one of his staff displayed a picture on the conference room's optical screen. A new technology, the screen eliminated optical feedback and generated a sharper picture than the old 'high definition' screens. Captain Galloway was an extremely professional officer who had come up quickly through the surface warfare community as a destroyer commander. The polar opposite of his boss, Captain Galloway was still upwardly mobile in the U.S. Navy.

"What have you got on this group, Jim?" Rear Admiral Barnaby asked, turning to look at his intelligence officer.

Captain James Spence moved to the podium. Admiral Barnaby was pretty sure if anyone ever looked up "nerd" in the dictionary, they would find Captain Spence's picture; he was tall, thin and wore thick-rimmed glasses. Although he couldn't wear a pocket protector in uniform, Barnaby guessed that Spence wore one with his civilian clothes. As he spoke, Captain Spence used his laser pointer to indicate the important characteristics of the ships, "The flagship of the force is the PLAN *Long*, which will be pier-side at Bremerton, along with their Type 903 oiler *Qinghaihu.*" Although Naval Base Kitsap had been created in 2004 by merging Naval Station Bremerton with Naval Submarine Base Bangor, both were often still called by their previous names.

Captain Spence continued, "We don't know a lot about the Type 081, as the *Long* is the first ship in the class, but we believe it is very similar to a French *Mistral*-class LHD. We expect it has the transport capability for a reinforced battalion of between 500-800 troops, somewhere between 40-50 vehicles and a mix of about 20 helicopters. It also has a well deck that can hold a variety of landing craft, but we expect it will probably have four Type 726 *Yuyi*-class air-cushioned landing craft."

"From the operations we've seen," he added, "it looks like they have two or three Z-15 helicopters, which are medium-lift, twin-engine helicopters that can hold 16 people. The *Long* will also have eight or nine Z-8 helicopters. These are indigenously produced versions of the French Aerospatiale SA-321 Super Frelon heavy transport helicopter. This helicopter can carry up to 38 combat-equipped troops. Finally, we believe it will also have eight or nine Z-10 attack helos. This helicopter is a knock-off of our Cobra attack helo, but it has a very capable internal cannon and can carry a variety of rockets and missiles. Of note, the Z-10 can carry air-to-air missiles, so it is a threat in the air war, as well as the ground war."

Rear Admiral Barnaby looked at his watch and asked, "Is that all?"

"Well, no," Spence said, pushing up his thick-rimmed glasses so he could refer to his notes. "We don't know if it will have any aboard, but the *Long* can carry the Type 63A light amphibious tank. Not many countries build amphibious tanks, but China has one, and it's pretty good. Its predecessor, the Type 63, was designed for river-crossing operations on inland rivers and lakes, but the 63A can be launched from amphibious ships six miles or more offshore. The 63A has a fully-stabilized 105mm rifled gun that is manually loaded and can fire a variety of high explosive and anti-tank ordnance, including an anti-tank guided missile developed from the Russian 9M117 Bastion. This missile has a maximum range of 5,000 meters and a hit probability of over 90% against stationary targets. Of note, this missile can also be used against low-flying helicopters. The tank also has a 7.62mm coaxial machine gun and a 12.7mm machine gun mounted on top of the turret."

Admiral Barnaby rolled his eyes. "Is there anything it can't do?" he asked.

"Actually, yes," Captain Spence replied. "Its one weakness is that it has very thin armor, as its developers had to keep the overall weight as low as possible to help keep it afloat, so it is fairly vulnerable to just about any of our anti-tank weapons."

"And that's it?" the admiral asked, looking at his watch again.

"Almost," Spence finished. "The ship also has a 76mm gun and four 30mm close-in weapon systems. That's it."

"Okay, so the LHD is a pretty capable platform. What about the destroyers?"

Spence switched to the next slide. "One destroyer, the PLAN *Kunming*, will be pier-side at Naval Station Everett and the PLAN *Changsha* will tie up in Tacoma. Apparently, the *Changsha* has some spare parts for the Chinese SAIC Automobile factory in Tacoma. I guess whoever owns SAIC must have some serious horsepower with the Communist Party to get them to deliver it for them, but I'm told the assembly line is down until it gets here."

"Why not send it by aircraft if it's so important?" the logistics officer asked.

"I'm not sure. It had something to do with the pressurization of an aircraft messing up the calibration of the whatever-it-is, as well as the thing being heavy and awkwardly-sized. Once they tie up to the pier, the Chinese are going to deliver it to the plant with the destroyer's helo."

"What do we know about the weapons systems on the destroyers?" the operations officer asked.

"Like the flagship," Spence briefed, "the destroyers are the first two ships of a new class, so we don't know as much as we'd like. We do know the class has a really good 130mm gun, a remote-controlled 30mm gun, 6 torpedo tubes and a close-in weapons system. The Type 052D also has a brand new vertical launching system for surface-to-air missiles, cruise missiles, anti-submarine missiles and anti-ship missiles. We don't know much about it yet, but it appears to be more advanced than anything we've seen from the Chinese. What I'm personally more worried about is that the Chinese military talks about the Type 052D as 'Aegis.' Similar to our Aegis-radar equipped ships, it appears they have a phased-array system which may allow their warships to share tracking and targeting data over their datalink systems. We don't know if this is true or not, but if it is, you might never see the ship shooting at you until missile launch, as a second ship could be providing the tracking and targeting info."

Although he didn't comment on the not-so-subtle, "That sucks," that could be heard from one of the junior officers sitting in a group in the back of the room, the admiral replied, "Well, happily we're not at war with them, then," while frowning back toward the source of the interruption. Looking back at the operations officer, he asked, "What have the geniuses at the State Department signed us up for during their visit?"

"So far, not too much," Captain Galloway said. "We have been invited to a formal dinner onboard the *Long*, and we are supposed to provide a couple of softball teams to play the crew of the *Kunming*. Apparently, they have two teams that have been trying to learn the game. The Chinese think their teams are pretty good and have challenged the crews of any of the ships in port there to a game. As it happens, there are a couple of fields that sit next to each other on Fletcher Way at Naval Station Everett and two ships currently in port."

The voice from the back of the room said in a stage whisper, "It's almost like they planned it that way."

Now it was Commander Galloway's turn to frown at the back of the room. "Yes, they probably did. Can you imagine anything better than coming to the U.S. and beating us at our own game? First they 'turn over a new leaf' and say they want to be 'good people' and improve diplomatic relations. Then they show up and beat us in softball. Lots of great PR for them, eh? They're in a no-lose situation—if they lose the game, they weren't expected to win anyway, and we're bad hosts for beating them; if they win, then everyone makes fun of us."

"Well, we can't very well say "no," either," the admiral said. "The ships at Everett, they're the *Shoup* and the *Ford*, right?" He referred to the USS *Shoup* (DDG-86) and the USS *Ford* (FFG-54). "They each need to come up with a team to play the Chinese. John, please let them know."

"I will, sir," Captain Galloway said, sounding about as unenthused as he expected the commanding officers of the two 'lucky' vessels would be.

"Okay, anything else we need to do for the visit?" the admiral asked, anxious to leave for a job interview with one of the local defense contractors. "I've got another meeting in 15 minutes I need to go to."

"Well, sir, if they're hosting us on their ship, we probably need to put together some sort of shindig for them," Lieutenant Bill Weathersby, the admiral's protocol officer, said.

"Great idea, Bill," the admiral said as he headed toward the door, "You're in charge of setting it up for me. Please make it happen and keep me updated on your progress."

"Yes, sir," the lieutenant replied, mentally vowing that he was never, EVER, going to open his mouth again.

Mt. Garfield, WA, June 3

"Thanks again for coming," Sara said. "I know we should probably be studying for final exams, but I had cabin fever and needed to get outdoors. Besides, it's the first day the temperature has climbed to 75 degrees, and it's just too nice to study."

"That it is," Erika said. "With all the warm weather we've been having, the snow is finally gone from the mountains so it's a lot easier to hike."

Sara was happy that Erika had agreed to come up to the mountain with her. She had wanted to explore Mt. Garfield for a long time and was excited to finally get to do it. Sara had done an internet search and was amazed at the amount of "Garfield" summits there were in the United States. For a man that had held the presidential office for just 200 days before being assassinated, there were five Garfield Mountains, seven Garfield Peaks and four Mt. Garfields.

She didn't know much about the rest of them, but this one, located about 35 miles east of Seattle, was good enough for her.

At only 5,519 feet of elevation, it was not the tallest peak around, but its exposed volcanic rock facings were impressive as they jutted out from heavily timbered foothills. With five separate peaks and several lesser crags, it was visually and spiritually appealing to her. Although all the peaks had been climbed, very little of the mountain's lower areas had ever been explored. To Sara, not explored meant not destroyed by human beings; she knew she could hike around and not have to be disgusted by the beer and soda cans, candy bar wrappers and the rest of the normal refuse people left behind when they camped out. The base of the trailhead was a case in point; when they parked the car there, they saw that someone had used it as a target range. Old CDs used as skeet shooting targets littered the area, as well as milk jugs on sticks and bullet casings on the ground.

They left the trail as quickly as they could, intending to go west of the peaks to a place known to the locals as Infinite Bliss. A saddleback of volcanic rock in the midst of the wooded area, it offered a great view of the local region. She wasn't sure it was really 'infinite bliss,' but she had heard the view was pretty nice. Several hours into the hike/climb, they arrived at their destination and were enjoying the view when they noticed they weren't alone.

"Hi, ladies," the stranger who suddenly appeared at the overlook alongside them said. "It's a beautiful day for a climb, eh? This is one of my favorite views." He didn't approach them or do anything to intimidate them, which would have been easy since he was a big man. Sara saw he was tall, tanned, and very well-muscled. Not the kind of muscles that weightlifters get, but the kind you get from a *lot* of physical activity. He was also kind of cute, with big blue eyes, although in an "older" sort of way; he was probably almost her dad's age. He was also armed, she noted, with a rifle slung on his back next to his pack. While it wasn't unheard of to climb or hike armed, as there were poisonous snakes and other dangers, it was certainly uncommon. Still, he didn't give the impression of danger, just quiet competence.

"I love the view," Sara agreed. "Do you come up here often?"

"I live close by," the man said. "My name's Ryan."

"Hi, Ryan," Erika said. "My name is Erika and this is Sara. You live here in the forest? I thought this was national forest?"

"I have an apartment in Seattle, but I used to be a Navy SEAL," he said, looking uncomfortable. "When budget cutbacks sent me home a couple of years ago, I needed some time to readjust to civilian life. Being out here gives me peace of mind and lets me focus on some of the finer things in life."

Ryan smiled, "Well, I didn't want to scare you, but I was going by and heard you up here, so I thought I'd swing by and say 'hi.' I like to know who's around." He tipped his cap. "However, I do have to be going, so have a good day and be safe." He turned and started off in the opposite direction from which they had come.

"Well, that was interesting," Erika said after he left. "He sure was cute, but kind of intimidating. I don't think I'd want him to be mad at me."

"I get the feeling he can take care of himself," Sara said, "even without the rifle he was carrying."

Naval Base Kitsap, WA, August 10

"Welcome to Naval Base Kitsap," LT Bill Weathersby said to the advance team from the Chinese Navy. Their fleet was currently in Vancouver, but three of its officers had flown down to Seattle to liaise with the staff of Naval Region Northwest and see the bases hosting the ships. LT Weathersby had sent the admiral's driver to pick up the Chinese officers and bring them to the base at Bremerton, saving him a trip and 30 minutes of conversation with them. They were meeting in the admiral's conference room so Weathersby could spread out all the information he had for them.

"Thank you very much for hosting us," Commander Gao Qiang, the executive officer of the PLAN destroyer *Kunming,* replied. Short and slight of build, Commander Gao was able to project an air of confidence many sizes bigger than he actually was. "We are very excited to be here."

"Your English is very good," LT Weathersby said. "You've obviously been to the United States before, correct?"

"Indeed," Commander Gao said. "I attended college here in Seattle at the University of Washington, so I am somewhat familiar with the area, although I never made it onto any of the military bases."

"Well, we're very happy to have you here," LT Weathersby reiterated, "and it'll be my pleasure to show you around. If you have any place you want to go or see, please let me know. We'll also make sure you have all of the services you need for your ships at their individual piers. If you need anything special, please let me know so we can get it for you."

"Well, we'd like to see where you're going to have us tie up our ships," Commander Gao said. "I understand my ship is going to be at Naval Station Everett up the coast, so we can play softball against the teams from the ships there. We will be pulling into port on the 18th. Is that still correct?"

LT Weathersby nodded. "Yes, that is still correct. As I understand it, your teams will be playing teams from the destroyer USS *Shoup* and the frigate USS *Ford*. They have played a couple of practice games, and you probably want your better team to play the *Shoup's* team. As their crew is a little bigger, they had more people to draw from, and their team is better. I heard they won pretty handily over the *Ford's* crew."

"Will the *Changsha* still be going to the Port of Tacoma so we can make our delivery?" Lieutenant He Fang, the *Changsha* operations officer, asked.

"Yes, it has all been arranged for you to go to the Navy Pier on the Hylebos River on the 18th," LT Weathersby confirmed. "We have also talked with the air traffic control facilities at McChord Air Force Base to coordinate your flight to the SAIC facility. McChord Air Force Base was consolidated with the Army's base at Fort Lewis in 2010; they are now known as 'Joint Base Lewis-McChord,' so you may hear it called that, too. Here are the radio frequencies McChord is using, and the procedures they would like you to follow." LT Weathersby handed him the paperwork.

"Thank you very much for arranging everything. Do you have a phone number I can call if there are any questions?" Lieutenant He asked.

"That's in there, too," LT Weathersby replied.

"And the *Long* and *Qinghaihu* will still be pulling into Bremerton on the 18th?" Lieutenant Commander Lin Gang, the air operations officer from the *Long,* asked.

"Yes," LT Weathersby answered, "both ships will be at Pier D at the Bremerton Naval Station. I have a set of charts that show how to get there, and what the water depths are enroute."

Lieutenant Commander Lin, a tall and studious-looking man, bowed. "Thank you very much," he said. "Do you have the guest list for who will attend our dinner on August 19th?"

"Yes, I do," LT Weathersby replied. "Governor Shelby and his wife will be able to attend, as will Representative Bennett and his wife. It also looks like the majority of Admiral Barnaby's staff will be there, as well as the commanding officer and executive officer from Naval Base Kitsap and their wives. Almost everyone who was invited will be able to attend, and they were all very happy to be included. Speaking of which, Admiral Barnaby would be very honored if your admiral and as many of your officers as are able could join him at his house on August 20th for a party to commemorate your visit here."

"We would be delighted," Lieutenant Commander Lin said. "Although I will have to confirm it with him, I'm sure my admiral would be happy to attend. My admiral also asked me to coordinate some logistical movements while we are here. With our ships separated at three different bases, he was wondering if we would be able to fly our helicopters between the ships so we can move supplies and people back and forth. It is quite a long drive from Bremerton to Everett, although it is not very far as the raven flies, as I believe you say."

"The bird is a crow," Commander Gao corrected, "but the point is valid. The admiral has asked my commanding officer to be present for several planning sessions for our upcoming port visits; it would be a much more economical use of his time if we could fly him to the *Long* and back. We would also like to be able to use our landing craft to move around some supplies and renew our certifications. Would that be all right?"

"I imagine that can probably be arranged," LT Weathersby said. "I will confirm that with my chain of command and get back with you."

"Actually, do you know what would also be very helpful?" Lieutenant Commander Lin Gang asked. "I believe the local air traffic control (ATC) facility is in Seattle, correct?"

"I don't know," LT Weathersby said with a shrug. A ship driver by trade, air operations were not his forte.

"I think the local ATC agency is called "Seattle Control," LCDR Lin said. "It would be very helpful if we could get a tour there for our air traffic controllers so that they could talk with the ATC personnel. If we could get a tour at about 1300 on the 19th, our controllers would be well prepared for coordinating our operations while we are here. Not only that, but by seeing the equipment in operation, our sailors will understand what your controllers are looking at, which will help our controllers better interface with yours."

"I realize Sunday afternoon isn't the best time for a tour, but we'd like to do it as soon as possible once we pull in to avoid any airborne misunderstandings with our helicopters," LCDR Lin continued. "By doing it at 1300, we also won't have to disturb the dinner later that afternoon."

"I will try to get it set up," Weathersby said. He was worried about the Chinese using the opportunity to spy on the American ATC facilities, but the request made sense; if the Chinese were going to be conducting flight operations in the Seattle area, it was imperative they know how to contact ATC, and what procedures they should be following.

"Thank you," said LCDR Lin. "That would be most helpful. Do you suppose the ATC personnel would mind if a couple of wives attended, as well? I know the men involved, as they work for me, and two of them have wives who work for the auto manufacturers in the area. They were hoping to spend some time with them while we are here. It is not a problem if they can't, but I know the wives had planned to meet with their husbands while we were in port."

"I'll see what can be arranged." Weathersby indicated the table with several piles of papers. "We've also taken the liberty of putting together some other trips and tours you might be interested in, if you'd like to take a look."

Guangzhou Interbay Assembly Plant, Seattle, WA, August 17

The plant was closed for a three-day weekend so workers could attend the trade show at the convention center. The members of the Guangzhou Military Region special forces had to come to work, though, and it was most definitely *not* business as usual. The second and third shift operators had pulled the first three special containers into the plant the night before and had emptied them. All the ammunition they contained was now down in the basement of the plant, which had been transformed into its true purpose: a sound-proofed firing range.

Colonel Zhang watched as the members of the second and third shifts worked on re-honing their skills with their combat rifles. As he walked down the range with Lieutenant Colonel Peng and Captain Chou Min, he looked at the targets his men were using and decided he was satisfied with the results. Not happy, but satisfied. "Their marksmanship is not as good as it used to be," he noted. "It is obvious they haven't been able to practice recently."

Lieutenant Colonel Peng nodded as he walked along next to his commanding officer. "We moved all the non-special forces personnel to the first shift a couple of weeks ago so our second and third-shift troops could start shooting again. The remaining special forces personnel on the first shift are going to be a little rustier than these, but they will get a chance to shoot tomorrow morning."

Colonel Zhang nodded. "Make sure they get an extra allotment of ammunition so they can get the practice they need," he told his second in command. "Do you suppose any of the other workers have figured out this is a rifle range?" he asked.

"I don't think so," Peng said, having had more contact with the daily workers than Colonel Zhang. "Some of the architects and builders wondered why we needed a storage room that ran the length of the building, but most were satisfied with the explanation that we had a wide variety of equipment and spare machinery to store here." He motioned down range. "It's good to finally have all the extra equipment moved back to the first floor so we can use it as it was intended."

The three officers walked back upstairs. Colonel Zhang looked out to the storage yard. It was full to overflowing, although most of the vehicles seemed to be the new J-Van. "You seem to have a disgraceful backup in inventory," Colonel Zhang said to his transportation officer, Captain Chou. "Do we have enough vans?"

"Yes sir, we do now," Captain Chou said. "Thank you for 'forgetting' to schedule the transporter train to take them to market, or we would not."

"They are all appropriately configured, too," Lieutenant Colonel Peng said. Each van used a modular system for its interior, allowing its owners to reconfigure it for a variety of seating or cargo options. "All the vehicles have been configured with the 'Maximum Bench Seating Option,' and have bench seats that run the length of the van with room for storage down the middle."

"And this configuration is big enough to seat twelve soldiers with all of their combat gear?" Colonel Zhang asked.

Lieutenant Colonel Peng nodded. "We brought one into the plant last night and re-tested it. The storage space is tight for holding the 12 soldiers' packs, but it will work. The only problem we had was the head of marketing. She wanted to know why all 200 of these vehicles were painted black."

Washington State Convention Center, Seattle, WA, August 17

With four separate ballrooms totaling 45,000 square feet, the Washington State Convention Center could accommodate groups of up to 3,500 in a general session. The Convention Center also had 61 meeting rooms, which gave an organization hosting a conference an opportunity to have numerous breakout sessions. It was an excellent site to host a conference, and Captain Liu Fang was a little disappointed he wouldn't be able to enjoy it.

But only just a little, because Liu had worked his whole life for this moment. The son of one of the first special forces soldiers, he had been raised in the special forces and taught to believe that it was the best, and only, place for him. Setting his sights on that goal, he had studied English because he knew that one of the main missions of the special forces was reconnaissance behind enemy lines. His father had told him many times the Americans would have to be dealt with eventually; he wanted to be ready.

He had excelled during his special forces training, which normally had a dropout rate of 75%. Although most trainees were unprepared for the 10 kilometer (6.2 mile) swim, he had prepared for it by swimming at least 25 kilometers a week for the two years before he reported for training. He was still just getting warmed up when he reached the finish line, completing the arduous event over two minutes ahead of the second place finisher.

He had been selected to join the Guangzhou Military Region's Special Forces unit, 'The Sword of Southern China,' just like his father. He was proud of his unit, China's first regiment to be truly triphibious. Just like the American SEALS, they were trained to conduct operations under the sea, in the air and on land. He was also proud of his abilities and the part he was to play in the coming operation. When he had suggested this conference as a means of getting his troops into the country, he had never expected that the conference, and his resulting responsibilities, would grow to the extent they had.

As he stood overseeing the check-in of the IAMA conference attendees, he laughed at the Americans showing up like sheep for the event. With over 3,000 attendees (not counting the 'special guests' from China), it was a major event, and he had already heard people talking about how they hoped there would be many more conferences like it. While his staff had lined up discussions on many interesting topics, including his own scheduled lecture on language barriers, Captain Liu rather doubted that in a couple of days they would want more conferences 'just like this one.' He smiled. No, probably not.

Looking at the paperwork he had just been handed, he saw that over 500 people had already checked in, and there were lines in Rooms 307, 308, 309 and 310 as attendees continued to arrive. New production and concept import automobiles were positioned in the South Galleria and Rooms 303-306 on the Third Level. A number of exhibitors and vendors had already set up their displays in 4E and 4F, and on the Skybridge. The main conference rooms 4A and 4B would be used for the initial convocation and…other things.

Washington, D.C., August 17

"How are the plans proceeding?" President Jiang Jiabao asked.

"Everything here in Washington is moving forward according to plan," Fung Qiang, the ambassador to the United States, said. "I just heard from Colonel Zhang in Seattle, and almost everything is proceeding on track there, as well. Our warships are on their way down from Vancouver as scheduled. They are conducting a joint exercise with several Canadian and United States' ships today, prior to pulling into port tomorrow. That is as expected." He paused. "Most of the civilian ships are also on schedule to enter port as planned, although one ship, the *M.V. Erawan*, experienced some engine problems that required it to reduce its speed while the mechanical issues were resolved."

"Will they make it to port on time?" the president asked.

"Yes, Mr. President, they will," the ambassador answered. "The plan was built with a little extra time in case something like this happened. Even though the *Erawan* is running a little behind timeline, she will still be in port when required."

"Good," the president said. "Let me know if anything changes." He looked at his aide. "What do I have planned for tomorrow?"

His aide, Han Min, consulted his notes. A small man, he was full of energy and kept detailed notes on the president's schedule. "Your schedule starts at 0800," he said, "with a presentation from law enforcement officers and the U.S. military on non-lethal riot control. Apparently, they have a wide variety of presentations lined up for you with lasers, chemical agents and sonic blasters."

"While I'm sure the U.S. is doing wonderful things with their toys, and that the Americans are on the cutting edge of crowd control, it will be difficult to appear to care about the presentations," the president said with a yawn. "To do so will challenge my acting skills to their fullest. The ability to use non-lethal means to control crowds, clear streets and subdue individuals is all very nice, as is the Americans' belief in the value of a human life; I, however, simply don't have the time, money or attention to waste on them. Life is cheap, and if people want to protest in the middle of the street and not move when they are told to, a bullet in the head is an even cheaper solution."

The president sighed and shrugged. "I will go see the presentations because that is what is expected; however, if I had been in charge in 1989, I would have told the tanks to run over the man who stood in front of them in Tiananmen Square. If you want to stand in front of moving tanks, it is better to take your genes out of the gene pool by running you over. You are obviously not smart enough to help the Party." He sighed. "All I can hope for is that maybe they will have some new variations on tear gas or pepper spray we can try out."

"Yes, sir," Han Min said, consulting his notes again. "After several hours of non-lethal crowd control, you will have lunch and a couple of hours of meetings with the U.S. President, where you will probably have to waste more time listening to him talk about improving human rights." He looked up at the president. "I'm sorry, sir, but not only did the Americans place it on the agenda, they made human rights the first item."

"That is all right, Min, I know it is not your fault," the president said. "I will make it through by thinking about the pictures our soldiers will take while they are driving their tanks down the streets of Seattle and Tacoma. Won't those look nice on TV! If any Americans think *these* tanks will stop just because someone stands in front of them, they will be sadly mistaken." Yes, the president thought, I will make it through the events of tomorrow and, yes, I will pretend to care. But I will care a lot more about what happens the day after.

Pier 57, The Port of Seattle, WA, August 18

Captain Hon Ming watched with great satisfaction as his ship, the cruise liner *Henna*, tied up to Pier 57. This was the third time he had made the trip, and things were going much more smoothly this time. Unaccustomed to having a bigger cruise ship come to Pier 57, the Americans did not have enough people pier-side to tie it up correctly on their first visit, and it had taken some effort and a great amount of shouted instructions to get enough people. While they waited for the Americans to assemble all of the workers required, the *Henna* had backed out of the pier area to wait offshore in the Puget Sound. Unfortunately, while they were waiting, they had drifted a little too far south and had come a lot closer to the Seattle-Bainbridge Island Ferry coming into Pier 52 than he would have liked. Although there really wasn't *that* much danger of a collision, both vessels were massive. It took time to stop the ferry and to get the *Henna* moving, and the fastest way to lose your Captain's stripes was to have your ship hit another one. He preferred to stay a good distance from the traffic lanes.

Things seemed to be going smoothly this time, even more so than their last visit. He could see enough people on the pier to tie the ship up correctly. He even thought he saw the woman who was the Head Customs Inspector for this area of the port. On their first visit, she had taken two hours to get to the ship, even though he had made sure all of the appropriate people were notified and the appropriate forms filled out (in triplicate!) prior to their sailing. Oh, how the passengers had screamed waiting for her arrival! There were so many things to do and see within a few blocks of the pier, and no one was allowed off until they cleared customs. On his last visit, she was only 15 minutes late, and the passengers didn't have as much time to complain about their delay in going ashore.

He hoped everything would run as smoothly with Customs as it seemed to be with everything else. Familiarity breeds complacency, and they were no longer the "new thing." Once you've seen something a few times, you really stop noticing it. He hoped that was true with both Customs and Immigration on this visit; if they were looking closely, they might very well notice the overwhelming majority of the passengers were men. He had a good cover story for why that was, of course, but didn't want to use it unless he absolutely had to. That was, after all, why they had done this twice before, so no one would look at them as closely.

He looked back to the pier and could see a line of busses waiting on Alaskan Way. The Los Angeles Dodgers' baseball team was in town for the second game of a three-game series with the Seattle Mariners, and the cruise ship had acquired 200 tickets for the game. Peng Jun Jie, a native Chinese ballplayer, had just come to the United States from the Japanese Nippon Professional Baseball League, like many others before him, and the Chinese were looking forward to seeing him play.

Looking a little further to the right, he could see Elliot's Oyster House on the next pier. He had visited Elliot's on his last trip and knew it had excellent seafood. Since he planned for the ship to stay later so the passengers could attend the baseball game, he knew he had time to go to Elliot's for dinner. He was looking forward to some king crab legs, and, if something unforeseen happened to make the ship stay in Seattle longer, he would be able to make it back over to try the Dungeness crab, too!

Naval Base Kitsap, WA, August 18

With much fanfare, the PLAN *Long* and PLAN *Qinghaihu* pulled up to Pier D at Bremerton Naval Station. The *Qinghaihu* pulled up first and was the closest to land; the *Long* pulled in behind her with her stern facing the sea. Like many amphibious assault ships, the *Long* had a stern that folded down. This allowed water to come in and lift the smaller assault craft inside that carried the troops and equipment to the beach. In effect, the *Long* functioned like a car ferry, except that her well deck carried boats that could drive in and out. In the case of the *Long*, it also carried Type 63A amphibious tanks onboard that could exit the ship via the well deck and swim their way to shore. By tying up to the pier 'nose in,' the Chinese were able to use the ship's well deck and the smaller boats she carried, as had been previously approved by the Americans.

Naval Station Everett, WA, August 18

Located on the northeast side of the Puget Sound, Naval Station Everett was 15 miles north of Seattle. Home to the USS *Abraham Lincoln* aircraft carrier, as well as several smaller combatants, it allowed easier access to the Pacific Ocean than the naval facilities at Bremerton or Bangor. Naval Station Everett was also a lot closer to Seattle, resulting in a better quality of life for most of the people who worked on base. It also wasn't very far to the Mt. Baker-Snoqualmie National Forest and other wilderness areas, for those people who liked their life unspoiled by civilization.

Billing itself as the United States Navy's most modern facility, Naval Station Everett had about 350 sailors and civilians assigned there, as well as another 6,000 personnel stationed onboard the ships home-ported there. The majority of these were onboard the *Abraham Lincoln*, which was currently on deployment, so there were 5,000 fewer personnel at Everett when the PLAN *Kunming* pulled into port and tied up at the pier. Everett's port facilities formed a giant "U," which projected off the end of Spruance Boulevard like an enormous tuning fork. The *Kunming* was on the inside of the "U" on the southern pier, behind the USS *Ford*. Captain Tang Ping, the captain of the *Kunming*, could see the destroyer USS *Shoup* on the other side of the "U" from them.

This is going to be a lot easier than we initially planned, he thought to himself. The absence of the American carrier simplified things greatly for the sailors of the *Kunming*. When the planning for Dragon's Bite was in its initial stages, he had not seen any way possible for his ship's complement to carry out the tasks given to them, even with an augment of soldiers from the People's Liberation Army. As ships are designed to hold the minimum number of personnel required to effectively operate them, and no more, the *Kunming* would not have been able to carry the significantly greater number of troops the operation would have required if the carrier had been in port. He smiled to himself. It was nice when the enemy simplified your tasks for you.

Interlude Five

"Defense of Taiwan Planning Analysis"

Current Political Situation – Rising Nationalism

The tremendous growth of a national Taiwanese identity, encouraged by its current ruling party, has upset the political balance between Beijing and Taipei recently. Survey data from the most recent polls indicated most of the island's citizens regard themselves as "Taiwanese" (77 percent) or a mix of "Both Taiwanese and Chinese" (22 percent). It is unlikely that it has escaped the attention of Beijing that only 1 percent of Taiwanese citizens regard themselves as "Chinese." As recently as December, 2008, the number claiming to be solely Taiwanese was only 51 percent, indicating a large upswing in nationalism...

Chinese Missile Forces – Opening Devastation

In the event of a war with Taiwan, China is expected to use all the missile forces it has at its disposal. A surprise barrage of over 1,000 cruise and ballistic missiles will likely herald the onset of an attack, overwhelming the air defense capabilities of the island, cutting every military runway and destroying any unprotected aircraft on the ramps. It is expected the initial assault will wipe out nearly all of Taiwan's air defense capabilities. Additional missiles are expected to target the United States' surveillance, communications and navigations satellites overhead, denying and degrading the United States' command and control capabilities…

The Air War – Continued Destruction

The People's Liberation Army Air Force has long held a quantitative advantage in fighter aircraft; its new J-10, J-11, and J-20 aircraft now give it at least a qualitative balance, if not an edge. With its missile forces wiping out the majority of Taiwan's air defense capabilities, Chinese fighters will be able to deliver precision-guided munitions and additional cruise missiles where needed to destroy defenses and prepare the island for invasion…

The Conclusion – Chinese Invasion of Taiwan

The only way China can control Taiwan for the long-term is to successfully invade and occupy it. To do so, it must not only have the means to transport its soldiers, but it must also have control of the sea in order to get its forces to Taiwan's shores. Having recently upgraded all of its transport capabilities, China now has enough sealift available to get its soldiers quickly to the island. With control of the air, Chinese aircraft can patrol forward, sinking United States' shipping with advanced anti-ship missiles, while Chinese *Kilo*-class submarines conduct coordinated attacks on U.S. aircraft carriers with SS-N-27 Sizzler missiles. These missiles cruise at three times the speed of sound at an altitude of 30 feet…

- U.S. Department of Defense Classified Analysis

August 19
Red Tide Morning

Beijing and Guangzhou China, 0500 China Standard Time (0200 PDT)

The two China Air flights to the United States, China Air 779 and China Air 780, were ready to taxi for takeoff when a number of armed soldiers came onto the flights. The passengers were told that someone had just called in a bomb threat and that, as a precaution, there were to be no transmissions of any kind—a cell phone call could set it off. The soldiers quickly hurried the passengers off the plane, but instead of going back up the ramp to the terminal, they were ushered down a staircase and into a holding room where their cell phones were taken from them.

As they filed down the stairs, an even larger group of soldiers were walking up the steps and into the plane. "That's strange," one passenger said to another, "that's a lot of armed men to look for a bomb."

One of the soldiers passing by smiled at them and said, "There are a lot of places we have to look, and it is imperative we find it as quickly as possible." This made good sense to the passengers, who proceeded down to the holding room, while the soldiers continued onto the two planes.

Fifteen minutes later, the airplanes took off on their non-stop flights. Their destination: Seattle-Tacoma Airfield.

The Port of Seattle, WA, 0600 Pacific Daylight Time

The assistant port operations officer looked at the schedule for the day's activity at the port. "Geez," he said. "It's a regular stinkin' Chinese invasion."

The port operations officer looked out the window of the Port of Seattle Headquarters building, located at Pier 69 on the waterfront in the center of Seattle. From the window, he could see the majority of the port, from the cruise ship terminal located two miles to the north on down to the cargo terminals located two miles to the south. As befit his position, his office was tastefully decorated with a variety of nautical pictures and paintings. "What do you mean?" the port operations officer asked.

"Well, in addition to all the Chinese naval vessels that pulled in yesterday at the naval bases, we've got four Chinese commercial vessels coming into port today, and another car carrier going into Tacoma. No wonder we're losing the balance of trade with China; the Pacific Northwest is doing all it can to import the entire nation of China."

"I think what you really mean," the port operations officer said, "is that, unlike the rest of the country, we've got job security. What ships are coming in today?"

"It's going to be busy at Pier 91. Not only do we have the Holland Cruise Lines' *M.V. Oosterdam* leaving this afternoon, we also have the China Shipping Container Lines' *M.V. Xin Qing Dao* car carrier coming into port, as well as the China Navigation Company's *M.V. Erawan* bulk freighter."

"Couldn't one or the other of those have gone to one of the other terminals?" the port operations officer asked.

"Unfortunately, no," said his assistant. "Both of them have things for the Chinese car factory at Interbay; the car carrier is loaded with cars for the showroom and the *Erawan* has some heavy machinery for the plant. It's better to have them come into 91, where they can easily get it to the factory without having to drag it all the way through downtown Seattle." He continued, "In addition to those two, the China Shipping Container Lines *M.V. Xin Beijing* freighter is coming into Terminal 30, where they normally offload. This is one of their big ones, over 1,100 feet long and carrying 7,450 containers. Finally, China Ocean Shipping Company's *M.V. Hanjin Kingston*, a big container ship, will be docking at Terminal 46 today. "

He paused. "Oh, yeah, the Chinese cruise ship, the *Henna*, is still at Pier 57. It was supposed to leave last night, but broke down. They hope to have it repaired and out of here by this evening. I spoke with the captain of the ship, and they have some high ranking people on board; there is a lot of pressure for him to get underway as quickly as possible and back on schedule. He's doing everything he can to get it fixed ASAP. Still, between here and Tacoma, that makes *six* Chinese ships in port this afternoon, assuming the *Henna* doesn't get underway earlier."

"And that," the port operations officer said, looking at the *Henna* from his window, "is what I call true job security."

"I still think it looks like a red tide is coming in," the assistant grumbled.

Guangzhou Interbay Assembly Plant, Seattle, WA, 0700 Pacific Daylight Time

Having donned his uniform, Zhang was once again 'Colonel Zhang' as he watched the distribution operation proceeding as planned. The plant was still closed, and his regiment had formed up inside it by companies, except for the people detailed to act as sentries at the doors. The third shift operators the night before had pulled the last two special containers into the plant and emptied them. Their contents, Chinese army uniforms, were now laid out on tables that ran halfway down one side of the plant, and the companies were taking turns getting their uniforms and going down to the firing range to get their ammunition. They were a little shorter than he'd hoped they would be on some things, but the rest of what he needed would be unloaded from the *M.V. Xin Beijing* in the Port of Seattle later that day. They had plenty of ammunition for their QBZ-95 rifles and QSZ-92 pistols; what they lacked was more rocket-propelled grenades (RPGs) and other explosives. As long as they didn't get into too many firefights, they would be okay.

As the squads walked by him, he saw that they were excited and ready to go. They should be, since many of them had been in the United States, waiting, for years. Each of the squads had 10 men: a Type 69 RPG gunner (the Chinese version of the venerable Russian RPG-7 rocket-propelled grenade launcher), as well as seven infantrymen equipped with 5.8mm QBZ-95 assault rifles, one soldier with a 5.8mm QBZ-95 light support rifle and one armed with a 5.8mm QBU-88 sniper rifle.

His men and women represented a very proficient combat force, all the more so since they were unexpected, especially the women. Unlike other nations, the United States included, China had started allowing women into its special forces units a long time ago, a fact that he was looking forward to exploiting later in the day.

Zhang watched as the men and women who were not already in uniform began driving J-Vans into the plant, where they were quickly loaded with the supplies his troops would need in the hours to come.

August 19
Red Tide Afternoon

Approaching the *M.V. Oosterdam*, Seattle, WA, 1200 Pacific Daylight Time

Senator Jack Turner and his family drove south on 15th Avenue West toward the northern piers of Seattle's harbor where the Holland America cruise ship *M.V. Oosterdam* waited. Jack was looking forward to their cruise and spending some quality time with his wife and children. The junior senator from Oregon knew he should probably have stayed in D.C. to continue working on the latest budget impasse, but this trip had been planned for months, and he didn't want to lose the money he had invested. The cruise was a week-long trip to Alaska and back with stops in both Alaska and Victoria, British Columbia. He was looking forward to seeing Alaska, but he knew the vacation would be a success in his children's minds as long as they saw whales somewhere along the way.

"What's going on there?" his 14-year-old son Joey asked as they passed a massive building covered in streamers. The sign read 'Guangzhou Interbay Assembly Plant.'

"I think that's the new Chinese auto plant," Jack replied. "Guang-hoo, or something like that. I remember when they built the plant. Everyone was happy to have the plant and the jobs, but I think they built it on a golf course, which annoyed some of the locals."

"Why is it decorated like that? Is that what a car plant normally looks like?"

"No," Jack said, having seen his share of automobile facilities while working on the Senate Subcommittee on Housing, Transportation and Community Development. "I think it must be because the Chinese fleet is visiting here this week."

"That's cool," Joey said. "Will we get to see them?"

"I don't think so," Jack said.

"Bummer."

Pier D, Naval Base Kitsap, WA, 1215 Pacific Daylight Time

LT Weathersby and his driver, Petty Officer First Class Tim Smith, met the group of five uniformed Chinese sailors as they walked down the gangway from the PLAN *Long*, led by LCDR Lin. After quickly introducing everyone, the group began walking toward the parking lot across the street. As they reached the end of the pier, they saw two Asian-looking women waiting, who ran forward and jumped into the arms of two of the men as they approached. "I guess they're happy to see them," Weathersby said to LCDR Lin.

"I expect so," LCDR Lin said. "With our work-up schedule and their need to be here to work at the plant, they haven't seen each other in almost two years. Even for the families of sailors, who are used to separation, that is still a *really* long time. I know the men are looking forward to seeing their kids again, too, after the tour." He winked. "After some quality time with their wives, first, I am sure."

LT Weathersby laughed. "No doubt!" he said. Looking up, he saw that the women were leading them toward two black vans parked in the "Z" Parking Lot across Wyckoff Street from the pier. "Do you have enough transportation? I have a driver and a bus set up."

"Actually, the two women have enough room for all of us," LCDR Lin said. "That is one of the benefits of working for an auto maker; access to cheap transportation. I think these are two of the new vans that GAC just started producing."

"Do you know where you are going?" LT Weathersby asked.

LCDR Lin chuckled, "Google Maps and MapQuest are wonderful things. Not only do the women already have directions, I'll bet they printed out satellite imagery of the building's parking lot, so they know where to park. I've already talked with our point of contact at the facility and confirmed our time there, so we're all set."

"So you don't need any transportation or for me to go along?" LT Weathersby asked.

"No," LCDR Lin said, "I think we are okay. If you're interested in seeing the ATC facility, you're certainly welcome to come along with us, but please don't feel like you need to babysit. The two wives have been here two years and are very familiar with the area." He paused, considering, then smiled. "Of course, if your admiral has detailed you to come along with us to make sure that we don't plant listening bugs at the facility or do something spy-related while we're there, you are welcome to come along." He chuckled and pretended to look around furtively. "I am, of course, a most untrustworthy individual!"

"No," LT Weathersby said, "I wasn't along to keep you from spying, but to make sure you had transportation and got there safely. If you don't need me, I'll go get ready for the dinner tonight."

"We are good," LCDR Lin said, shooing him off. "I am not expecting any problems." He paused and said cheerfully, "Have fun at the dinner; I know they spent a lot of time planning and preparing for you!" The Chinese started getting into the two vans.

"All right then, have a good tour!" LT Weathersby said before walking off with Petty Officer Smith.

Once they were out of earshot, LT Weathersby looked at Petty Officer Smith. "Okay, I'm not spying, much, but the admiral wanted to know. What did they say when the women joined them?"

"Typical stuff you'd say to your spouse after a cruise, sir," Petty Officer Smith said. "I missed you, it's so good to see you, can't wait to be alone, blah, blah, blah."

"Thanks," LT Weathersby said, "Maybe they were on the up-and-up, after all."

"If they're not," Smith replied, "they're good actors. They sure sounded like people that were getting lucky tonight."

Vancouver International Airport, Vancouver, Canada, 1252 Pacific Daylight Time

"*Vancouver Control,*" the pilot radioed, "*this is Air China 306.*"

"Air China 306, *go ahead,*" Vancouver Air Traffic Control (ATC) replied. The controller looked at his readout and saw that *Air China 306 Heavy* was a 747-400 aircraft. The Extended Range model of the venerable 747, it had a range of 7,670 nautical miles with a full load, which was much more than needed for the 5,838 nautical mile flight from Beijing to Seattle. He didn't think fuel was an issue, but he knew some of the Air China aircraft were old and not well-maintained. He hoped *306* wouldn't be a problem that would ruin his day.

"*This is* Air China 306. *We are currently at the DUGGS intersection and are having some problems with our navigation equipment. It's a beautiful day up here today, though, and we can make it the rest of the way to Seattle visually. We'd like to follow J502 to HARDY and then J590 to Vancouver and then J5 to Seattle. Our instruments still seem to be functioning, but we would like to follow the coastline, just in case.*"

"*Roger that, 306, you are approved as requested,*" the Vancouver ATC controller replied. He breathed a sigh of relief. Although *306* might have an instrument problem, they already had a solution that seemed workable. There weren't that many other airplanes in the area at the moment, so he wasn't worried about re-routing the aircraft as requested.

"*Thank you, Vancouver Control,* Air China 306, *out.*"

359 Nautical Miles Northwest of Vancouver, Canada, 1252 Pacific Daylight Time

The pilot of *Air China 306* smiled at his co-pilot. "See?" he asked. "No problem. I told you it would work. Tell them you have a problem, but don't ask for any assistance. As long as they don't have to do any extra work, they're happy to let you do whatever you want."

Over their other radio, the co-pilot transmitted "*We are a 'go.'*" In reply he heard rapid transmissions of "*Two,*" "*Three,*" "*Four,*" "*Five,*" and "*Six*," as the other five aircraft acknowledged they had heard his call.

Looking at his instruments, all of which were functioning perfectly, the pilot saw they were running a little ahead of schedule. He pulled the throttles back slightly to compensate, and the Y-20 Kunpeng heavy lift aircraft slowed slightly. Looking over, he saw that his wingman was slowing down to match him. His wingman was close by and not radiating any of his electronics; he doubted Vancouver Control had any idea the second plane was even there. Nor were they supposed to.

Downtown Seattle, WA, 1300 Pacific Daylight Time

Section 333 of the Communications Act of 1934 states that 'No person shall willfully or maliciously interfere with or cause interference to the radio communications of any station.' This law prohibits the marketing or operation of cell phone jammers in the United States, except in the (very limited) context of official use by the federal government.

What the two *Henna* passengers were doing on top of the Renaissance Seattle Hotel, therefore, was illegal.

Private Lau Jie looked at his partner, Senior Sergeant Cheng Yong, as he set up the jammer. It was the fourth one they had placed so far. "How long do you think these will last?" he asked.

"I don't know," the senior sergeant replied, "but they will probably be found before too long."

"What is the point, then?" Private Lau Jie wanted to know. "These things are *heavy!* Surely Colonel Zhang knows that too?"

"Yes, he does," Senior Sergeant Cheng Yong replied; "in fact, he is planning on it. The Colonel thought it would be useful at the start for the American phone service to be cut off for a while, in order to create confusion and help keep everyone guessing about what was really going on in the area. It is good for operations security." He paused, connecting a wire, then added, "But after that, it is better to give them back their service."

"If that is the case," the private said, "why bother cutting it off at all?"

"Because, if the Americans do not have cell phone service, they can't upload photos of our tanks or troops to the internet and prove we are in Seattle," Senior Sergeant Cheng Yong answered. "If we keep the photos out of the news media for a while, the American government won't have as much information on our movements or order of battle, which will hamper them if they try to send in soldiers to stop us." He paused while he started the motor on the jammer, then continued, "There's no way that we could do away with all phone communications from the area, and even stopping cell phone coverage over the long term would be hard. Seattle has too many cell phone towers and other antennae. There are 900 registered antenna towers in the metropolitan area, and most of these carry cell phone traffic. If you add in all of the towers that would have to be disrupted in Tacoma, as well, it wouldn't be possible to take out all of the cell phone service long-term. However, if you only want to shut it off for, say, 10 hours or so, *that* is possible, which is why we're up here today."

He gestured to the northern part of the port. "The jammers we're placing will stop cell phone usage in this area, and then, once the

Erawan pulls into port, these jammers will be augmented with the heavy jammers the ship is carrying."

"Will the jammers make the Americans' phones explode?" the private asked.

"I wish they would," Senior Sergeant Cheng Yong said, "but they won't. They just send out stronger radio waves on the same frequencies the cell phones are using, overriding them. The interference disrupts the signal from the phone to the tower and the tower to the phone, rendering them unusable. In most cases, the cell phone owners won't even know their phones are being jammed; their phones will just look like there's no signal." He gestured to the city, "Right now, there are four other teams setting up jammers, just like we are. These little ones are 200 watt jammers, each of which will block out coverage within about 1/3 of a mile radius."

"They're not *that* little," the private complained. "I had to carry this one up here."

"Stop whining," the senior sergeant commanded, "it's only 70 pounds, so it's not that big. Besides," he said, standing up as he finished, "the view is outstanding!" From 29 stories up, the men had an excellent view of the city and could see much further than the seven block radius that no longer had cell phone service.

Softball Fields, Everett Naval Station, WA, 1300 Pacific Daylight Time

Commander Gao Qiang watched his teams getting ready to play while inspecting the rest of the naval base located to the south of the softball fields on Fletcher Way. Most of the naval bases he had seen in his career had been rather dingy affairs, built over long periods of time. While one style might have been in fashion when a base was first built, other styles came and went, usually leaving a mish-mash of building exteriors, in addition to the industrial look of warehouses and ship support facilities. As all major naval bases were built on salt water, rust was a constant enemy of any fleet, regardless of its nationality. Unless a lot of time and money was spent on upkeep, the facilities on the waterfront generally developed at least an orange-red patina of rust, if not a fullfledged case of it.

That wasn't the case with Everett Naval Station. Located on the west side of the city of Everett, Washington, the naval station's facilities were all built in the same style and painted the same colors. It gave a sense of peace and 'oneness' that most ports didn't have, appealing to his Buddhist senses. Judging by the plastic climbing structures in the fenced off area behind the building to his right, even the child care facility matched the rest of the naval station's edifices.

Laid out together on Fletcher Way, the two softball fields faced southwest and southeast with bleachers in between. Bleachers also lined Fletcher Way on the north side of the fields with a barracks facility to the south. On the other side of Fletcher Way, a parking lot supported both a marina across the street and the softball fields; part of it had been blocked off for their use.

It was a beautiful day for a game and, even though he didn't know much about the sport, he was looking forward to seeing how his teams performed. On the eastern field his "B" team was lining up against sailors from the USS *Ford*. Watching the Americans getting ready for the game, Commander Gao didn't think the contest would be much of a game. Even though fairly new to the game of softball, his team threw the ball with precision; the Americans looked more like they were playing "fetch" than "catch," as half of the pairs were retrieving overthrown balls at any given point. Perhaps they were just trying to make his team overconfident, Gao thought. They couldn't really be this bad at their own national sport, could they? Looking at them, he didn't think it was a ruse. Most of the players didn't look like athletes, including many who had pot-bellied stomachs.

It was a different story on the other field. The Americans there gave every indication of being proficient at the game. Two of the men on the team in particular were large and athletic, and they were going around to the others, watching them throw and correcting perceived flaws in their throwing motions. Noticing his interest in them, one of the Americans next to him started talking to him.

"You may win the game against the *Ford*," he said, "but you're going to lose this one. The *Shoup* team has two people on it who played college baseball. The captain of the team, Lieutenant Raul Espinosa, had a scholarship to Georgia Tech University to play baseball, until he hurt his shoulder and had to quit. The other guy, Petty Officer Brad Davis, played Division 3 college ball and then some semi-professional baseball in Texas before he decided to enlist in the Navy. They've been working with the guys the last couple of weeks. I don't think you have much of a chance against them."

"We shall see," Commander Gao replied. "Our sailors have been working very hard and hope to bring much honor to the People's Republic today. Baseball is not unknown in our country, and it has seen considerable growth since one of our players got hired to play professionally here." He looked at where the "A" team was warming up. Although they didn't have the physical size of the Americans, they threw the ball accurately and with good velocity. "You may be surprised."

The umpires arrived, and the teams moved to their respective benches. There were good crowds supporting the teams on both fields; Commander Gao knew the games had been highly advertised. He had seen trucks from several television stations in the parking lot earlier and didn't have to look far to see the camera crews in action. They were probably filming the public relations event for their nightly news, but he expected their stories would be...pre-empted. "The news will be very full tonight," Commander Gao told the man next to him with a chuckle.

The mayor of Everett walked out to the pitcher's mound of the western "A" field with the *Kunming's* Commanding Officer, Captain Tang Ping. The public relations people must be playing this up for all they are worth, thought Commander Gao as he noticed the wireless microphone in the mayor's hand. Looking around, he saw several speakers had been set up so everyone could hear what the mayor said.

"I would like to take this opportunity to welcome our guests from the People's Republic of China," Mayor Tom Green said. "We are very happy to have you visit our city. We hope you will have time to get out and see the sights while you are here; I know our folks have tried to line up some great tours for you. I'm looking forward to some good softball here today and have told our boys to be good hosts and not go too hard on you." He smiled as a few people in the stands chuckled at his joke.

He handed the microphone to Captain Tang, who knew a challenge when he heard one. "We are very happy to be here," he said. "Thank you very much for your gracious welcome and for arranging trips so my sailors can see all of your wonderful sights." He smiled.

"I, myself, hope to go many places and see many things while we are here."

"As some of you are aware," he continued, "the People's Republic just had our first baseball player, Peng Jun Jie, hired by an American team, the Mariners. What you may not know is that this has caused American baseball to grow in popularity in the People's Republic. Our teams have trained for this match and are looking forward to giving you our best efforts. Do not worry about going 'too hard' on us, for we will be doing everything possible to beat *you*. In fact, I would like to propose one of your American 'friendly wagers' to you on the outcome of the game on this field. Whoever's team loses has to take the winner out to dinner tomorrow night." He handed the mayor the microphone.

Commander Gao knew that this had been arranged earlier, so he wasn't surprised with the challenge, although he agreed with his Captain's annoyance. When the mayor had called the ship to welcome them, he had let it slip that he didn't think the Chinese had much of a chance to win the softball games, arousing the ire of his commanding officer. While neither Commander Gao nor Captain Tang knew much about the game, having had other things to attend to prior to their departure from the People's Republic of China, neither of them wanted to have the efforts of their men disrespected by someone from another country. Commander Gao looked forward to the mayor's disrespect being paid back in full, regardless of whether or not he had to take Captain Tang out to dinner.

"You're on!" the mayor said, acknowledging the bet. He smiled as if he could already taste his victory. "Now, if you would do the honors?"

"Certainly," Captain Tang said. Looking at the crowds gathered in the bleachers, he shouted, "Play ball!"

Seattle ARTCC, Seattle, WA, 1300 PDT

"Good afternoon, sir," LCDR Lin said to the portly gate guard who met them at the security checkpoint as they turned into the ATC facility. "We are here to see Mrs. Barbara Morgan, the Air Traffic Manager. Along with the van behind us, we are the group from the Chinese ship *Long*. I believe we are expected." He handed the guard his ID.

The guard looked at his clipboard. "Yes, you are," he said. "Please park in the lot to the left and go to the main door. I will have someone meet you there."

They parked the vans in the indicated lot and walked to the door of the facility, where they were met by a tall, brunette woman who appeared to be in her early 50s.

"Welcome," the woman said. "I'm Barbara Morgan, Seattle Center's Air Traffic Manager. In this position, I am responsible for air traffic control throughout the northwestern United States. Our airspace encompasses nearly 300,000 square miles, including all of the state of Washington, most of Oregon, and portions of Montana, Idaho, Nevada and California. We have nine different approach control facilities, a Class B airport in Seattle, and four Class C airfields at Fairchild Air Force Base, Whidbey Island Naval Air Station, Portland International and Spokane International. We also have about 25 smaller Class D airfields that have tower facilities and 15 Class E airfields that don't."

"Wow," LCDR Lin said, bowing. "I think we've come to the right place to find out everything we need to know about air traffic control in the area."

"Yes," Mrs. Morgan said with a laugh, "indeed you have." She turned to the guard who was stationed at the door and picked up their visitor badges. She looked at the 11 people in front of her and frowned. "I was under the impression there would be eight of you; six naval personnel and two civilian wives, but it seems you brought five women."

LCDR Lin nodded. "When the wives of our sailors told their friends there would be single men with their husbands, several of them asked to join us. It was nice for them to be able to speak Chinese to single men again." He bowed. "It is my fault for not telling them "no." As a military man, I understand completely about security, especially in so important a facility. If they are unable to join us due to your regulations, I will simply have them wait in the cars; it is no problem."

Mrs. Morgan considered his request for a moment before saying, "No, that's okay. It is a warm day out, and I'd hate to make them wait in the car." She turned to the guard and asked for three more badges.

"Thank you very much," LCDR Lin said. "I greatly appreciate it."

As she handed out the badges, Mrs. Morgan told them, "These IDs must be kept in plain sight and worn somewhere between your hips and chin. Security is very important in the facility and is ensured by a variety of cipher locks and personal IDs. Because of this, you *must* be accompanied by a Federal Aviation Administration employee at all times; everyone must stay with the group. This is a bigger group than we normally give tours to; please help me out by paying attention and staying close."

LCDR Lin looked at the group and nodded. "We will," he said.

"I also need all of you to turn off your cell phones for the time you are here," the facility manager instructed. "We will be seeing some sensitive electronic equipment on the tour and stray emissions could literally have catastrophic effects."

LCDR Lin nodded as he turned off his cell phone. "We have the same policies," he said with a smile. "It will be quite satisfactory to have everyone's cell phones off while we are here."

"Thank you," she said, smiling back. She opened a cipher-locked door. "If you would follow me, I will show you the facility, and then we can talk about how to integrate your aircraft into our system."

Softball Fields, Everett Naval Station, WA, 1325 Pacific Daylight Time

Many friends and families had come out to support the American teams, and about 150 Chinese nationals had driven up from the SAIC factory in Tacoma. The alcohol was flowing, as many of the Americans had brought coolers of beer to the fields. One enterprising group of sailors from the USS *Ford* had gone so far as to bring a keg to the game, which was matched on the Chinese side by the 20-foot U-Haul truck the SAIC men had used to bring their own drinks and snacks. While Commander Gao was greatly in favor of the Americans drinking as much as they wanted, he was monitoring the alcohol intake of his men to ensure they didn't overindulge. While almost all of his sailors carried around cups or cans of beer, so they would appear to be enjoying the festivities, most either sipped them or dumped them out when they went to the bathroom. There also seemed to be an unusually high incidence of beers getting accidentally knocked over. Commander Gao was sure it appeared everyone was having a good time.

He smiled. His teams were doing as well as he could have hoped. Although only a couple of innings into the game, both of his teams had leads on their American rivals. At 8-1, his "B" team already had a good lead on the sailors from the USS *Ford*, who were lucky to have scored that one run. A walk, followed by an error by the *Kunming's* shortstop, had put an American runner on third base, where he had been driven in by the only well-hit ball so far by the *Ford* sailors. The ball was caught in center field, but it was deep enough for the runner to return to the base and score after the ball was caught. Commander Gao expected continued success on that field, especially since a couple of the USS *Ford* outfielders had started carrying their beers with them to the outfield. The Americans didn't seem to be trying too hard to win; if anything, it almost looked like they were going out of their way to lose. They did, however, give every impression they were having a lot of fun.

It was a different story on the western field, where his "A" team clung to a narrow 3-2 lead. The two players from the USS *Shoup* who had played college baseball were much more serious about the game and were exhorting their comrades to do their best. They had also scored both of their team's runs. Already down 3-0 in the bottom of the first inning, Petty Officer Davis had hit a triple that bounced off the fence in center field. Although he probably could have scored, he was held at third base because their team captain, Lieutenant Espinosa, was up next. LT Espinosa got the pitch he was looking for and hit the ball so far it not only cleared the left field fence, but put out a window on the first floor of the barracks next to the field. Their pitcher would have to be a lot more careful with them the rest of the game, thought Commander Gao, if they were going to have a chance at winning.

Seattle ARTCC, Seattle, WA, 1330 Pacific Daylight Time

"Thanks," John Thomas said, as his relief sat down at his radar console. "I really need to hit the head." Despite having left the U.S. Navy five years previously, the former special operations air traffic controlman still used the word "head" to mean a bathroom. A former Senior Chief, his orders were terminated early in the sequestration process as the Navy looked for easy ways to trim billions of dollars from its budget. He had retired to Seattle to get away from it all, and he had picked up a job at the ARTCC to make some extra money. With 21 years of guiding aircraft to targets in a high-stress environment (i.e., one where people were actively trying to kill you), he found the environment of an air traffic control facility to be far less stressful than most of the other people who worked there.

John walked out of the dark radar room, holding the door for a large group of visitors walking in. He recognized the Chinese naval uniforms on the six men—one officer and five enlisted, he noted automatically. They were accompanied by five women, who also looked Asian. He remembered hearing the Chinese Navy was in town and decided they must be spying on the American air traffic control system. The Chinese Navy personnel were probably still learning how to operate the new aircraft carrier they had just put into service. He held the door for them and then shut it securely, forgetting the visitors as his original purpose reasserted itself.

Returning to the radar room, John opened the door to find a woman holding a gun to the site manager's head. As his eyes scanned the room, he saw that all of the women visitors had drawn pistols from their bags, and some of them were arming the men in uniform, as well. "If I could please have everyone's attention," the uniformed Chinese officer said in a loud voice. "You are now open under new management. I require nothing more from you than to continue to do your jobs. Please know that the men and women around you are experienced air traffic controllers who know your procedures. Anyone who tries to give out warnings over the radio will be shot. Anyone that doesn't do what they're told will be shot. Just do your jobs, like you normally would, and you will all be released unharmed at the end of your shift. I give you my word—"

He stopped suddenly as he saw John standing open-mouthed in the doorway. Reacting instantly with combat-trained reflexes, John dove back out the door and started running up the corridor. He heard the door slam back open as someone came after him.

John ran around the corner and stopped at the bathroom. He had never understood why it needed a cipher lock since they were already behind cipher-locked doors (was someone worried about him taking a classified bowel movement?), but he thought that he could use it to his advantage. He quickly worked the combination and slipped inside; unfortunately, a Chinese woman came around the corner and saw him before he could shut the door.

He knew he'd been seen; he didn't have much time. He pulled out his phone and turned it on. The woman began beating on the door, and the phone's boot-up seemed to take forever. It became ominously quiet outside as the phone finally reached the "ready" screen. A hole appeared in the lock mechanism as he dialed his friend's number, and he heard a bullet ricochet past him. Damn, he thought, they've got silencers too. So much for attracting the attention of the guard downstairs. This obviously wasn't his lucky day.

A second and third hole appeared while the phone dialed. There was a pause from outside the door as the line connected, followed by a slam as the woman kicked the door. Perspiration appeared at his temples; John could tell the door wouldn't take more than another kick or two before it gave. Finally, he heard "Hello?" He'd never been so happy to hear a man's voice.

"Ryan," he said, "it's John." The door gave way as it was kicked again, and the woman walked through the doorway. The way she moved, and the ease with which she had defeated the door told John that she was a professional. "We need your help. The Chinese are at the facility and we've been taken over—" His pleas ended in a grunt as the woman fired three shots from her silenced pistol, two to his chest and one to his forehead.

The woman picked up the phone from where it had fallen on the floor. "Honey," she said in a voice she knew would be heard on the other end, "you're drunk. Quit fooling around and come back to bed." She purred. "That's better…"

She ended the call before the person on the other end could ask any questions. Placing it on the floor, she stomped it into hundreds of tiny, and very inoperable, pieces.

Pier D, Naval Base Kitsap, WA, 1345 Pacific Daylight Time

The party was in full swing in the Officer's Mess onboard the PLAN amphibious assault ship *Long*. The Mess was a large dining room where the ship's officers normally ate their meals; for the evening's festivities, all the tables had been moved to the perimeter or removed to create enough space for the attendees.

The American guests had arrived between 1300 and 1315, as requested, except for Governor Shelby and his wife. Typical American politician, thought Admiral Zhao Na; the governor had to be late, just to show he could. It would not affect their timeline as they had planned for the delay; in fact, based on his experience with American politicians, he had expected it! Everything was well within tolerances when the governor showed up at 1330. In attendance were the staff of Navy Region, Northwest, the commanding officer of Naval Base Kitsap, Senator George Shelby, Representative Matt Bennett and all of their spouses. The only person who didn't make it was the executive officer of Naval Base Kitsap, who had a fever of 102 degrees and had stayed home in bed.

Admiral Zhao tapped a spoon to his glass to get everyone's attention. "Ladies and gentlemen," he said, "welcome to the Dragon, which is what *Long* means in our language. Thank you very much for coming to our party. My officers and I are very happy you were able to make it here this afternoon. As many of you know, the *Long* is the newest ship in our Navy and one that we are very proud of. I'm sure there has been a lot of discussion in the United States about the capabilities of this ship, as I've already had many people ask me about different aspects of its ability to project power ashore. I'm happy to tell you our senior military council has authorized me to give you a demonstration of some of its capabilities." Admiral Barnaby looked at his intelligence officer, Captain Jim Spence, raising his eyebrows in anticipation. Admiral Zhao continued, "If you will all follow me topside, I think you will find this demonstration very exciting."

He walked out of the Mess and led all of the guests up the three flights of stairs to the aft end of the flight deck. Four Z-10 attack helicopters and two Z-8 heavy transport helicopters already had their rotors spinning on the forward half of the flight deck. As the guests watched, 70 troops with full combat gear and rifles came running out of the ship's superstructure and sprinted to the waiting Z-8 helicopters, which lifted off and flew away to the north. Seconds later, the four Z-10 helicopters also lifted off, headed toward the northwest. As the noise of the rotors faded into the distance, the guests could hear and feel motors operating at the aft end of the ship. Walking to the stern, the guests were surprised to look down and see the back of the ship had been lowered. They were even more surprised when four landing craft, each loaded with a tank, came shooting out of the well deck. The landing craft were followed by six additional tanks that came swimming out of the well deck on their own. Three of them turned to the left, and the other three turned to the right.

Coming ashore near Wycoff Way, the three tanks that went to the left turned around and pointed their guns at the submarines nested together to the east of Pier B. The three that went right also came ashore near Wycoff Way and turned and pointed their guns at the aircraft carriers tied up to the piers.

As the tanks came to a halt, armed men began racing down the gangway toward the pier, while more armed men began issuing forth from the ship's superstructure and running toward the group at the stern of the ship.

"That's all very impressive," Admiral Barnaby said, looking somewhat nervously at the display of Chinese power, "but where are those helicopters going?"

Admiral Zhao smiled. "They are going to capture the nuclear weapons storage facility at Bangor and sink all of the submarines there. After all of the planning and practice they've put into this, it should be quite exciting for them to actually get to do it for real."

"You're joking!" Admiral Barnaby gasped, "You can't be serious! That would be an act of war!"

"Of course it is an act of war," Admiral Zhao said, looking at his watch. "It is now 1410 and we have been at war for 10 minutes already." He nodded to the soldiers surrounding the Americans, their weapons drawn, and laughed. "It would seem that so far you are losing quite badly."

He addressed the lieutenant leading the troops. "I believe our guests have had enough fresh air for now. Take them below to their new quarters." He looked back to Admiral Barnaby. "These men have been ordered to shoot you the first time you look like you are going to do something stupid. You don't even have to do it; you just have to look like you're contemplating it. Don't test them. Just go where they direct you, relax, and you will live to see your families again. If you do otherwise, *you will die.*"

Terminal 91, Port of Seattle, Seattle, WA, 1350 Pacific Daylight Time

Major Chin Haung stood at the side rail of the China Navigation Company's *M.V. Erawan* bulk freighter and surveyed the pier. With both the freighter *Era-*

wan and the car carrier *Xin Qing Dao* on the west side of the pier, and the Holland Cruise Line ship *M.V. Oosterdam* on the east side of the pier, it was very crowded, with people milling about its entire length. Neither of the two Chinese ships had cleared Customs yet. The massive car carrier *Xin Qing Dao* had pulled in first. Its crew hadn't had any problems tying up, but they hadn't been able to get the ship's gangway mounted and secured to allow the Customs inspector aboard. Major Chin could see the Customs agent on the pier with a briefcase, no doubt full of the interminable American forms. He looked more and more annoyed as time went by.

Appearing to give up on the *Xin Qing Dao*, he started walking down the pier to the *Erawan*, frowning slightly as he looked up and saw the rotors on the helicopter on the bow of the ship start to turn. Waving his hands as he ran toward the gangway onto the *Erawan*, he yelled, "You can't do that! You haven't cleared Customs yet!"

Major Chin moved to intercept him at the end of the gangway. As the Customs agent ran aboard, still yelling, the major grabbed him by the front of his shirt, jerked him out of sight and slammed him into a wall, stunning him. He shoved his pistol under the Customs agent's chin. "What were you saying we couldn't do?" he asked.

The agent's eyes grew large in shock and fear. "I…um…you can't…um…not cleared Customs…" he mumbled.

Major Chin waved the five special forces soldiers forward from where they had been standing out of sight. "Go!" he said. Dressed in merchant marine sailors' clothes, they walked off the ship as if they had every right to be doing so. They did not appear to be armed and they weren't…aside from the knives they had in scabbards up their sleeves.

"Take this man and put him in the brig," the major said to the other soldiers waiting there. Having turned the Customs agent over to the soldiers, Major Chin immediately forgot about him and went back to the rail to watch the progress of his troops. As planned, they fanned out and proceeded down the pier, stopping in the vicinity of the five security guards at the end. When they were all in position, he gave them a simple command of "Go" over the radio. Within seconds, all five members of the port security were down, with the soldiers assuming their positions.

Looking at the men assembled behind him, he said, "We have bowed before the Americans for too long. Now is our time for revenge. Attack!" The wave of men rushed forward.

Softball Fields, Everett Naval Station, WA, 1355 Pacific Daylight Time

"This is almost too much fun," Commander Gao Qiang said to his operations officer as he watched the softball game on the western field. The executive officer of *Kunming* had just checked the score of the other game, and he knew both of his teams were winning with only a couple of innings to play.

"Yes, sir," Lieutenant Commander Wong Chao, his operations officer, replied. "I will be sorry to leave and miss the ending."

On the eastern of the two fields, the Chinese "B" team was easily handling the team from the USS *Ford*, and was ahead 17-5. He didn't expect the score would get any closer, as several members of the Ford team were visibly intoxicated. On the western field, though, the game was very much in doubt. The Chinese were only ahead by a run, leading 8-7. The two college baseball players on the USS *Shoup* team continued to make a difference; their leadership and the instructions they were giving their teammates were both paying dividends. With two more innings to play, the Americans might very well come back and win, as both of their marquis players had already hit home runs in the game and would be coming up to bat again at least one more time.

LT Espinosa had hit four balls over the fence so far, although two of them had been foul. In an effort to reduce his effectiveness, the *Kunming's* pitcher had started throwing LT Espinosa pitches on the very outside portion of the plate so he couldn't pull them as easily. LT Espinosa had retaliated by switching sides of the plate after two pitches in his last at bat. The pitcher, who had never seen this before, was caught unaware. He threw the same pitch, now on the inside of the plate, to LT Espinosa, who crushed it into the play yard of the day care center beyond the right field fence. The line drive was going so fast it would surely have killed a young child if it had hit one; fortunately, it was Sunday afternoon, and the yard was vacant.

As he watched the game on the western field, Commander Gao silently agreed with his operations officer; it would have been nice to watch the last couple of innings of the "A" game. The cell phone the Americans had given him buzzed, confirming that his time had run out. It was nice that Everett was over 15 miles away from downtown Seattle, he thought, so they could still use the phones. And, although they might very well have been bugged, it was nice of the Americans to give them the phones in the first place to coordinate their attack plans. He answered the phone to find his commanding officer on the line.

"We need you back at the ship," the CO said, giving him the code phrase that meant they were a "go."

"I'm on my way," he replied.

Looking at the field, he saw the teams were changing sides. Commander Gao waved to the Chinese stands. "Let's go get a beer while they change," he said in English.

About 40 men joined him in walking over to the U-Haul. It was turned so no one could see the men removing the fake wall in the interior, exposing the racks of Chinese assault rifles behind it.

Naval Station Bangor, WA, 1358 Pacific Daylight Time

The four Z-10 Fierce Thunderbolt attack helicopters swept in on the unsuspecting submarine base from the south. Each of the helicopters mounted a 25mm M242 Bushmaster chain gun the Chinese had reverse-engineered and adapted for helicopter use. Developed to defeat the frontal armor of Western tanks, the auto-cannons on the helicopters devastated the submarines in port as they flew up the coast, stopping at every pier to destroy the submarine tied up there. They spent extra time on the submarine in the dry dock at the Delta Pier, as it would be the easiest to repair since it was out of the water. Not only did they shred it with their chain guns, they also fired two HJ-10 anti-tank missiles that left immense holes in its side. Similar to the U.S. AGM-114 Hellfire missile, the missiles were equipped with high-explosive anti-tank (HEAT) warheads to defeat modern tank armor; they were equally effective on the hull of a submarine. The helicopters swept past, leaving the shredded submarines in their wake.

Having completed the easiest part of their mission, they turned back south toward a building standing by itself in the middle of a huge pock-marked field. Just as Fort Knox was once the repository for America's gold reserves, Bangor was the repository for almost one-quarter of America's nearly 10,000 nuclear weapons, and the pockmarks in the field each represented a storage silo for a nuclear weapon. This made it the largest nuclear weapons storehouse in the United States, and possibly the world. Over 2,300 nuclear warheads were housed at Bangor for the Trident ballistic missiles and Tomahawk cruise missiles carried by its submarines. While the overwhelming majority of these were the 100 kiloton yield W76 warheads for the Trident II missiles in use on the *Ohio*-class ballistic missile submarines, there were also 264 W88 warheads at the facility. The most sophisticated weapon in the U.S. nuclear stockpile, the W88 had a yield of 475 kilotons, nearly thirty times greater than the atomic bomb used on Hiroshima.

As the Z-10 helicopters came to a hover around the building, the two Z-8 helicopters approached from the south. They landed close by and troops spilled out of both sides. Rather than go with finesse, the lead helicopter positioned itself in front of the building's door. The troops stayed back as the Bushmaster on its nose started to spin and then fired 20 rounds through the door, ripping it from its hinges and killing the two sailors stationed behind it. "*We're in,*" said the leader of the ground forces over his tactical radio as the troops began to pour into the building.

Beijing, China, 0459 China Standard Time (1359 Pacific Daylight Time)

Lieutenant Colonel (LTC) Huang Mong cracked his knuckles and grinned in anticipation. LTC Huang was the Brigade Commander of the 1st Hacker's Brigade, a clandestine arm of the People's Liberation Army, which was tasked with probing and penetrating enemies' computer networks during peacetime, in preparation for assaulting them during war. A veteran of over 20 years of computer hacking, he was looking forward to the crowning achievement of his life—the complete shutdown of the United States' power supply system.

He and the men and women under him had been probing the cyber defenses of the United States for many years and had established a presence in a huge number of computers throughout the U.S., both military and civilian. It was laughable how lax the Americans' computer security was, he thought. By simply typing in a wife's name or child's birthday (both of which were easily accessible on Facebook and other social media sites), you could easily break many peoples' passwords and, once into one system, you were often able to breach some of the systems connected to it.

That was how he had gained access into the computer network of power distribution giant Entergy, where he had shut down the lights during Super Bowl XLVII. He had originally planned to turn off the lights of the Louisiana Superdome right at the start of the game, but somebody noticed his original backdoor into the system and closed it the day prior. After nearly 24 hours of constant work, his team was close to penetrating it again at the start of the game, but it wasn't until just after halftime they finally broke back into the system. Even then, someone noticed their attack as soon as they started turning off the power to the Superdome. The unknown administrator had kicked them back out of the system, and they had only been able to turn off half of the lights in the stadium. Huang appreciated the administrator's efforts, even if he was chastised for allowing it to happen, and had made a copy of the tricks the administrator had used to prepare for today's attack.

The most annoying thing about the preempted Super Bowl attack was that, coming just after halftime as it did, the American politicians were able to say that the mega-star's flashy performance at halftime had over-taxed the Superdome's circuitry, causing the failure. Not only did he not get any credit for the attack, most Americans were blithely unaware one had even taken place. Even his cousin, a customs inspector in Seattle, didn't know he had been responsible for the power failure.

That wouldn't be the case today.

He laughed as he thought about the times he had allowed himself to get caught by cyber security as he probed their systems—the fools thought they had stopped him, but they had only stopped what he had allowed them to see. His finger poised over the "Enter" key, he was ready to make the lights go out all over the United States. By causing spikes throughout the country, he hoped to fry the Americans' transformers and circuit breakers. He would then use the cascading failures and additional spikes to take down the rest of the power net in the United States. He wasn't sure how long it would last or how far he would get, but if he could black out the key military and civilian nodes, he would be very happy. Others in his unit would take down internet servers, communications facilities and banking networks. It was a very organized cyber attack, the likes of which the world had never seen.

He counted down, "Three."

"Two."

"One."

"Lights out! This is it! Take them all down now!"

His men and women began typing on their keyboards, and systems began to fail all across the United States and throughout the rest of the world. LTC Huang looked at his monitor, smiled, and pressed the key that would unleash his own brand of chaos. He had named his program, 'Anarchy.'

Terminal 46, Port of Seattle, Seattle, WA, 1359 Pacific Daylight Time

Similar to ongoing events at the *M.V. Erawan*, the Customs inspector boarding China Ocean Shipping Company's *M.V. Hanjin Kingston* was also met with a pistol to the head and escorted below. 856 feet in length, the huge container ship had just docked at the southern end of Terminal 46 in downtown Seattle. The *Hanjin Kingston* was similar to the *Erawan* in that it had gone through a similar modification process. Although it still looked like a container ship from the outside, complete with several hundred 53' containers stacked along its deck, its interior had been modified to carry troops, in this case the 1st and 2nd Battalions of the 144th Mechanized Infantry Division's 489th Mechanized Regiment.

Like the soldiers of the 372nd Amphibious Regiment onboard the PLAN *Long*, these soldiers were members of the 42nd Group Army, and it was not the first time the unit had the fought Americans. The 42nd Army had been part of the initial Chinese force that crossed the Yalu River in October of 1950 to help defend North Korea, and it had fought the United States' Eighth Army for the next two years.

Unable to defeat the Americans in the Korean War, the members of the 42nd Army were hoping for a better showing this time.

First off the ship were the men and women of the 1st Battalion of the 489th Mechanized Regiment. The 1,000 men and women of the battalion were organized into six operational companies of about 150 soldiers each, as well as a Headquarters Company that oversaw the operations of the battalion. Having practiced disembarking the ship many times during their preparations for the operation, the soldiers quickly formed up and began leaving the pier area at a jog; the lone exception was Company A, which dispersed throughout the pier area to set up a perimeter and provide security.

The first company to form up, Company B, went immediately to the southern end of the port facility where the United States Coast Guard Cutter *Midgett* (WHEC-726) was docked. Most of the 24 officers and 160 enlisted crewmen were not onboard at the time, and the duty section sailors onboard were completely unprepared for the 150 soldiers who swarmed aboard. Immortalized on the cover of the 1979 Jefferson Starship album *Freedom at Point Zero*, the *Midgett* was built to enforce fisheries and drug interdiction laws. Its sailors weren't armed, and it was captured without loss of life on either side; overwhelmed by the heavily-armed Chinese soldiers, the crew of the *Midgett* surrendered without firing a shot.

The soldiers of Companies C and D proceeded south past the *Midget*. Company C attacked the Coast Guard Station Headquarters building, while the men and women of Company D continued down the Coast Guard pier to where the Coast Guard Cutter *Healy* waited. The soldiers of Company C quickly overran the duty personnel in the drab, gray concrete building and secured it without loss of life. Unarmed and unexpectedly faced with an overwhelming number of armed soldiers, the Coast Guard personnel could do nothing but put their hands up in surrender.

Several of the *Healy*'s crew witnessed the Chinese assault on the *Midgett* from across the narrow inlet between the piers, so the *Healy*'s sailors were marginally better prepared to withstand the assault force than the crew of the *Midgett*. Unfortunately, 'marginally better prepared' only meant that they had 30 seconds notice rather than none at all. Even worse, the *Healy* was an unarmed polar icebreaker, and it had neither been designed nor equipped to repel boarders, especially heavily-armed ones who outnumbered its crew. The crew's acts of defiance were limited to trying to pull up its gangway so that the Chinese troops couldn't get onboard and locking its exterior doors while the crewmen and scientists onboard tried to call for help.

Despite the limited amount of preparation time, the crew almost succeeded in detaching the gangway from the ship before the Chinese soldiers arrived; however, they were forced to stop when one of the Chinese riflemen fired a warning shot past the crewmen's heads. The sound of the ricochet whining off the side of the hull was sufficient to stop all efforts, and the Chinese troops quickly came aboard. One of the Chinese soldiers carried a number of breaching charges; it did not take him long to blow open one of the doors, and the soldiers quickly infiltrated the interior of the ship. Although the crew completed several phone calls before the Chinese burst in on them, the calls were made to the Coast Guard Station offices, which were already in Chinese hands. The crew of the *Healy* did not succeed in raising the alarm.

While the 1st Battalion secured the Coast Guard facilities to the south, the 300 soldiers of Companies A and B of the 2nd Battalion got into the 30 black vans prepositioned at the pier for their use and proceeded out of the port facility. Heading east on South Atlantic Street, they made good time to 1st Avenue, with Company E of the 1st Battalion stopping traffic for them in the first two blocks. Reaching 1st Avenue, the convoy diverged, and ten vans continued east onto Edgar Martinez Dr., while the other 20 turned left onto 1st Avenue. Ten of those vans stopped in the first block of 1st Avenue, while the other ten turned right at the first light onto Royal Brougham Way, where they stopped. As the last vehicle moved into position, a signal was given, and soldiers began exiting the vehicles simultaneously.

Captain Ma Gang, the company commander of Company A, 2nd of the 489th, paused as he got out of his van and surveyed his surroundings. There were quite a few people on the sidewalks who stopped and stared at the large number of armed, Asian men getting out of identical vehicles, as well as the two other companies who could be seen coming around the corner at a jog. Some appeared concerned, while others looked quizzical, wondering if they were in the middle of a movie scene being filmed. Some, correctly, even looked frightened and started moving away from the heavily-armed men. None, however, seemed to be a threat to his ongoing operation. How these people became world leaders was beyond him, the captain thought.

Shrugging, he turned back to his objective. He could hear the cheering from inside as he marched toward the gates of Safeco Field, home of the Seattle Mariners.

Terminal 30, Port of Seattle, Seattle, WA, 1359 Pacific Daylight Time

The China Shipping Container Lines freighter *M.V. Xin Beijing* pulled into Terminal 30, where it normally offloaded. Over 1,100 feet long and carrying 7,450 containers, the *Xin Beijing* was one of China Shipping Container Lines' biggest container ships. In addition to the containers on its deck, it also carried the 3rd and 4th Battalions of the 489th Mechanized Regiment.

As a mechanized force, the two battalions were normally equipped with armored personnel carriers and infantry fighting vehicles for transport and combat. For this operation, though, there was no easy way for them to be reunited with their combat transportation, nor were there enough of the black GAC vans available for them to use; beyond a mere handful for emergency use, all of them were gainfully employed elsewhere. The initial planning stages had taken this possibility into account and had devised an alternate means of transportation.

While Companies A and B of the 3rd Battalion provided security around the port facility, the engineers went to the southern portion of the port, hot-wired the semi-truck cabs staged at the port and drove them back to where the ship had tied up. As each container came off the ship, it was attached to a cab and loaded with troops, for the solution to the transportation problem had been to make modified containers. A simple and elegant solution, each container had the combat seating used in transport aircraft mounted to both sides of its interior. There was enough room for a platoon of troops to sit on the webbing on each side of the container, with room in the center of the container between the two platoons for the soldiers' packs.

The containers were quickly unloaded from the ship, with the troops waiting in formation on the pier. As each container was attached to its cab, it was loaded with two platoons of soldiers and sent on its way. The trucks were able to negotiate the Seattle roadways faster than their APCs would have, while blending in with the normal traffic. The 3rd and 4th Battalions of the 489th Mechanized Regiment deployed to their positions throughout Seattle without anyone even knowing they were coming.

White House State Dining Room, Washington, DC, 1700 EDT (1400 PDT)

As could be expected at a State Dinner, the food had been outstanding, Chinese Ambassador Fung Qiang noted. The Chinese had coordinated with the United States for it to be a traditional American "supper" with the first course starting promptly at 1600. Right on schedule, the d'Anjou pears with farmstead goat cheese, fennel, black walnuts and white balsamic had been served at 1601, followed by the second course of poached Maine lobster with orange glazed carrots and black trumpet mushrooms at 1620. After a palette cleansing lemon sorbet, the main course of dry aged rib eye with buttermilk crisp onions, double stuffed potatoes and creamed spinach was served at 1640. The ambassador had to laugh at the irony of the wine choice served with the main course, a 2005 Quilceda Creek cabernet 'Columbia Valley;' the winery was located in Snohomish, Washington…just a couple of miles to the north of Seattle. They probably wouldn't be getting many more bottles of this label for a while, he thought with a grin.

It was a shame the Chinese President couldn't have been here, the ambassador thought; he would have savored the irony. As planned, though, he had "fallen ill" earlier that morning and canceled the rest of the morning's and afternoon's scheduled events. He hadn't even been able to make the State Dinner planned in his honor; the ambassador was attending in his place. The president couldn't have attended the dinner; he wasn't in the country anymore. He had snuck out of the embassy and onto an Air China flight earlier that morning. He was already more than halfway home, well out of reach of any American retribution. Of course, that left everything to fall on the ambassador's shoulders, but he found himself curiously looking forward to the role he had to play in today's events. Over the course of history, there were very few people who had the opportunity to say and do what he intended.

The dessert was just being served at 1700 when the lights went out. There was a short scream, and a crash as a platter of old-fashioned apple pie with vanilla ice cream dishes hit the floor. After the space of a heartbeat more, the backup generators came to life and normal lighting was restored.

Standing up, the ambassador got the attention of the President of the United States and said simply, "Mr. President it is my duty to let you know we are at war."

United States of America, 1400 Pacific Daylight Time

The power failed at 1400.

It didn't matter where you were; if you were using anything electrical at 1400 Pacific Daylight Time, it stopped working within a few seconds of that time. A few areas that were not attached to the power grids of the United States continued to function, but for more than 93% of the people in the United States, the power went out at 1400. People in Canada fared slightly better, as only 64% of Canadian citizens lost power, largely because Canada was far more rural than the United States. If you lived in one of the major metropolitan areas like Toronto, Montreal or Ottawa, the power ceased at 1400. Vancouver, British Columbia, located 140 miles to the north of Seattle, was particularly hard hit; almost all of its citizens lost both power and landline phone service, as well.

For people within the electricity generation and distribution industries, this outage was not as much of a surprise as many others might have thought. With electricity usage skyrocketing for the past couple of decades, the aging electrical infrastructure was ripe to fail, as had been noted in the aftermath of many super storms that rocked portions of the United States. In many cases, it had been weeks (and sometimes months) before the power was restored to all of the customers in the affected areas.

Politicians had discussed fixing the system for a long time, but hadn't made any substantive progress. In 2007, President Bush signed legislation to modernize the energy grid, and a little improvement was made during the initial years of the Obama administration. Then sequestration hit, and the money needed to make significant progress was siphoned off to prop up Medicare, Social Security and a variety of other entitlement programs. The electrical power distribution system was on its last legs, prone to failure and unable to support itself. It could not withstand the knockout punch the cyber warriors gave it.

In 2009, national security officials stated publicly that the U.S. electrical grid had been penetrated by agents of China, Russia and other countries. The officials believed the spies had mapped out the power grid and were well aware of both the critical nodes, and what it would take to knock them out. Although the potential saboteurs hadn't damaged the system, they had left behind software programs, some of which security officials later found. It was surmised, correctly, that these programs would be used in the event of a war to turn off portions of the U.S. power grid. While American officials worried periodically in the press about attackers taking control of electrical facilities, especially nuclear power plants, behind closed doors they worried non-stop.

They had already seen catastrophic examples of what was possible. In 2000, a water treatment plant in Australia was rigged by a disgruntled employee to release over 200,000 gallons of sewage into nearby parks and rivers, and onto the grounds of a major hotel. In 2008, the power equipment in several regions of Brazil was compromised by cyber attack, with extortion demands for ransom sent to officials shortly thereafter. With over 70,000 cyber security breaches occurring yearly in the United States, it wasn't a matter of 'if' the power grids would be compromised; it was only a matter of 'when.'

Congress had spent billions in secret funding to try to protect government networks. They didn't spend enough.

Washington State Convention Center, Seattle, WA 1400 Pacific Daylight Time

The power went out at almost exactly 1400 on Captain Liu Fang's watch. Along with the lights, the air conditioning also shut off, leaving the main conference hall not only dark but quiet. After a very brief pause, just long enough for people to start to talk nervously, the emergency generators fired up, and the lights and air conditioning came back on. The Guangzhou People's Symphony Orchestra had ceased playing about 15 minutes prior and had stacked all of their instruments in the back of the conference room near the Skybridge over Pike St. The orchestra had then gone into rooms 4C-3 and 4C-4 to change. Captain Liu had listened to them playing earlier and had been very surprised; they were actually quite good, far better than he would have expected under the circumstances.

In fact, all aspects of the conference had gone very smoothly (including his own lecture on overcoming language barriers in international trade), and he expected that, had the conference ended at 1350, most of the attendees would have gone home with good memories of the conference, as well as a lot of good information learned from it. Up to this point, there was no indication the conference was anything other than what it seemed; the lectures and round table discussions were all well-attended and had the right people moderating them. There was certainly no lack of exhibitors; all the available space was taken up with a variety of new import automobiles, as well as foreign automakers' new concept cars. He saw several he hoped would be sold in China in the near future; assuming he survived the next couple of weeks, he wanted one!

Liu surveyed the room from the front podium. The divider between main conference rooms 4A and 4B had been removed, turning it into a massive 80,000 square foot room. At the moment, it was filled with over 3,000 conference attendees, sponsors, and a variety of other support and staff people, who had come to hear the keynote address. In an effort to get the maximum attendance possible, Liu had ensured the conference's program specified that all of the exhibitors and vendors would have to close their displays and shops at 1345, and had sent around security to make certain they had.

Looking at the first couple of rows, he saw the chief executive officers (CEOs) of several foreign automakers, the CEO and chief financial officer of the Ford Motor Company and the CEO of General Motors. Ford had been trying very hard recently to expand its market share in China (with over a billion citizens, it was a huge market American automobile manufacturers *still* had not made any inroads into), and all of the Ford brass had come to the conference to score as many points as possible with not only his company, but also with the rest of the Chinese automakers represented.

Tapping on the microphone to get everyone's attention, Liu said, "It appears power has been restored, so if everyone will please take your seats, we will get started." He waited a couple of moments until the room quieted and then stared pointedly at the Ford CEO, who was talking loudly and animatedly with a representative in the row behind him. Eventually, someone tapped him on the shoulder, and he turned around and focused on Liu. If he felt in any way chastised for holding up the other 2,999 people, he did not give any indication of it.

"I would like to thank you very much for coming," Liu said. "More effort than you know has been put into the preparations for this conference." He looked to the back of the room and saw the members of the orchestra coming out of their changing rooms, now dressed in camouflage uniforms and holding Chinese assault rifles. "Unfortunately," he added, "it is time for the conference to come to an end. While many of you know me as Mr. Liu Fang, my real name is *Captain* Liu Fang of the special forces of the People's Republic of China." A confused babble broke out in the audience. He allowed it to go on for several seconds and then pulled out his pistol from under the podium and fired a round into the ceiling. Complete silence ensued.

Having regained everyone's attention, Liu continued, "Now, you will notice some members of my unit have taken positions at the doorways. Their orders are to do nothing, as long as you stay in your seats." As the attendees looked around the room, they could see at least two soldiers in every doorway, with rifles pointed at the crowd. The soldiers looked serious and intent on their jobs. "Anyone who gets up and tries to approach the doors will be shot without warning," Liu continued. "Anyone who does not do what they are told or causes a commotion will be shot without warning. Do not test my soldiers *or you will die.*"

"I am sure many of you are wondering what is going to happen to you," Liu said, "and I am happy to tell you that the answer is nothing, assuming you do as you are told. Right now, soldiers from the People's Republic of China are securing the cities of Seattle and Tacoma. We neither want these cities, nor do we intend to stay in them. What we do want, however, is to reunify the breakaway province of Taiwan with the rest of our country. Right now, our military forces are currently reincorporating that province. We are here today, not to hold you as hostages, but to ensure the goodwill of your nation in allowing our efforts to proceed unopposed."

"If we're not hostages, then let us go!" the CEO of Ford shouted.

Captain Liu frowned. "It is rude to speak when someone else is talking. The next person who interrupts me, or speaks without being spoken to, will be subject to discipline." He paused to ensure he was understood. "Now, if everyone does as they are told, you will be released at 2300 tonight. Until that time, you should stay in your seats and follow instructions. I know it is legal for some people in this country to carry concealed handguns. Your first instruction is, if you are in possession of a concealed weapon, you are to pass it down to the end of the row where one of my troops will take it. This will keep anyone from trying to be a hero and getting his friends and neighbors killed. Believe me when I say all of my troops have been told to shoot anyone who looks like he is resisting. While you may kill one or two of us, the rest will return fire on full automatic, killing not only you, but many other people around you, as well. There is no reason to do this, as you will all be released, unharmed, in less than nine hours."

He saw one pistol make its way to the end of a row. He frowned again. "Really? Only one? I highly doubt that. This is your one chance to turn in any weapons you have. If you are later found with one, you will be shot as an enemy combatant. Please be aware that you will have to go through a metal detector in order to go to the bathroom. If you cannot hold it for nine hours, you better turn them in now." Several more pistols were turned in.

The Ford CEO motioned to one of his group, a large man wearing an ill-fitting suit, who pulled out a pistol and passed it down to the end of the front row.

"I hope that is all, for your sakes," Liu said. "Now, sit back and get comfortable, because we are going to be here a while. You may talk quietly with your neighbors, if you would like, but everyone needs to remain seated. We will start bathroom breaks shortly, but until then, stay seated and remain calm, and everything will be all right."

Terminal 91, Port of Seattle, Seattle, WA, 1401 Pacific Daylight Time

The Chinese troops poured like water from the *Erawan* onto the unsuspecting Washington pier. Although the transport looked like any other bulk carrier, the inside had been gutted during its last overhaul and replaced with living space for troops. From the outside, it maintained the image of a somewhat sloppy, long-haul freighter (right down to the rust spots along its sides, which had been encouraged to grow during that same overhaul); it was, however, the transport for a battalion of Chinese troops.

Having been stacked like cordwood for the majority of the two-week trip, the soldiers' joy at being free of the confines of the ship was apparent in the way they sprinted down the ramp of the ship and began setting up a rapidly increasing perimeter. Major Chin Haung inspected the deployment with watchful eyes, and he liked what he saw. The heavens above knew they had practiced this enough; he expected nothing different.

Although the major spoke perfect English, as his grades from Stanford would attest, most of his soldiers were less fluent. All of them, however, knew the rudiments of the language, especially words like 'down on your stomachs,' which they used to secure the long-shoremen who had been waiting on the pier to unload the 'freighter.' Although they spoke in English, one woman watching was neither mentally nor emotionally prepared to have dozens of armed men in uniform come running toward her, and she stared blankly at the tide of men as they swarmed past her. Her ears heard the commands of "Get down!" but her mind stalwartly refused to process the information. She never saw the butt of the rifle which hit her in the head, knocking her to the ground unconscious. Unfortunately for the private wielding the rifle, the jarring of it hitting the woman's head caused his finger to slip inside the trigger guard. In spite of orders to keep the safety of his rifle 'on,' he had taken it off in his excitement, and the trigger pulled, firing off a round. Although it didn't hit anyone or anything important, it did serve notice that something was going on.

Major Chin frowned as he heard the report of a QBZ-95 rifle firing. The success of the operation required speed and surprise, and he did not want to alert the Americans to their presence before he had to. Looking up the pier to the *M.V. Xin Qing Dao*, he could see the side and stern ramps coming down as planned. Quickly scanning the rest of the pier, he could see that his troops had secured the length of Pier 91, including the capture of the *M.V. Oosterdam*, a cruise ship of the Holland America Line. As one of the 'higher-end' cruise lines, he was sure there would be some excellent hostages aboard. He grinned at the thought of the fun they might have with them.

Whidbey Island Naval Air Station, WA, 1403 Pacific Daylight Time

Whidbey Island Naval Air Station was the Navy's biggest air base in the Pacific Northwest and home to all the tactical electronic attack squadrons (the aircraft that jammed enemy radars and communications). In addition to the EA-18G Growler electronic attack squadrons, NAS Whidbey Island was also home to four maritime patrol squadrons and two reconnaissance squadrons. It was a fairly busy base, although it appeared quiet to the pilot of *Air China 306* as he flew over at an altitude of 10,000 feet.

Having reached the turning point, the pilot transmitted the word, "*Now!*" over the radio and banked his aircraft to fly parallel down the length of the taxiway below him. As *Air China 306* reached the drop zone, he pushed the button in the cockpit that turned on the green light in the back of the aircraft. Seeing the light illuminate, the jumpmaster waved to the troops lined up in the open doorway. "Go!" he yelled, "Go! GO! *GO!*" and the soldiers threw themselves out of the airplane. All of the aircraft's 158 troops came down along the ramp area in front of the airfield's hangars, putting them in a perfect position to secure the base operations building and control tower, as well as to form a guard over the aircraft on the ramp. The aircraft would have been very valuable to the U.S. Navy's efforts to counter the Chinese attacks, both at home and abroad; it was important to take control of them early on.

Air China 306's wingman waited a few moments after *306* made its turn and then made a 90 degree turn to the left. The wingman flew down Ault Field Road, dropping his load of 158 troops on an easterly heading. Once on the ground, three of the platoons were responsible for securing the gates to the base on Saratoga Street, Langley Boulevard, and Charles Porter Avenue, while the rest of the troops would advance on the airfield from the south, helping to secure the patrol squadrons' hangars.

Control Tower, Whidbey Island Naval Air Station, WA, 1403 Pacific Daylight Time

"**D**o you have your scope back yet?" Chief Air Traffic Controlman Bill Stevens asked his trainee.

"Almost," Air Traffic Controlman Third Class Ed Brown replied. "Just give me a second more."

Right at 1400, all of the power had gone out in the tower. Looking out across the base, Chief Stevens couldn't see any other buildings that looked like they had power, either, so he supposed the power was out base-wide. While the emergency generator had kicked on, and they now had power in the tower, getting the scope back and regaining situational awareness was taking a little longer.

Their radar scopes were almost online when a shadow went past. Looking up, Petty Officer Brown saw a man in a parachute drift by the tower window. The chief had his back to the window, though, and didn't see him.

"Umm, Chief...is there supposed to be a parachute drop today?" he asked. "Someone just parachuted past the window, and it looked like he was in full combat gear."

"No, there isn't," Chief Stevens said, spinning around. "There isn't supposed to be anything going on this afternoon." Looking out the window, he saw a line of men in parachutes running the length of the taxiway, about to touch down. "What the hell?" he asked.

"Is this some sort of drill?" Petty Officer Brown asked.

"There's no drill scheduled," Chief Stevens said, "and there's *no way* they would run a surprise drill where people parachuted onto the airfield without telling us; it's too dangerous." He had a bad feeling, which was confirmed when some of the men started running toward the tower, holding their rifles at the ready. "Make sure the door is locked," he instructed.

He picked up the phone. Dead, damn it!

"What do we do?" Petty Officer Brown asked. They had a big binder of procedures to follow in the event of an emergency, but the procedures in the binder were for things like aircraft malfunctions or emergencies with the tower equipment. There weren't any pages labeled, "What to do in the event of an airborne assault."

"Stack anything you can find against the door," the chief said. "I've got a call to make."

Control Tower, Naval Air Station Fallon, NV, 1403 Pacific Daylight Time

"**D**amn it!" Chief Air Traffic Controlman Dan Hamilton swore. "Hurry up and get those scopes back up. We have a strike package that will be back in 10 minutes." He looked down as his cell phone beeped. It was a text from one of his best friends, Bill Stevens, who he had known for a long time. The text from Bill said, "Emergency call. Pick up." As he finished reading it, the phone rang.

"Hi Bill," he said. "We're kind of busy here right now. We just had a major power failure and we've got an air wing strike package that will be back in about 9 minutes."

"I need you to listen to me," Bill Stevens said. "We also just had a power failure *and now we are being invaded!* We just had at least 100 men parachute in. They're now organizing, and it looks like they are taking over all the hangars. I don't have long—at least 10 are headed this way!"

"WHAT?" Chief Hamilton asked. "Are you sure it isn't a drill?"

"The power goes out at both our bases at the same time, and now there are armed men here?" Chief Stevens reasoned. "I don't think so!" There was a loud crash. "I don't have long," he said. "They're breaking down the door!"

"Does anyone else there know?" Chief Hamilton asked.

"No," Chief Stevens said, "all of our phones are out. Even if they did, there wouldn't be much they could do. There are hundreds of armed men on the base." Another crash could be heard, louder than before, followed by several voices shouting in the background. "Holy shit!" Chief Stevens exclaimed. "A fucking Chinese transport just landed on our runway! We need help here right now! You are—"

Rifle fire could be heard in the background, and the call ended abruptly.

Pier 57, The Port of Seattle, Seattle, WA, 1403 Pacific Daylight Time

The power went out, and Captain Hon Ming looked up from his plate of Dungeness crab at Elliot's Oyster House and over to where the cruise liner *Henna* was tied up. For all intents and purposes, nothing was going on over at the *Henna*. Looks weren't deceiving; nothing really *was* going on—all the troops the ship had brought to Seattle had departed earlier that morning, leaving him with nothing better to do than have lunch. The ruse with the broken motor had gone exactly as planned. No one expected Chinese maintenance procedures to be 100% effective, so no one was surprised when he reported to the port authority that the ship had broken down at the pier, just like it had done the last time he came to Seattle. Captain Hon was a proud man and ran the proverbial 'tight ship;' the cruise liner was meticulously maintained, and all of the maintenance procedures were followed to the letter (or better). It had pained him greatly to break the port motor (again) and then to have to tell the Americans "his" ship had broken down (again).

But the Dungeness crab made it all worthwhile, he thought with a smile.

Terminal 91, Port of Seattle, Seattle, WA, 1404 Pacific Daylight Time

Major Chin watched the rest of the 1st and 2nd Battalions of the 467th Mechanized Regiment stream off the *Erawan*. Companies E and F of the 1st Battalion joined with Companies E and F of the 4th Special Forces Battalion to continue securing the *M.V. Oosterdam*. Looking toward the *M.V. Xin Qing Dao* car carrier, he could see the ramps were down and the first of the ZBD-08 infantry fighting vehicles (IFVs) were rolling off. The rest of the 1st Battalion was securing the port facility and unloading both *Erawan* and the *Xin Qing Dao*. The 2nd Battalion was ashore, waiting for its IFVs and armored personnel carriers (APCs) to roll off the *Xin Qing Dao*. They mounted up and headed out as quickly as the vehicles came off the ship. Everything proceeded according to plan.

The IFVs and APCs had been loaded onto the *Xin Qing Dao* last, so they were the first off. With so many objectives to secure in Seattle, getting the maximum number of troops into position as soon as possible was the highest priority. If the initial objectives could be secured, they wouldn't need the heavier armored vehicles and surface-to-air defenses. Today, anyway. The major had no doubt they would need those capabilities eventually, but he doubted the Americans would be able to mobilize their combat power for at least a couple of days. By then, most of the city would be secure, and all of the appropriate defenses emplaced. There would be plenty of time to unload the armored brigades as the afternoon wore on.

As he watched, the helicopter onboard the *Erawan* lifted off, carrying something underneath it. An odd-looking piece of equipment, a civilian might have thought the machine dangling from the helicopter was some sort of weird ray gun. The equipment had a ten foot long trailer with a generator on its back, and on top of the generator was a large, tapered metal object that spanned the length of the trailer and then extended another two feet beyond the end. The large piece of metal was about eight inches thick at the back, narrowing down to about four inches at the front with wire spiraling up its length, giving it the look of a gun. He could see a thin plume of smoke from the generator; it was obviously already in operation.

He smiled. There would be no cell phone calls to report the helicopter or the piece of gear it carried; the machine was a massive 800 watt, trailer-mounted cell phone jammer that wiped out all cell phone signals within a 10 mile radius; this one jammer was now blacking out all of the Seattle metropolitan area. He saw another jammer, just like the one being carried by the helicopter, lined up on the deck and ready for transportation to Tacoma. He chuckled. Anyone that needed to make a cell phone call in Tacoma had better make it soon.

White House Red Room, Washington, DC, 1705 EDT (1405 Pacific Daylight Time)

Not wanting to have the discussion in the State Dining Room, the president had taken the Chinese Ambassador, along with his closest National Security Council advisors, and gone into the Red Room next door. The Red Room was one of three state parlors on the first floor of the White House. It had served over time as a parlor and a music room, and had traditionally been decorated in shades of red; the current carmine color did nothing to decrease the president's ire.

"What the hell do you mean 'we're at war?'" he asked.

"That actually was imprecise," the ambassador said. "My apologies; I was overly excited. What I meant to say is that my country is currently engaged in combat operations to recover our breakaway province of Taiwan. These operations started a few minutes ago and are in accordance with our rights under international law. The People's Republic of China is the legitimate government of China, of which Taiwan is a part. We exhausted all the peaceful means at our disposal to recover Taiwan; today our military forces will recover it by force."

"Are you saying our nations are at war?" the president asked.

"I am saying nothing of the sort," the ambassador replied. "We have not declared war on Taiwan. There is no need. It is not a foreign government; it is part of China. We are simply conducting military operations to recover part of our territory that has been governed by a foreign power for far too long. We certainly have *not* declared war on the United States, nor do we intend to unless provoked. Should you declare war on the People's Republic, we of course will have no option but to reply in kind. While I cannot tell you all of our plans, I have been authorized to tell you our forces have been prepositioned to deny any sort of response on your part.

132 | CHRIS KENNEDY

Anything short of complete acquiescence with our plans to recover Taiwan will go poorly for the citizens of the United States."

While he was talking, a man entered the room, crossed to the National Security Advisor and whispered in his ear. When the Chinese Ambassador paused, the National Security Advisor spoke to the president. "Sir, we have confirmed reports that power has failed nation-wide. The power failure we experienced is not contained to the area, but has affected all three of the power grids in the United States. Most of Canada is experiencing a power outage, as are most of our alliance partners. We also have reports of a variety of other governmental service failures, as well as failures in the 9-1-1 emergency system. It looks like we're being attacked on a variety of cyber fronts!"

The president turned back to the Chinese Ambassador. "I thought you said you hadn't declared war on the United States!" he seethed through nearly closed teeth.

The ambassador shrugged. "I have no idea what you are talking about. Certainly, the failure of your antiquated systems cannot be attributed to our nation. Our focus today is on Taiwan, not on your domestic issues."

"I don't believe you," growled the president. "There's no way all of these things happened coincidentally with your invasion of Taiwan. It's obvious you are lying, and if you're lying about that, what else are you lying about?"

The president turned to the head of his Secret Service security detail. "I need information, Bill, not worthless platitudes, and it's obvious the ambassador isn't going to give it to me. Take him to the Green Room and keep him there. I'll need to speak with him later, but first I need to find out what's really going on."

The Secret Service leader spoke into his wrist microphone, and two agents detached themselves from the walls where they had been waiting anonymously and walked over to the ambassador. "Sir, if you would come with us, please?" one of them asked.

The ambassador stood up on his own, then stopped and would not move any further. The agents began to physically herd him toward the door. "You cannot hold me against my will!" he cried. "I have diplomatic immunity! I demand to be returned to my embassy immediately!"

The president looked up and smiled. "I wouldn't dream of making you go out on the roads right now," the president said. "With the power out, you might get into an accident. I fear for your safety on the roads, so I am offering you a place to stay until things calm down. Also, some citizens might get the wrong-headed idea that China is behind these failures and want to cause you harm. No, for your own safety, we'll keep you right here at the White House where we can protect you." He waved to the secret servicemen, and the ambassador was ushered out.

"Okay," the president said turning to face his advisors, "what do we know?"

The senior advisor spoke first. She was responsible for strategic initiatives, intergovernmental affairs, political affairs and public liaison. "We're still gathering information, Mr. President," she said, "but it appears a wide variety of governmental services have failed, not just the power grid. In some places, water and sewage are out, too, and much of the internet appears to have gone away."

The president looked stunned. "What do you mean, 'gone away'?" he asked.

"I mean that sites that used to be available aren't there anymore. Most governmental sites, especially, have gone offline. Even Google is offline! We're trying to figure out what happened, but we depend on the internet for much of the information we need to figure these things out. That information isn't available to us at the moment, so we're having to fall back on old-fashioned things like phone books. Have you even seen a phone book recently? Most phone companies aren't even making them anymore! And now the phone service is out in many places, too! I can't give you information I don't have!" Her voice had risen over an octave during her answer, and it appeared to the president that she was starting to lose her grip.

"Okay, okay," he said, trying to calm her down. "Get with your staff and see what you can find out. We'll obviously need FEMA involved as soon as possible." The Federal Emergency Management Agency had been created to oversee emergency management for disasters; he was sure it would be needed everywhere and at once today.

"Okay," said the president. "What else?" Calming the senior advisor had the unintended effect of calming himself down. His temper was back under control, and he was ready to lead.

"I called the Chinese Embassy," the chief of staff said, "but I didn't have any luck. After being told the Chinese president wasn't feeling well enough to talk on the phone, they finally confessed that he had 'flown home for treatment.' He couldn't have come to the dinner tonight because he went back to China either yesterday or earlier today. I guess that makes sense. If they were planning on invading Taiwan, he'd want to be back in China to oversee the attack."

The president looked to the Secretary of State. "I want to talk to him," the president said. "Now." The Secretary of State left to oversee the task. The president turned back to the chief of staff. "We're going to need everyone here to deal with this," he said. "Get the vice president back, ASAP." The vice president was currently in Iowa looking at the latest crop failures caused by the ongoing drought. The chief of staff said something to one of his staffers, who left to take care of it.

The president turned to his senior military advisor, the Chairman of the Joint Chiefs of Staff. "Obviously, I'll need options, as soon as they're available. Dust off the 'Defense of Taiwan' scenarios and see what forces we have in the area to support them. I'll want a full briefing in two hours." He knew this wasn't enough time to put together a complete response plan, but he could feel things sliding away from him. He felt sure that if the U.S. didn't respond soon, Taiwan would be lost.

The Chairman nodded his head. "Yes, sir, my staff is already working on that. We'll have something for you at 1915. It won't be the best, but it will give you enough info to start making decisions."

The president addressed the Director of National Intelligence (DNI). "How likely is it the Chinese are responsible for these power failures and the other service malfunctions?"

"I'd say it's damn likely," the DNI replied. "We've known for years that the Chinese have been mapping our power networks, as well as the rest of our service utilities. My worst nightmare is an Al Qaeda attack along these lines, because we know they've been trying to do it for the better part of 17 years. We've caught them sniffing around electrical generation and distribution facilities, emergency phone system services, water storage and distribution, and gas and nuclear generation facilities. If Al Qaeda has been working on it, you *know* the Chinese have, and their guys are much better funded and equipped. We haven't seen anything so far like a reactor going super-critical or a dam suddenly opening its floodgates, but we *have* seen electrical substations hit with hundreds of thousands of volts simultaneously, shorting them out completely. It will take a long time before we can put them back in operation. If this is the Chinese, and I firmly believe it is, I don't think they will cause a nuclear meltdown or wipe out our first responders' 9-1-1 system; if they did and we could prove it, they know we'd come after them with everything we have at our disposal. Power generation and distribution, though, has been a legitimate target since it was developed. In fact, that was the first thing we went after in Iraq, because it hampered their command and control efforts."

"Kind of like what it's doing to us right now," the president said.

"Just like what it's doing to us right now," the DNI confirmed.

"Okay," the president said, "does anyone have anything useful?"

The room was silent.

Blair Terminal, The Port of Tacoma, Tacoma, WA, 1405 Pacific Daylight Time

For more than 35 years, the Port of Tacoma had served as a port-of-entry into the United States for the automobile industry. With the addition of SAIC, there were now 10 manufacturers using Tacoma's port facilities to transship automobiles, including major manufacturers like Isuzu, Mazda, Mitsubishi, Suzuki, Ford, and GM. It was not unusual, therefore, for the China Shipping Container Lines Co. (CSCL) *M.V. Xin Fei Zhou* car carrier to pull into the Blair Terminal Facility, as that was the normal terminal for automobile onload and offload.

The *Xin Fei Zhou* was the second ship of the CSCL to bear that name, and was a brand new ocean-going car carrier. One of the new breed of large car and truck carriers, the *Xin Fei Zhou* was a "roll-on/roll-off" ship with both a starboard side ramp that folded down so cars and trucks could drive off the ship from its interior, and a ramp at the stern of the ship on the starboard side, so vehicle offload could be greatly expedited. At 656 feet in length and 105 feet wide, the *Xin Fei Zhou* could carry 5,501 cars across the ocean at nearly 20 knots. As the ship pulled up to Blair Terminal, the Auto Warehousing Company employees expertly tied it to the pier. Situated across Port of Tacoma Road from the U.S. Customs Office, it only took a few minutes for the Customs Officer to arrive at the ship; however, the ramps were already in motion, even though the gangway was not in place yet.

The Customs Officer was the first person across the gangway once it was secured. "What is the meaning of this?" he asked. "You can't begin to offload until Customs is complete!"

Stepping onto the ship, he was forced to a sudden stop as a large caliber pistol was shoved in his face by a man in a military uniform. The man was short and stout, and he held the pistol with an air of competence. "I think we will use a different procedure today," the military man said, "assuming that is all right with you?"

The Customs Officer mumbled something that might have been "Okay," as he tried to scurry back onto the gangway and off the ship, but it was hard to tell in his haste.

The man with the pistol, Captain Du Jun, looked at his superior, Major Pan Yan and said, "Sir, I don't believe there will be a problem if we skip Customs today. Our only problem is that we will need someone to clean the deck. It appears the American wet himself in his haste to leave."

"Somehow, I didn't expect Customs would be a problem," Major Pan replied. "Thank you for not shooting him and making an even bigger mess."

"Won't he go and call his superiors, though?" asked Captain Du Jun.

"Of course he will try to," responded the major, "just like the longshoreman who are currently trying to do the same." He pointed to the pier where at least 15 of the 20 men and women in sight had their cell phones out and were pressing their buttons.

"Judging by their confused expressions, it looks like their cell phone service stopped working," the major continued, "and really, what good would it have done?" He nodded toward the starboard amidships ramp, and the first Type 99 tank charging down it, along with the first two companies of troops whose mission it was to secure the port facilities. "We have the surprise we need for the mission, and we were running behind schedule due to the incompetence of the ship's captain." He smiled. "Besides," he finished, "I planned for this."

The first tank reached the pier, and its 125mm main gun traversed until it was pointing at the Customs Office. Smoke belched from the muzzle of the gun as it fired one round, blowing half the building apart.

"I don't think he will be a problem," the major said.

As they had planned and practiced, it only took a few minutes until the first group was ready to get underway, and Major Pan watched as the first convoy left the pier. Ten Type 99 tanks led the group. They represented an effective fighting force all on their own, as they were as good as any main battle tank in the world, on par with even the U.S. M1A1 Abrams. The Type 99 showed a mixture of Russian and Western influence in its design and technology, with a hull similar to the Russian T-72, but with a Western-style angular welded turret. With a 125mm main gun and the ability to fire the locally-produced version of the AT-11 anti-tank guided missile, it had tremendous offensive firepower; it also had a 12.7mm heavy machine gun for the tank commander and a 7.62 mm coaxial machine gun as a secondary armament.

Although not quite as top-of-the-line as the Type 99 in most respects, the 10 Type 98 tanks bringing up the rear were still very capable tanks in their own right. Together, the twenty tanks represented far more combat power than anything else in the region. They would be hard to stop unless the Americans could bring in their air power.

The group brought both the HQ-9 and the PGZ-95 combat systems for when the American air power arrived. The HQ-9 gave the group a medium to long-range surface-to-air missile (SAM) capability. Its guidance systems were on par with the U.S. Patriot or Russian S-300 missile systems, with missiles that could fly at Mach 4.2 out to their maximum operational range of 125 miles.

The HQ-9 battery that followed the tanks consisted of a truck-mounted acquisition radar, a truck-mounted engagement radar, a command post truck, six transporter/erector launchers (TELs) with four missiles each and three support vehicles. The radars represented a new generation in Chinese air defense. Gone were the days of reliance on missiles launched from static, fixed sites; the HQ-9's highly mobile radars now gave it the ability to hide, then 'shoot and scoot.' By moving after a launch, it was much better able to evade the aircraft trying to destroy it. The system used a huge missile with a 400-pound warhead. Even near misses would probably be fatal.

The PGZ-95 self-propelled anti-aircraft vehicles that followed the missile system each held four 25mm cannons that fired 800 rounds a minute and four infrared homing missiles effective to almost 11,500 feet. The system could also be used against ground forces, as its guns could be brought to bear on them. As good as it was against aircraft, it was nothing short of devastating against most light armored fighting vehicles or troops in the open. The PGZ-95 battery consisted of six anti-aircraft vehicles led by a command vehicle and three resupply trucks.

Ten ZBD-08 armored fighting vehicles followed the anti-air systems. The ZBD-08 had better armor than its predecessor, the ZBD-04. The front of the hull and the turret could withstand hits from 30mm rounds, while the sides could stop 14.5mm rounds and the rear 7.62mm. The turret included a thermal imaging gun sight and was armed with a 100mm main gun, a 30mm cannon and a coaxial 7.62mm machine gun. Each of the ZBD-08s transported seven armed soldiers in addition to its crew of three.

The 52 vehicles drove out of the port facility through the main gate. It was less than two miles to I-5 and then a short, 20-minute drive to McChord Air Base where they had a runway to capture.

Sea-Tac Airfield, Seattle, Washington, 1405 Pacific Daylight Time

"Is your system back up yet?" Patrol Officer Juan Mendez asked, leaning on the ticket counter.

"Not yet, no," Stacy Hough replied, looking at

her screen and wishing he would go away. The petite blond Delta ticketing agent could tell the patrolman cared more about ogling her than he did about whether her system was functional or not, as the policeman always stopped by to chat. She didn't mind *too* much when there weren't any lines, because she thought he was kind of cute, but it got to be annoying when she was busy. Like now.

The early afternoon had been a hectic one at Seattle-Tacoma Airfield even before the problems started. The 17th busiest passenger airport in the United States, Sea-Tac served 31 million passengers a year and moved more than 346,000 metric tons of air cargo annually, so there really weren't many 'dead' times. Things went downhill when the power failed, even though Sea-Tac had backup generators, which quickly kicked in and restored power.

"You've got power back, right?" Mendez asked, still looking more at her cleavage than her screen.

"Yes, I've got power," Stacy said, "but the ticketing system hasn't come back up since the power came back on." The airport had an extensive Airport Emergency Plan, and all of the staff members were well-trained and practiced in following its procedures. Normally, the procedures ensured that critical services were expeditiously restored. She was frustrated because this time they weren't.

"I've tried re-booting the system a couple of times since the power came back on," Stacy said. "We've all tried," she continued, indicating the other ticket agents, "but it's almost like the internet isn't working anymore; none of our programs can log into the central servers, no matter what troubleshooting procedures we try. We can't even get *onto* the internet to do things like a Google search; it's almost as if the entire internet is down."

Mendez laughed. "I doubt it," he said. "Maybe it's just that your router is down or got corrupted with the power fluctuation," he suggested. "I hear that happens sometimes." He was not a computer expert, but was happy to pretend to be one if it allowed him to stay and talk to her.

"No, it's worse than that," Stacy said. "Not only are our automatic ticketing systems not functioning, all of us lost our cell phone service, too. Right after the power came back on, everyone's phones went out."

"Really?" Mendez asked as he pulled out his personal cell phone. "That's strange. Do you all have the same cell phone provider?"

"No," Stacy replied, "we have three different providers, but none of them work. It's almost as if we've been cut off from the rest of world. It's kind of creepy."

"Don't worry," Mendez said; "I'm here to protect you. Huh, my phone is out, too. I don't know what could be causing it, maybe sun spots or some other kind of interference, but I'm sure there is a good explanation for what's going on." He pulled out his walkie-talkie. "I'll try to call dispatch and find out if they know."

"I don't know," Stacy said with a shrug. "All I know is that I can't do my job, and the passengers are starting to get annoyed. There's *nothing* I know of in the Emergency Plan for a complete loss of communications capability."

"Let me see what I can find out," Mendez said. He spoke into his walkie-talkie, "Sea-Tac Comms Center, Patrolman 235."

There was no reply from the Communications Center, so he tried again. "Sea-Tac Comms Center, Patrolman 235, over."

Mendez looked confused. "Hmm, that's weird," he said. "I've never called them and not gotten a reply before. They must be really busy with the power outage." He smiled at Stacy. "I'm sure that everything will be worked out shortly." Even though he tried to sound convincing, Stacy didn't think he had totally convinced himself.

Before Stacy could reply, there was a sound like an explosion from the direction of the runway, and she felt a rumbling through the floor.

"What the fu…I mean, what the heck was that?" Mendez asked. He tried to use his walkie-talkie again. No luck.

Stacy saw one of the other policemen jog past. "What's going on?" she yelled.

"No idea," he yelled back, without stopping. "I'm going to the Communications Center to find out!"

"Umm," Stacy said to Mendez, "shouldn't you be doing something, too?"

Before Patrol Officer Mendez could say anything, the fire alarm emergency strobe lights began flashing, and the audible warning signals began sounding their nerve-jangling horns. With almost no delay, the Airport Communications Center began broadcasting on the terminal's public address system, "Attention in the airport, this is the Seattle-Tacoma Emergency Management System. At this time, the airport is closed for an emergency, and all travelers are to exit the terminal building and go to the parking deck across the street. Please walk, DO NOT RUN, to the parking deck across the street. You will be given additional instructions and information there. The Port of Seattle Aviation Division has implemented its Emergency Coordination Center at the Parking Deck, Level One. All emergency personnel should assemble there. All personnel and passengers MUST leave the terminal at this time."

"That sounds like the bomb threat emergency procedure. The airport's director must have implemented the Incident Command System," said Mendez. "Hey! Everyone needs to leave now!" he yelled.

Stacy started walking quickly toward the parking deck. With none of her equipment working, there wasn't any need to shut anything down, and she only needed to hear the word 'bomb' once. The message began repeating, and the few members of the Port of Seattle Fire Department and Port of Seattle Police Department who were in sight started directing all of the staff and passengers to evacuate the terminal building. Stacy knew their efforts were hampered because neither their cell phones nor their walkie-talkies were working.

She was almost to the door when men and women in camouflage uniforms began pouring from the bathrooms and the stairwells. With many military bases in the area, Stacy was familiar with all the various United States' military uniforms. These appeared different.

She looked back to see Patrol Officer Mendez drawing his pistol as he yelled, "Who are you guys?" Her confusion turned to horror as one of the camouflaged soldiers fired, and a line of red splotches walked across Mendez' chest as he was blown backward by the bullets. Stacy sprinted for the exit.

USS *Shoup* (DDG-86), Everett Naval Station, WA, 1405 Pacific Daylight Time

This sucks, thought Lieutenant (Junior Grade) Tim Wallace, who had the misfortune of being the Duty Officer for the USS *Shoup*, as he stood on the quarterdeck of the ship. Everyone else gets to go to the softball game to drink and have fun, and I'm stuck here. Not only that, I'll probably get called to drive some of the drunks home, too. Won't that be fun?

Wallace sighed. Another hour and a half until he would be relieved. By then, the game would be over, and everyone would probably have dispersed to the bars. Hopefully, he could change quickly, meet them out in town and salvage at least a piece of the afternoon.

He gazed down the pier and noticed four Chinese sailors walking in the direction of the destroyer, singing in Chinese. They appeared to be quite drunk, supporting each other as they stumbled down the pier. The softball game was the place to be, he thought, watching the Chinese sailors walk up the wrong pier toward his ship. None of them seemed to notice or care that they were walking up the wrong gangway. "Hey," he called as they started up; "this isn't your ship; this is the *Shoup.*" The sailors pointed at him and laughed as if he had said something funny, and they continued talking to each other in Chinese.

"What's so funny?" he asked with a touch of exasperation as they reached the top of the gangway where he waited with the Petty Officer of the Watch.

"Your security," one of them said in fluent English. A large caliber pistol materialized in his hand, inches from LTJG Wallace's nose.

As Wallace looked around, he saw that all four of the sailors now had pistols, two of which were pointing at him, while the other two pointed at Petty Officer Mathis. Suddenly, the Chinese seemed very sober, too. "Quickly!" the sailor with the most gold on his insignia said to Petty Officer Mathis. "Who is in charge here?"

Petty Officer Mathis, stunned at the turn of events, stammered, "Uh…our commanding officer's name is—" He stopped suddenly as the Chinese sailor pistol-whipped him in the temple, knocking him to the deck.

"No," the sailor said, turning to face LTJG Wallace as he smiled. "We are in charge. Do you understand that?"

"Yes," LTJG Wallace said, his eyes large with fright.

"Good! The sooner you understand that, the easier it will go for you." The Chinese sailor paused, then asked, "Who is the senior officer onboard right now, and how many people are currently on the ship?"

"Uhh...the commanding officer is aboard. I...umm...don't know how many crew...," LTJG Wallace stammered, "just a few." Normally, almost 1/3 of the 380 officers and crew would have been onboard the 509' *Arleigh Burke*-class destroyer, but the commanding officer had allowed the majority of them to go to the softball game in the interest of public relations. At the moment, there probably weren't more than 60 personnel onboard.

The sailor answered, "Good. Then take us to your bridge and do not try anything heroic or we will shoot you." Faced with a no-win situation, LTJG Wallace turned to lead them to the bridge.

USS *Ford* (FFG-54), Everett Naval Station, WA, 1405 Pacific Daylight Time

At the same time LTJG Wallace was being forced to the bridge of the USS *Shoup*, five Chinese sailors in uniform were walking up to the gangway of the USS *Ford*, an *Oliver Hazard Perry*-class frigate. The Duty Officer, LT John Musselman, saw them coming, carrying two large, brightly-wrapped packages. The packages were obviously heavy, he thought, as it took two sailors each to carry them. The fifth Chinese sailor was obviously their officer, as he appeared different in both dress and manner. "What do you suppose this is all about?" LT Musselman asked his Petty Officer of the Watch.

"No idea, sir," Damage Controlman First Class Esteban Ramirez responded. "Is it your birthday? Those look like birthday presents."

"Nope, my birthday's in January," LT Musselman said as the Chinese sailors reached the gangway and started up it.

Reaching the Quarterdeck at the top of the gangway, the officer saluted and asked, "Permission to come aboard?"

"Permission granted," LT Musselman said. "Can I help you with something?"

"Yes, you can," he answered. "I am Lieutenant Sun Xiuying, and I have a couple of packages for your commanding officer and executive officer, from my commanding officer, Captain Tang Ping. Would they happen to be aboard?"

"The commanding officer is aboard, but the executive officer is ashore at the softball game," LT Musselman said. "Would you like me to call him?"

"Yes, please," LT Sun responded. "I am supposed to deliver this to him so that it doesn't get lost in transit. The contents are very valuable."

LT Musselman stepped away from LT Sun, picked up one of the ship's phones and dialed a number. When the person on the other end responded, LT Musselman talked to him in a muted voice, too low for LT Sun to hear what he was saying. LT Musselman turned back to LT Sun and said, "He will be here in a minute."

Commander Steve MacGuinness entered the Quarterdeck a couple of minutes later to find five Chinese sailors standing at attention

148 | CHRIS KENNEDY

behind two large boxes. A tall man with flaming red hair, he was naturally loud and outgoing. "Hi," he said. "I'm Commander Mac-Guinness. Can I help you?"

"Yes sir, you can," answered the Chinese officer. "I am Lieutenant Sun Xiuying, and I have packages for both you and your executive officer from my commanding officer, Captain Tang Ping. They are something special we brought from China for you. He asked us to bring them to you. We are supposed to wait until you open the packages to make sure you get it and not someone else."

"All right," Commander MacGuinness said. He tore off the bright paper and ribbon and found a sealed box underneath the wrap. He worked off one edge of the tape with a fingernail and pulled it off. Opening the box, he found four strange-looking rifles. They did not appear to be of U.S. manufacture as the magazines were located behind the trigger assemblies. "What is—?" he started to say, but as he looked up, he realized all five Chinese sailors had drawn pistols and were pointing them at the three Americans. He changed his question in mid-sentence to, "What is the meaning of this?"

"It is simple," LT Sun said. "We are taking over your ship."

Red Square, The University of Washington, Seattle, WA, 1407 Pacific Daylight Time

Sara walked with Erika through Red Square on the warm, late summer afternoon. Unlike many best friends that go to college together and quickly part ways, they were still not only roommates, but also the best of friends. They had even decided to attend the B-Term Summer Session together. As both of them were Art majors, they continued to live together in McMahon Hall.

"Do you have time for lunch?" Erika asked. "I didn't bring anything to snack on while I studied, and I'm *starving!*"

"I'm not hungry," Sara said, "but I have time to have a drink while you have lunch. I've still got a couple of days until my first exam, and I need a break from studying for a bit. I've been at Suzzallo Library since about 8:00 this morning. Let's go up to Finn Mac-Cool's, and you can have lunch while I get a drink."

"Sounds good," Erika said. "They probably won't even be carding yet."

The plaza was almost deserted as they walked across it, as Sara would have expected for a Sunday afternoon during summer school. There wasn't a cloud in the sky, so she was surprised to see a shadow go past her. Looking up, Sara was shocked to see two rows of parachutes coming down in a line running the length of Pierce Lane from Red Square through the Liberal Arts Quadrangle. "That's something you don't see every day," she said to Erika as they stopped and looked up at the parachutists.

"No, never," Erika agreed as the parachutes drew closer. "With all the multi-story buildings in the area, I can't believe people would intentionally try to parachute onto campus."

"No kidding," Sara said. "It looks like several of them are trying to come down here in Red Square, too. Why don't we get out of the way? I'd rather not have one of them come crashing into me, especially since it looks like they're wearing a lot of gear."

"Yeah," Erika said as they walked past a few other people who were gawking up at the parachutists. "Going to the hospital will *not* get me fed any time soon."

"That's weird," Sara said, looking back. "Not only do the parachutists have an awful lot of gear, they also look like they're in uniform. You haven't heard of any sort of exercise going on, have you? It's too late for the Fourth of July and too early for Labor Day."

Erika looked back, too. "Not only are they in uniform, they've got guns!" She sounded scared, Sara thought. Come to think of it, Sara was starting to feel a little nervous, too.

"Hey, Sara," Erika asked, "do you remember that movie we saw where Russia invaded the U.S.? Didn't they parachute in just like this? What do you suppose is going on? Do you think we're being invaded?"

"I think the movie was Red Dawn or something like that," Sara replied, always the calmer of the two, "and I doubt it. Maybe it's the Army or National Guard doing some kind of practice thing, and they just missed where they were trying to go. Still...maybe we should be going."

They broke into a trot and started to go around the corner of the Odegaard Library. Looking back, Sara stopped as she saw the first man, obviously a soldier, land in the square. Jettisoning his parachute, he unshouldered his strange-looking rifle and fired several shots into the air. "Everyone get down!" he yelled in a strange accent.

The noise of the rifle being fired broke the confused reverie of the students watching the soldiers, and Sara watched as the students hurried to get on their stomachs. All except for one student. She didn't know the large black man who refused, but she listened in surprise as he said, "You can't tell me what to do. It's a free country!"

"Yes, I can," the soldier said, flipping the safety of the rifle back to the off position. "It is no longer free." He leveled the rifle and fired a three round burst. The man was thrown backward as the high-velocity rounds hit him in the chest.

"Anyone else?" the soldier asked.

Sara and Erika took off running around the corner, away from the madness.

Safeco Field, Seattle, WA, 1407 Pacific Daylight Time

Captain Ma Gang walked into the PA booth along with three of his soldiers. He was in no hurry, as he knew no one was leaving the stadium; they had brought locks and chains and had secured the entire facility. Nor was anyone making a cell phone call to alert the police or their friends to their problem. He had seen several people trying to make calls, frustration on their faces. The cell phone jammer appeared to be doing its job.

He looked out of the press box window. The sun was shining, and it was a beautiful day at the ballpark. In fact, it was far too nice a day to have so many empty seats. As he was walking in, he had heard it announced that there were 18,145 people in attendance. With a seating capacity of over 47, 000, they had hoped for more hostages than that, but the Seattle Mariners remained mired in their decades long slump (they hadn't won the division since 2001), and attendance was low, even for a beautiful Sunday afternoon. Still, over 18,000 people were going to get a little more than they bargained for today.

M.V. Oosterdam, Pier 91, Port of Seattle, Seattle, WA, 1408 Pacific Daylight Time

The cruise should have left an hour ago, but the Holland America ship *M.V. Oosterdam* still sat on the west side of Pier 91 due to mechanical difficulties that had prevented it from getting underway. Due to several recent mishaps where cruise liners had experienced malfunctions at sea that turned ugly, the cruise ship's Captain had decided to stay pier-side while the crew worked to fix it. The passengers had been told it was a minor malfunction that would only delay them a short time and would not affect their itinerary in any way. The ship was holding a 'Pre-Sail Party' at the Sea View Pool on the Lido Deck, with free cocktails as a way of keeping tempers in check. Jack and his wife Janet had decided to stay in their cabin and have a drink there; not only did they not feel the urge to fight their way through the crush of people seeking free booze, they were able to have a drink in their cabin, courtesy of the ship's Captain. When they arrived, there were already two bottles of the ship's signature Chardonnay chilling in ice buckets, with a note to welcome the senator and his family aboard. It's good to be king, the senator thought.

Jack knew his children didn't mind missing out on the party; they were in the cabin next door, preparing to go to sea by texting all of their friends while they still could. Jack wondered what they'd do without their cell phone connectivity during the cruise, but then chuckled as he thought about the grief he could give them over their expected withdrawal symptoms. Having refreshed their glasses, Jack and Janet stepped out onto the balcony of their suite. As they surveyed the port area, Jack noticed armed men in uniform coming from the freighter on the east side of the pier.

Within seconds, they spread out across the pier at a run. Jack saw some of them come onboard the ship, and he *knew* it had to be a

Homeland Security drill. In the last round of budget talks before he left Washington for the cruise he had signed a bill that cut government funding to several agencies; the Department of Homeland Security (DHS), with all of its inefficiencies, was one of the organizations that bore the brunt of the cuts. It would be just like the Director of DHS to put together an impromptu drill, the senator thought, just to inconvenience him in return.

More than a little annoyed that no one had briefed him on the drill, Jack decided to go down to the cruise ship's gangway to see what was going on. "Janet, stay here with the kids," he directed. "I'm going to go see what those Homeland Security assholes are doing to delay our cruise even further."

USS *Shoup* (DDG-86), Everett Naval Station, WA, 1409 Pacific Daylight Time

The Commanding Officer of the USS *Shoup*, Commander Jane Wiggins, stepped onto the bridge of the USS *Shoup* to find three Chinese sailors pointing pistols at her watchstanders. "What the hell is going on here?" she asked.

"It is quite simple," their leader, a Grade 6 Non-Commissioned Officer (NCO 6), said. "My name is Hu Yan, and we have taken over your ship. Now, we have no desire to hurt or kill any of your sailors, but if you do not do exactly as I say, we will kill as many as we need to make our point."

"I'm not sure that three of you can hold the ship," CDR Wiggins said. "You may be able to kill a few of us, but my men and women will overpower you in short order."

"That may be true," the NCO 6 said, "but there are more of us aboard than what you see here. We left another of our group at the entrance to your ship, and I just saw more of my countrymen arrive." While the *Shoup's* CO had been talking, Hu had seen four black vans driving down the pier toward the ship. "I don't need to tell you how many are aboard, but you can be sure the ones who just got here are heavily-armed, and we have enough onboard to do the job."

"What is it that you want from us?" CDR Wiggins asked.

"Easy," the NCO 6 said. "All you have to do is leave."

USS *Ford* (FFG-54), Everett Naval Station, WA, 1410 Pacific Daylight Time

The group of sailors led by CDR MacGuinness and PLAN LT Sun reached the bridge of the USS *Ford*. Although the group had started out with seven people when it left the quarterdeck, it had grown to ten by the time it made it to the bridge. The group had come across several American sailors along the way, and they had been forced to come along. While four of the PLAN sailors covered the other four Americans with their rifles, LT Sun spoke with CDR MacGuinness.

"Commander MacGuinness, I have no desire to be melodramatic like your American movies, but we can either do this the easy way or the hard way. The easy way is you get on the ship's intercom and tell your people to leave the ship. How you do that is up to you. From the time you start talking, your people will have five minutes to exit the ship. Anyone we find onboard after that will be shot. Not wounded, not captured, but shot dead. Their deaths will be on your head." He looked out the bridge window. "Now, in case you get any delusions of resisting, I think you should know a number of heavily-armed special forces soldiers came onboard from the vans that just pulled up." He pulled CDR MacGuinness to the window so he could see the last of the men coming onboard in full combat gear.

"That is the easy way," he continued. "You talk, everyone leaves, and no one has to die. If you refuse, the hard way is we kill you, right here, right now, and then go about the ship, exterminating everyone as we go. The result is the same for us, although a lot more bloody for you. In the end, though, we *will* take over this ship." He smiled at the commanding officer. "So, which way is it going to be?"

"What am I supposed to tell my sailors?" CDR MacGuinness asked, stalling for time.

"As I said," LT Sun answered, "I don't care what you tell them. The truth would probably work as well as any story you can concoct." He looked at the Americans' name tags. "Tell them we have taken over the ship, and if they don't leave it immediately, Chinese sailors will shoot you, LT Musselman and the three other sailors we have on the bridge. Please also let them know that, while we will let everyone off the ship who leaves in the next five minutes, anyone we see with a weapon will be shot on sight, as well as anyone remaining after the five minutes is over."

Stepping over to LT Musselman, he put the barrel of his pistol next to LT Musselman's temple. "Your five minutes starts now," he said, looking at his watch. "You'd better hurry."

CDR MacGuinness knew he was out of time and options. He picked up the microphone for the ship's intercom system and began talking.

M.V. *Oosterdam,* Pier 91, Port of Seattle, Seattle, WA, 1411 Pacific Daylight Time

Senator Jack Turner arrived at the gangway of the *Oosterdam* to see a sailor in a foreign uniform pointing a strange-looking rifle at the Holland America staff assembled there. Most of them had their hands in the air. "What's going on here?" he asked in his most officious and aristocratic voice. "Why wasn't I told there was going to be an exercise today?"

"This is no exercise," a man behind him said. "We are taking over this ship." As Jack turned, he could see the man was also in a foreign uniform, but had on some kind of officer's insignia. He also had one of the weird rifles in his hands and a pistol in a holster at his side.

"That's preposterous!" Jack scoffed. "As if a foreign country could come onto American soil and capture a fully loaded cruise liner. That's preposterous, I say. I know this is just another Homeland Security drill, and one that is directed at me because I voted to cut your funding."

"You are mistaken," the officer said. "Now, get back with the group over there." He used the muzzle of the rifle to indicate the Holland America staff.

"I certainly will NOT!" Jack cried. "I'm Senator Jack Turner! I'm tired of this shit, and I don't like your attitude." Stepping toward the officer, he said, "Now give me your badge number. I'll make sure you never work for the federal government again." He reached toward the officer to take his gun. To his surprise, the officer reversed the weapon, taking hold of it by the carrying handle on top and swung it at him. The butt of the rifle impacted his temple, and Jack folded like a marionette whose strings had been cut, unconscious.

The demonstration had served its point. As the officer looked back to the Holland America staff, he saw all of them now held their hands up. "Anyone else want to see if this is indeed a drill?" he asked. He paused a minute, contemplating what he had just heard. "Did he say that he was a senator?" he asked the staff. A couple of them nodded their heads.

"Good," the officer said. He looked at two of his men. "Why don't you take one of the boat's staff and see if you can round up the rest of the senator's family? When you find them, take them and the senator back aboard the *Erawan* and give them to Major Chin, with my compliments."

USS *Shoup* (DDG-86), Everett Naval Station, WA, 1415 Pacific Daylight Time

The commanding officer and the sailors from the bridge filed off the USS *Shoup* to find the rest of the crew milling about on the pier under the watchful eyes of four special forces soldiers. The commanding officer of the USS *Shoup*, Commander Jane Wiggins, asked, "What's going on here? You said we'd all be allowed to leave."

"And indeed you will," Hu Yan said, having followed them off the ship. "But first, we need three volunteers to show us how to use the radar systems."

"And if we decline?" asked the CO.

"That would be most unfortunate," he replied, "and we would probably be forced to start shooting your sailors until we found someone who could help us." He looked back up at the ship. "We would probably start with them."

Looking back at the ship, the CO could see three of her young, female sailors standing next to the rail on the side of the ship. She could also see three Chinese soldiers standing behind them with pistols to their heads. The sailors looked scared, and at least two of them had tears running down their cheeks. She didn't know what the soldiers had told her sailors, but it had obviously had a big effect on them.

"You wouldn't!" the CO said. "That violates all of the rules of warfare."

"Yes we would," he said, "and yes, that would indeed make me a criminal under international law. You are welcome to lodge a complaint with the International Criminal Court if you ever get a chance to talk to them. None of that is going to change what happens here over the next few hours. Now, would you be able to find someone who can show us how to use the ship's radar, or do we need to start shooting people?"

The CO paused, and all three of the Chinese soldiers cocked the hammers on their pistols. One of the female sailors started whimpering. "Okay," said the CO. "Take the guns off my sailors. We'll help you."

"I thought you might."

Softball Fields, Everett Naval Station, WA, 1417 Pacific Daylight Time

In the end, the softball game came down less to the bat of LT Espinosa or Petty Officer Davis than it did to the actions of two 13-year-old girls.

The Chinese team led 10-9 going into the bottom of the final inning, having scored two runs in the top of the inning to reclaim the lead. Both pitchers were starting to labor, and the quality of the game had gone downhill a little after Commander Gao left. In fact, both runners who scored in the top of the inning had made it onto base by walking and were helped along by an error on the *Shoup's* second baseman.

The team from the *Shoup* might have been down on the scoreboard, but they were by no means out of the game. They only needed one run to tie and two to win, which was well within their reach, as the top of their lineup, including their two big hitters, were up to bat.

Morale soared as the first hitter in their batting order walked. It was just as quickly crushed when the second hitter drilled a line drive at the second baseman, who deftly caught the ball and threw it to first. The runner didn't make it back in time and was thrown out for the double play.

The team from the *Shoup* was down to its final out, but had Petty Officer Davis up next, followed by LT Espinosa. The Chinese pitcher had seen enough of those two, and he intentionally walked both of them on four pitches each.

"Let's go guys!" shouted the XO of the *Shoup*, LCDR Ernie Griffin, "Remember the ship's motto, 'Through Perseverance Comes Victory!' You can do this!"

Looking scared and not up to the moment, the *Shoup's* #5 hitter went up to bat. He had one hit in his four at bats, but he also had two strikeouts on the day.

Looking up at her father, the XO, Adrienne Griffin said, "You know what we need, dad? We need a cheer. That always picks people

up!" Adrienne had been a softball player for seven of her thirteen
years, and her teams always did cheers to get each other fired up.
Along with her friend Abby, they started a song at the top of their
lungs:

> *"There was a little froggy, who sat up on a log,*
> *He rooted for the other team, he had no sense at all!*
> *He fell into the water, and bumped his little head,*
> *And when he came back up again, this is what he said!"*

The pitcher, not ready for the loud cheer, threw low. Ball one.

> *"Go, go go, go you mighty Shoup-ers!*
> *Go, go go, go you mighty Shoup-ers!*
> *Go! Fight! Win! Until the very, very, end!*
> *And then he fell back in again!"*

More people joined in. Looking annoyed, the Chinese pitcher
threw high. Ball two. The other game had ended and the players
from the *Ford* drifted over to see the score. Joining in, they helped
sing it even louder the second time through.

> *"There was a little froggy, who sat up on a log,*
> *He rooted for the other team, he had no sense at all!*
> *He fell into the water, and bumped his little head,*
> *And when he came back up again, this is what he said!"*

Completely off his game now, the pitcher threw behind the hitter. The catcher kept it from going to the backstop, but the runners advanced to second and third. Ball three.

"Go, go go, go you mighty Shoup-ers!
Go, go go, go you mighty Shoup-ers!
Go! Fight! Win! Until the very, very, end!
And then he fell back in again!"

The ball bounced six inches in front of the plate. Ball four and the bases were loaded. Unfortunately, that brought up Ensign Patrick Allen, who had struck out three times so far and grounded out weakly to the first baseman in his other at bat. Things looked grim. "Next song!" Adrienne yelled. She and Abby sang:

"Swing that bat and bash that ball, honey, honey!
Swing that bat and bash that ball, baby! Na, na, na
Swing that bat and bash that ball, round the bases, Yee-Haw!
Honey, I'll meet you at home!"

The pitcher had adjusted to the noise and threw the ball better this time. Ensign Allen gave a half swing, missing it by six inches. Not good; strike one. The girls sang louder, joined by a large portion of the crowd.

"Swing that bat and bash that ball, honey, honey!
Swing that bat and bash that ball, baby! Na, na, na
Swing that bat and bash that ball, round the bases, Yee-Haw!
Honey, I'll meet you at home!

One more time!"

Ensign Allen swung weakly again, missing it by even more. Strike two. The girls and the rest of the fans just sang louder.

"Swing that bat and bash that ball, honey, honey!
Swing that bat and bash that ball, baby!
Swing that bat and bash that ball, round the bases, Yee-Haw!
Honey, I'll meet you at home!"

Ensign Allen stepped out of the batter's box to listen to the cheer. He nodded once and stepped back into the batter's box, looking more determined than he had all day. Another ball came down the middle; this time he swung with all his might and hit it, driving the ball just over a leaping shortstop. The centerfielder was moving on the swing, though, and kept the ball from going through the gap.

He came up throwing. Petty Officer Davis had already scored, and LT Espinosa had no intention of stopping at third, even though the base coach held up his hands to hold him there. LT Espinosa knew it was all or nothing and kept churning for home. The relay at shortstop was perfect, and the throw reached home at the same time as the diving LT Espinosa. The catcher's glove came down and tagged LT Espinosa on the shoulder. The ump looked down and saw his hands were already on home plate. "He's safe! *Shoup* wins!" the umpire yelled.

The crowd went crazy and stormed the field to congratulate LT Espinosa and the rest of the *Shoup* players. Everyone was cheering and clapping, celebrating the great come-from-behind win.

The merriment was cut short by the sounds of gunfire as a soldier emptied half a magazine into the air. Stunned, everyone looked around to find the field ringed with armed soldiers. One stepped forward and said in a loud voice, "Good. You win. Now go home. We have captured your ships, and anyone who goes to the pier will be shot. Your captain will contact you. Now, GO!"

Faced with a squad of heavily-armed, angry-looking soldiers, the crowd rapidly dispersed. The glee of moments before had vanished.

I-5, South of Tacoma, WA, 1430 Pacific Daylight Time

No matter how many cars passed the convoy, it still amused PLA Captain Zhu Jing to see the looks of wonderment on the faces of the people who passed by. Not only was it strange to see such a large convoy of military vehicles on the road, he expected, the HQ-9 SAM vehicles in the convoy were painted in the PLA's blue pixilated camouflage, which very few Americans would probably ever have seen. The Red Chinese star *should* have been a giveaway that something was very out of the ordinary, and *very* wrong; he wondered how many people recognized it. Not many, he guessed, or none of the cars that passed him would have intentionally pulled back over into his lane of travel in front of the 125mm main gun of his tank.

The thought of a Chinese column driving down an American road was so alien, he finally decided, that most Americans wouldn't even remotely consider it a possibility. A student of history, he knew the continental U.S. hadn't been invaded in over two hundred years. After that long, it would be hard to imagine that it *could* ever happen. The joke is on you, he thought.

Although most Americans wouldn't have thought it possible, Captain Zhu had been dreaming about this drive for many years. He had been dreaming about driving his tank down the streets of Washington, DC, while patrolling the provincial capital of Urumqi, China, when riots broke out there in July, 2009. An enlisted man who had been a tank driver for ten years at that time, he had taken charge of his company of tanks when both of his officers were killed. In the ensuing three days of fighting, he had led the remaining 19 tanks in the company's rescue of the local commissar, earning him a battlefield commission to Second Lieutenant. Now, nine years later, he was a company commander in the 1st Armored Division of the Beijing Military Region. Many things had changed for him, but his dream remained. Even though he wasn't driving down the streets of Washington, DC, his drive down I-5 in Washington State was close enough.

They reached their turnoff and left the highway at Exit 125. This close to their objective, speed was of the essence. As such, he didn't stop for the red traffic light but proceeded to run straight over the small import car that did. "Hah! Japanese!" he thought as he crushed the car and its unlucky owner into a flat sliver of metal. He led the procession east to the main gate. The directions he had downloaded indicated he should use the left lane to stop and get a base pass, but he drove straight through the gate and past the two uniformed sentries who stared open-mouthed at him as he passed by. The first infantry fighting vehicle (IFV) behind him pulled over, and seven soldiers got out and secured the gate.

He continued down Fairway Road, bearing left onto Main Street. Two blocks after passing the softball fields, he took a left onto Tuskegee Airman Ave. and proceeded straight onto the airfield of

McChord Air Force Base. He led the rest of the Type 99's onto the ramp area where they parked next to the C-17 aircraft that had been staged in nice rows, making them easier for him to guard. "How thoughtful of the Americans," he mused. The IFVs peeled off, with half of them going to the base operations building, and the other half going to the tower facility at Hangar 4. Pulling up to their targets, the soldiers in the back jumped out and stormed the buildings. The airmen inside were neither armed nor prepared for such a lightning assault, and both facilities were quickly captured.

While his men were capturing the control facilities, the HQ-9 and PGZ-95 batteries set up their defensive positions, with the Type 98 tanks providing over watch fire support. The airbase was quickly secured...even though most people in the area didn't know it yet.

Five minutes behind them, this process was repeated at Fort Lewis, the army base located to the southwest of McChord Air Base. As there were many more combat-ready troops at Fort Lewis, including the 1st Special Forces Group and the 2nd Battalion of the Army's 75th Ranger Regiment, the force that crashed through the gate and took control of the administration building, armory and Gray Army Airfield was much larger in size. Thirty-one Type 99 tanks led the way, followed by 31 Type 98 tanks, 31 ZBD-08 personnel carriers and 30 of the new GAC J-Vans, each with 12 combat loaded troops. Bringing up the rear was a PGZ-95 battery, consisting of six of the tracked anti-aircraft guns, a command vehicle and three resupply trucks. All six of the PGZ-95 vehicles were in anti-surface mode; their turrets swiveled continuously, looking for something, or someone, to shoot.

Naval Air Station Fallon, NV, 1445 Pacific Daylight Time

Captain Jim 'Muddy' Waters was having a bad day. As the Air Wing Commander for Carrier Air Wing 2, he was also known as 'CAG,' and he had a lot to be angry about. His squadrons looked like they hadn't flown in months, the first full air wing practice strike had been nothing short of disastrous, with over half of his planes 'killed' on the practice range, and now he had some tower guy saying Whidbey Island was under attack? Didn't he have enough things going wrong without some moron starting outlandish rumors? There wasn't any way Whidbey Island could be under attack, was there?

"So you think this is for real?" he asked his Deputy, Captain Don 'Bambi' Heron.

"Well, I can't tell you for sure that it's real," Bambi replied, "but I can tell you *he* believes it's real. The tower chief said he was on the phone with the Whidbey Island tower operator an hour ago when the power went out. The chief at Whidbey said *their* power went out at the same time, and they had armed men parachuting onto the base. He also said a Chinese transport had landed there on the runway. Right before the call was cut off, the chief said he heard what he thought was gunfire."

"I asked Commander Meadows if any of his folks had heard anything strange from home," he continued. "He tried to call his wife, and she said she had just been turned away from the base's front gate by Asian-looking men armed with guns. I don't know if that corroborates the story, but even if it doesn't, there is still something seriously strange going on."

"You don't think Whidbey is doing some sort of Force Protection drill these people just didn't get the word on, do you?" asked CAG Waters.

"CAG, I'm as shocked as you are, but it sure seems like something is going on. If it weren't odd enough that both Whidbey and Fallon had power outages at the same time, I called back to Virginia Beach to see if they had heard anything, and *they* had just had a power failure, too. In fact, it looks like whole sections of the country got hit with simultaneous black outs. I don't know if we're being invaded," he repeated, "but *something* strange is definitely going on."

"It sounds like Whidbey is under attack, after all," CDR Fred 'Mighty Mite' Meadows said breathlessly as he came running in. "I had our officers call home to their spouses like you asked, Deputy, and two of them said they had seen 'hundreds' of parachutes coming down onto the base, and two other spouses have been turned away from the base by armed men. They were told the base is having a drill, but I've never heard of the base closing down like that for a drill. Also, one of the spouses said the weapons the soldiers at the gates were holding were *not* U.S. combat rifles. Apparently, the spouse is an avid gamer, and he said they looked like they were 'bullpups,' whatever those are."

"That's a rifle configuration where the magazine goes in behind the trigger assembly, rather than in front of it," Captain Heron said. CAG knew his deputy was a bit of a 'gun nut,' who enjoyed hunting. That enthusiasm had long ago earned him the call sign 'Bambi.' "If they are using something like that, they definitely aren't M-16s, and the soldiers are definitely *not* ours."

"Okay," CAG said, "you've convinced me that something is wrong, but I just can't believe the Chinese have taken over Whidbey Island. Who do we have flying on the next event?"

"The next event is pretty light," said Bambi, "since most of the aircraft were on the air wing strike that just landed. We have a pair of Rhinos and a Growler going to the Electronic Warfare Range and two Hornets going to the B-17 target for some bombing practice. There will also be a tanker available for them to get some airborne refueling practice."

As part of the air wing training and work-up cycle, all pilots had to prove they could conduct air-to-air refueling like they would have to do on cruise. At the carrier, there was always a tanker airborne whenever aircraft were flying. Not only would it be available to give pilots the extra gas they needed to complete their missions, but also to give extra gas to an aviator who was having problems landing on the carrier, so that he or she could make another couple of attempts. In order to take on fuel, the pilot had to maneuver his plane and stick a foot-long probe into a metal basket trailing on a hose from the refueling aircraft. Once plugged in, the tanker could pass fuel to the other aircraft. The Air Force used a number of modified transport aircraft as tankers; at the aircraft carrier, the tanker was normally an F-18 with a specially modified tank that let the pilot transfer fuel.

"Okay," CAG said, "let's re-task the Rhinos and Growler to go up north and take a look. They can fly up to the area around Tacoma and call them on the radio." 'Rhino' was the term used to differentiate the E and F variants of the F-18 Super Hornet from the C and D variants of the original F-18 Hornet. A modification of the notoriously short-ranged Hornet aircraft, the Super Hornet versions were a little longer, had a little more gas and were able to fly a little further than the original models. This made them a better choice to accompany the EA-18G jammer aircraft (the 'Growler') up towards its home base. "The distance from Fallon to Whidbey is about 800 miles. We can have them get enough gas from the tanker to get them there and back."

"They won't have any live bombs or missiles onboard," said Bambi, "but we probably still have time to make sure they have full ammunition loads for their guns."

"That's a good idea, Bambi," said CAG. "Make it happen." He looked at the Growler squadron's commanding officer. "Fred, I want you to lead the flight. Go up north, talk to the folks on Whidbey's Approach and Tower frequencies and check it out. Stay back from the field until you can confirm what's going on. Under no circumstances are you to risk any of the aircraft. If you even *start* to think things are getting squirrelly, haul ass and get back here. It's much better to get the word back here so that we can start trying to figure out what we're going to do. We're the closest force available; it will fall on us to get it done."

"Yes, sir," Commander Meadows said. "We'll take care of it."

The CAG looked at his Deputy, "Bambi, we'd better go ahead and cancel the rest of the flight schedule for the day. We need people to start looking at what our options are in case this all goes to shit on us."

Downtown Seattle, WA, 1503 Pacific Daylight Time

Sam Burton hated his cell phone provider and wasn't even sure why he still used it. He never seemed to be able to get a clear signal, much less the four bars he was promised, no matter where he went. He'd now gone over two hours without a signal. While he understood the big buildings in downtown Seattle could sometimes block signal reception, two hours was unacceptable! How was he supposed to conduct business when he was unable to make a call?

Just when he thought he couldn't get any more frustrated, he spied one of the cell phone provider's stores across the street. Not taking the time to go to a crosswalk in his fit of rage, he looked both ways and crossed in the middle of the block, causing two drivers to honk at him as they braked heavily and swerved to avoid him.

His mood didn't improve upon entering the store, as both of the people working there were already helping other customers, with many others waiting in line for both of them. Getting into the line of the prettier of the two, he stood fuming while he waited his turn. He didn't have to wait long before he noticed everyone else seemed to be having the same problem he did. Hah! It wasn't just his phone, like the provider always said. It was the provider's lousy service at fault, which he had *always* known was the culprit.

Sensing the growing frustration from everyone on the other side of the counter, the representative Sam was waiting for looked at all of the people in line and asked in a louder voice, "Is everyone having the same problem with not getting a signal?" Everyone replied in the affirmative, with varying shades of anger and annoyance. Pulling out her phone, Stephanie, as was noted on her name tag, saw her phone didn't have service either. "That's weird," she said. "I always have four bars here." She looked at her service partner. "It looks like we've got a pretty big problem; we better let the manager know."

Sam watched as she picked up the landline and dialed. "Hi Jim," she said. "This is Stephanie at the downtown store. We seem to be having a problem with reception in the area. I don't know if it is related to the power outage we had an hour ago, but nobody seems to be able to get a signal in the downtown area."

She listened intently for a few seconds and then replied, "No, I don't think there's anyone important in town. I know there's a conference at the convention center, but when *isn't* there?" She looked around the room. "Does anyone know if the president or vice president is in town?" Seeing only shrugs or negative responses, she said into the phone, "No, no one thinks there are any dignitaries here." She listened again for a bit then thanked the person on the other end of the line and hung up.

"My manager has no idea what's going on," she said. "He said it appears there is an active jammer in the area, because the cell towers seem to be working correctly, yet no one has a signal in the area. Sometimes the Secret Service will do that to defeat assassination attempts when the president is in the area, but it's illegal for anyone else to use a communications jammer. He's got all of our technicians working on the problem and assures me that the problem should be fixed very quickly."

Sam shrugged as he turned and walked out of the store. Typical techno-babble to justify crappy service, he thought. There was a store for his company's leading competitor near his house; he decided to stop and make the switch on his drive home.

172 | CHRIS KENNEDY

Blair Terminal, The Port of Tacoma, Tacoma, WA, 1505 Pacific Daylight Time

Captain Du Jun saluted and reported, "Sir, we have almost finished unloading. One of the last systems to unload, an HQ-19 missile transporter, is running a little late. They misjudged a low area of the deck and got stuck." Captain Du stood only a couple of inches over five feet tall, so he was forced to look up to talk to his superior who stood five feet, ten inches. Both weighed about 160 pounds; Captain Du was a bit on the stocky side, while his superior was rather thin.

His superior, Major Pan Yan, had left the *Xin Fei Zhou* and was watching the unloading operation from the pier. The smoke from the destroyed customs office had cleared, and all the longshoremen had been rounded up and sent home, leaving the pier occupied solely by the Chinese forces.

Major Pan was in charge of the forces deployed on the *Xin Fei Zhou*. Although the ship had been modified to carry military vehicles, the *Xin Fei Zhou* had originally been built as an automobile transport, and the conversion was "imperfect," at best. While the missile's cab fit well enough into the modified ship, the missile canisters it pulled were a little taller. There were some spots that had to be avoided, which was challenging because of the vehicle's large turning radius; apparently they had just found another low spot that wasn't previously surveyed. He was happy everything had, so far, gone relatively smoothly, but the HQ-19 was his best anti-aircraft system; not having it properly deployed was going to leave gaps in their air defense coverage. "What is the status of the system now?"

Captain Du Jun reported, "Because of the congestion in the ship, they lost some time trying to get a tow vehicle to it to pull it back out; however, one of the drivers suggested letting some of the air out of the tires, which would make it a little lower. This worked, and they were able to get the transporter the rest of the way out with no further problems. The canister that hit the roof was slightly damaged and will not be operable until the missile techs have time to check it out, but the other three canisters on that transporter should be fine."

"That was a good plan," Major Pan Yan said. "See that the person that spoke up is commended. Where was that system supposed to go?"

"That system was supposed to go to the northeast on the road the Americans call 'I-90,'" Captain Du Jun said, consulting his notes. "The jammed transporter also blocked part of the PGZ-95 anti-air battery that was supposed to go with it. Three of those vehicles were loaded in front of the HQ-19, so I sent them on ahead. They should be on schedule. I hope that was okay; I know you said to keep all of the systems together, but I thought it best to provide coverage as soon as possible for that valley."

"That was good initiative," Major Pan approved. "Besides, if they run into any trouble, the PGZ-95s are capable of defending themselves from any ground targets that give them problems; their 25mm cannon will make short work of any police or light armored fighting vehicles. As long as they don't run into heavy tanks, they should be fine; even if they run into tanks, they might still get lucky."

Seattle ARTCC, Seattle, WA, 1510 Pacific Daylight Time

The phone rang in the ARTCC radar room, and one of the special forces women picked it up. Her eyes had long ago adjusted to the dim lighting of the room. At an even five feet tall, she was of average height for a female in the People's Republic, and looked like a stereotypical Chinese woman. Mrs. Morgan was surprised, therefore, when the soldier answered the phone with a very Midwestern American accent. "Good afternoon," she said. "Seattle ARTCC radar room. May I help you?"

She listened intently for a few moments and then turned to LCDR Lin, covering the mouthpiece of the phone with her hand. "It's for the site manager. Our backup is here, led by Major Yang Wei. They are at the front gate, and the guard is asking if he should allow them in since his sheet only had one group coming to visit today."

LCDR Lin turned to Mrs. Morgan and said, "Remember, if everything goes well today, you will be released at 2330 tonight. If it does not, you will be responsible for a great many deaths, starting with all of your personnel in this room. I want you to tell the guard you forgot to put the second group on the access list. He is to let them in, but, because the first group brought extra people, he is supposed to check in the back of the van to make sure there are only 10 people this time." The special forces operative handed her the phone.

"Good afternoon, this is Mrs. Morgan," said the air traffic manager in a cheerful voice. "I'm awfully sorry, but yes, there is supposed to be a second group of Chinese visitors today. Their tour got added after the access list was put together, and I just forgot to let you know until now. I'm sorry," she repeated, "It's all my fault."

"No worries," the gate guard replied, "I'll pass the two vans through."

"Thanks," Mrs. Morgan said. "Oh, one last thing. They brought extra people in the first group, so we'll have to limit this group.

Please take a look in the back of each van and get a good head count. If they have more than ten, the extras will have to wait outside until the other group leaves."

"I will," the guard said.

"Thank you very much," said Mrs. Morgan, putting the phone back on its cradle. "No problems," she said, looking at LCDR Lin.

Seattle ARTCC Main Gate, Seattle, WA, 1515 Pacific Daylight Time

"You're all set," the gate guard said to Major Yang Wei, the passenger in the first van who was obviously in charge of this group. Although Major Yang appeared to be a short man, the guard thought he seemed very intense. "Mrs. Morgan said to let you in, but I need to open up the back of the vans and get a head count first. She said the first group brought too many people, and you were only allowed to have 10 at a time."

"That is fine," Major Yang said. "Be my guest."

Smiling his thanks, the gate guard went around to the back of the first van and pulled open the door. Looking in, he saw a large number of armed men. He couldn't get a good count of them; all he could focus on were the barrels of the three large rifles pointed at him within inches of his face. Two of the men were dressed exactly like him, and they squeezed past. "Get in the van!" one of them commanded with a southern accent as they slid past the guard, giving the word 'van' two syllables. The guard got into the van, and the new 'security guards' took his place at the gate, waving the vans through.

As the vans drove off to the parking lot, the new gate guards approached the car that had driven up behind the second van. The one with the southern accent spoke to the driver. "Ah'm terribly sorry, but the Center is closed for a drill, and probably will be for several hours. Y'all will have to leave."

The driver looked confused. "But I'm supposed to be going on shift here shortly, how do I get in to do my job?"

The guard shook his head. "Ah'm sorry, but we were told to not let anyone else in. There is a big group from Washington here to check readiness. They said the people who were already on duty would have to do a double shift to check their performance in the event of an actual emergency." He smiled. "They did say to tell everyone that you will still get paid for the day, though. Enjoy your day off!"

The man looked thoughtful as he began to consider how he might spend his day off. Surprising his girlfriend with a bottle of her favorite Shiraz would probably win him *big* brownie points, he thought. "Okay," he said, smiling. "Thanks for the information!" He drove off.

"Now wasn't that easy?" the security guard asked his partner in Chinese. "Just tell them they get money, and Americans lose all sense of duty."

"Shameful," his partner said in reply. "Simply shameful."

I-90, 15 Miles East of Seattle, WA, 1520 Pacific Daylight Time

Ryan O'Leary was confused. He had known John Thomas for a long time, and he was faced with two competing impossibilities. On one hand, John was drunk in the middle of the day and hanging out with a woman when he should have been at work. As long as Ryan had known him, John had never been someone to turn down either a drink or a woman (in fact, as a forward air controller, one of his favorite quotes was "call 'em in!"), but Ryan had just spoken to John last week and knew he was working the day shift. With his unflappable personality and many hours in combat, he was a priceless asset to the FAA's organization at Seattle Center, and he was someone who had already been chosen to train other controllers. John had recently told him that new recruit training was always done during the day, so he had been switched to the day shift from Wednesday to Sunday. The weekends were quieter, so more training could be completed. So…if John were drunk and with a woman, he was either skipping work, which was unlikely, or he had been fired, which was even more unlikely. He hadn't been fired.

The other possibility was even less likely. The thought that the Chinese had taken over Seattle Center was nothing short of ludicrous. How did they get there? What did they hope to accomplish? It made no sense. A *terrorist* takeover might have been possible, maybe even likely, in order to crash airplanes or something like that, but John hadn't said terrorists were there, he had said *the Chinese* were there.

Faced with two impossibilities and not getting an answer on John's phone, Ryan decided to drive into town to see for himself what was going on. If nothing else, it was a nice break from the firewood he had been chopping, and he could pick up some sorely needed supplies for the cabin.

As he passed the exit for Bendigo Boulevard on I-90, he was startled to see three self-propelled anti-aircraft vehicles heading in the opposite direction. They didn't look like any American systems he had ever seen; they looked like the ones in intelligence briefings that started out with "Here's what the bad guys have..." He looked again and saw the red and yellow star on the side of one. "What the hell?" he wondered. "Those aren't ours."

John's story had to be true, no matter how far-fetched, and he replayed the phone call in his mind. The coughs he heard at the end of the call must have been silenced pistol shots from a different type of silencer than the ones he had used. And if *that* was true, his friend was dead. With no further need to go into town, and a growing desire to get some revenge, he decided to see where the anti-aircraft guns were headed. If they were in North Bend, they were far too close to home for his liking. Taking the next exit, he turned around to go back in the other direction. The vehicles were only traveling at 30 miles per hour so it didn't take long for him to catch up with them. He slowed down to follow them, staying far enough behind them that they wouldn't see him. As they reached Mile 34, the vehicles turned off the highway. They didn't use an exit, they just went left and crossed the westbound lanes without regard for the oncoming traffic; Ryan watched as a BMW and a Ford crashed into each other when they swerved to avoid the massive anti-air guns. Ryan growled in the back of his throat; that's one more I owe them.

The anti-aircraft guns pulled into the Travel Centers of America parking lot and took up stations in opposite corners of the parking lot. Ryan followed the anti-aircraft guns across the median of the highway in his Jeep and pulled into Ken's Gas and Grocery across the street from the truck stop. As he pulled up to the gas pump, he saw the search radars turning on the backs of the vehicles; it appeared they had reached their destination. One of the Chinese soldiers had left his vehicle and was directing traffic to clear an open area near each of the anti-aircraft guns. When one of the truck drivers didn't come out to move his truck, the closest weapon system fired its guns at the truck, shredding it, before driving up and pushing it over.

Ryan saw the wanton destruction and his anger grew; he vowed revenge. Having filled up his Jeep, he also filled up the gas can he used for the generator at the cabin. Going into the store, he searched the shelves looking for glass containers, but didn't find many as the majority of products were in plastic containers. Knowing time was short, he purchased three medium glass jars of mayonnaise and a Styrofoam cooler and went back to the Jeep. He checked; the Chinese vehicles were still across the street. With a grim smile, Ryan drove behind the store where he would have a little privacy to work.

University of Washington, Seattle, WA, 1530 Pacific Daylight Time

Sara Sommers and Erika Murphy made it back to their second floor room safely, although Erika hurt her leg running from the soldiers. They had seen numerous soldiers in the distance after that, but none had come close enough to worry about. They had gone around the campus, rather than through it, heading north from Red Square on 15th Ave. NE and then turning east on NE 45th St. When they got to the high rise dorms, they sneaked into McMahon dorm through the pine trees behind it.

They both knew it was dangerous to come back to the room, but they didn't have any other options. They had spent most of the morning studying; the only things they had in their bags were books…which were of limited use against armed men. If they could make it to their room they could get their hiking packs and some dried rations. With food and a little camping gear, they could probably make it out of town and hike their way back home.

They had just finished packing their gear when they heard a commotion in the hallway outside their room. "Everyone out of your rooms!" a male voice yelled.

"They're here!" Erika cried.

"Quick, out the window!" Sara said.

They crossed to the window and threw their backpacks out. As they threw the second pack, there was a loud slam in the hallway as the door next to theirs was kicked open. "Go, Erika!" Sara urged.

"No," Erika said, "you go first. I hurt my leg and will need you to help me down."

"Okay," Sara said. "Hurry!" She pulled a chair to the window and swung her leg over the sill. She put her other leg out the window and then turned over onto her stomach to slide out. She slid down to where she was only holding onto the window sill and then dropped the remaining ten feet to the ground.

Erika followed her. As her first leg came out, there was a slam as someone kicked in the door to their room. Erika screamed and redoubled her efforts; she got her other leg over the sill and started sliding out the window. Before she could make it, an arm appeared around her midsection, and she was dragged screaming back into the room.

Grabbing the two packs, Sara started running for the woods. "Stop!" she heard a man yell from behind her. A shot rang out, and she heard the bullet go past her and slap into a tree. Before she could think to stop, she was among the trees, dodging them as she ran, and each one she passed provided additional protection from the men behind her. She slowed as she reached 45th Street again, not wanting to run out into the street.

Think, Sara, she said to herself. Realizing she owed her friend, Sara decided to stay and see what the soldiers were up to. Looping back around to the south, she stayed in the cover of the trees while she worked her way back to the high rise dorms. Coming down the Burke-Gilman Trail past the North Physics Lab, she could see a procession heading down Mason Rd., with soldiers shepherding what appeared to be students. Her guess was confirmed as she caught a glimpse of Erika in the group, hobbling along on her hurt leg.

She followed them to the south, staying hidden in the trees. Reaching the point where Wahkiakum Rd. ran alongside the intramural tennis courts, she realized she couldn't go any further without being seen. Looking down the street, she could see where the students were being taken: the Intramural Activities Building (IAB) next to Edmundson Arena where the school's basketball team played.

She paused to watch and heard a thumping noise. The beating sound got louder and louder, and a group of helicopters roared overhead, just above the tree line. She watched from where she was hiding as they flew over to the intramural complex. While four smaller helicopters remained airborne, flying back and forth around the area, two larger helicopters flew in and landed on one of the intramural fields. A group of 30 men came out of the IAB, with six of them pushing flatbed carts. The men approached the helicopters and pulled out six large boxes with the help of several men who were inside the helicopters. The boxes were each about six feet long and must have weighed several hundred pounds based on how many men it took to move them.

Even though they were heavy, the men quickly loaded the boxes onto the carts and pushed them back into the building. Sara knew she needed to leave; the longer she stayed only increased the likelihood she would be discovered, so she started working her way back to the north. If she could get to Conibear Shellhouse, she decided, she could "borrow" one of the sailboats there. It wouldn't take long to sail across Lake Washington to the mainland. Then she only had to worry about the 19-mile hike home.

Travel Centers of America, North Bend, WA, 1535 Pacific Daylight Time

Ryan carried two bags of groceries as he walked down 468th Avenue and turned into the parking lot for the Travel Centers of America. Two of the anti-aircraft vehicles were parked on the north side of the building, with the third in the southwestern corner of the parking lot. As he watched, two strange-looking black vans pulled into the north side of the parking lot, and soldiers wearing Chinese uniforms got out. Two squads of soldiers, too, he thought; wouldn't that just make this a *whole* lot more fun.

Coming from the east, the anti-aircraft vehicle in the southwest corner was in front of him, pointed away with its back toward the truck stop building. The soldiers were still congregating around the vans and guns on the other side of the parking lot; their view of the third vehicle would be blocked by the building. The lone vehicle was his best opportunity.

Moving toward the anti-aircraft gun, he got his first good look at it. The hull was mounted on a tracked armored chassis with an armored turret on the rear portion. It looked big enough for a crew of three: a driver, a gunner and the vehicle commander, and he could see a couple of raised hatches where they would get in and out. The vehicle was armed with four 25mm guns. Two were mounted on each side of the turret in such a manner they could be used against ground targets as well as aviation units; he would have to be careful around them. The vehicle was also armed with four short-range surface-to-air missiles and four smoke grenade launchers. All in all, it looked to him like a pretty badass air-defense system; it would be a significant loss if he could take it out.

As he crossed the parking lot, he stopped and pretended he was tying his shoe as a soldier carrying a handheld surface-to-air missile came around the Travel Center building. He set it down next to the vehicle and laughed at something a man exiting the vehicle said to him. They shared a couple of words in Chinese, and then both the men began walking back toward the other vehicles. That would only leave two people in the vehicle, at most, Ryan thought, as he reached the side of it. Ducking down, he pulled the three jars of napalm out of the shopping bags. He had emptied the mayonnaise out of the jars and filled them with gasoline, and then he had stirred in small pieces of Styrofoam until the mixture gelled to the right consistency. A couple of punctures in the lid with his knife gave access to the "fuse," a fuel soaked piece of his T-shirt. He lit them, jumped onto the deck of the vehicle and threw one through each of the hatches on the main body of the vehicle. Slamming the hatches shut, he jumped onto the turret and threw the third one into the hatch there, slamming it closed.

Slamming the hatches might not have been the best choice, as the metal-on-metal '*clangs*' drew the attention of a Chinese soldier coming from around the Travel Center building. Yelling something at Ryan in Chinese, he continued to run toward the vehicle as Ryan sprinted to the east, grabbing the surface-to-air missile from the ground as he jumped off the deck of the anti-aircraft gun. The soldier didn't pursue Ryan, going instead to the vehicle to see what Ryan had done. As the soldier reached the gun system, he was blown backward as the ammunition in the turret exploded from the heat of the napalm, bending the turret askew on the chassis with the force of the explosion.

Alerted to Ryan's sabotage by the sound of the blast, a cry went up from the soldiers on the north side of the Travel Center parking lot as Ryan ran across 468th Ave. toward the Edgewick Inn parking lot where he had left his Jeep. Seeing him running away, several of the soldiers fired shots in his direction, but he was too far away for them to get a good shot. Although he heard a couple of bullets go by, the majority weren't close enough to be a cause for worry. Looking over his shoulder, he could see a bunch of soldiers getting into the vans; that *was* a cause for worry.

A column of black smoke filled the sky over the Travel Center parking lot, and he could still hear ammunition cooking off as he gunned the Jeep south onto 468th Ave., racing away from the first of the vans pulling out of the parking lot. He wanted to go north, but that would have taken him past the soldiers and allowed the other two anti-aircraft guns to get a shot at him; that would have been fatal. He'd have to go around them to the west and then go north. The Jeep had a good head start over the van and more acceleration; he was already pulling away from the van as he turned west onto North Bend Way. He went about a mile, with the van in pursuit falling further behind, before turning north onto 455th Ave. He turned back to the east on 140th St., hoping the soldiers trailing him didn't have radios because he would be passing within about a quarter of a mile of the Travel Center on his way back east.

Unfortunately, the soldiers in pursuit must have called back, as the other van pulled up as he approached the intersection of 140th St. and 468th Avenue. It was going to be close. There were trees on both sides of the road, and the first van was behind him, so the only direction he could go was forward. He jammed the accelerator to the floor, and his speed neared triple digits as he rocketed through the intersection.

Only a couple of soldiers were in position to shoot at him, and bullets whined off and through his Jeep as he went past them. Several more bullets slapped into the back of his jeep as he sped off. Ryan had survived uninjured, but the Jeep wasn't so lucky. It had been hit in several places, and the engine started to miss. He kept the accelerator to the floor as he passed Twin Falls Middle School, hoping to coax as much speed as he could out of the Jeep before it died. He knew the van wouldn't stop chasing him, and he expected the soldiers in the other van would be coming after him now too.

He made it another mile, with the motor sounding increasingly worse, and then his speed began falling off. Knowing the Chinese would be upon him soon, he brought the car to a stop at the turnoff to Granite Creek Road, leaving it across the center of the road to block his pursuers. Grabbing the surface-to-air missile by its sling, he pulled his Savage Model 110 .30-06 rifle from the gun rack and jogged into the forest with his weapons. He had just found a good position at the top of a small hill when the first van drove up.

Sighting through the rifle's matte black scope, he focused on the driver as he stroked the AccuTrigger. The bullet hit the driver in the heart, a perfect kill shot, and the van coasted into a collision with the Jeep. As the van rebounded a short distance from the impact, Ryan switched his aim to the right front tire and flattened it.

Men started spilling out of the van on the opposite side from him. He took the time for one more shot, putting it through the grill of the van, before he withdrew to the northeast. He didn't know if the 165-grain softpoint would put the engine out of commission like it did a whitetail deer, but he figured it was worth a shot.

Fort Lewis Tower, Joint Base Lewis-McChord, Tacoma, Washington, 1545 PDT

"*Fort Lewis Tower,* Outlaw 65," the UH-60 pilot from the 2nd Battalion of the 158th Aviation Regiment (Assault) called. The Sikorsky UH-60 Black Hawk was a four-bladed, twin-engine, medium-lift utility helicopter.

"Outlaw 65, *Fort Lewis Tower, go ahead,*" the Chinese sergeant operating the tower radio replied in fluent English.

"Outlaw 65 *is a flight of 8 currently 16 miles to the southeast for a full stop,*" the helicopter pilot said, requesting clearance to land.

"*Roger,* 65, *winds are 320 degrees for 10. You're cleared to land, Runway 33.*" The Chinese sergeant looked at the U.S. Army soldier standing nearby in the tower, who was being held at gunpoint by a second Chinese soldier. "Who is *Outlaw 65*, and where is he coming from?"

The Army corporal didn't see any reason to lie or to keep silent. Even if he had, he had already seen resistance was futile; the Chinese soldier had killed his sergeant for refusing to answer his last set of questions. The corporal did not want to die, and he was too scared to think of anything other than the truth. "Outlaw flight is eight helicopters coming back from a weekend training operation at the Yakima Training Center."

"What is that?" the Chinese sergeant asked.

"It's a training center we use for maneuver and live fire training about 60 miles southeast of here near the city of Yakima," the American corporal said. "It's a really big training area. The helicopters were down there for some operations with a bunch of air national guard units."

"I see," the sergeant said. He picked up a walkie-talkie and said something into it in Chinese. He obviously got the answer he was looking for, because a broad smile covered his face. "We will be ready for them," he said.

Runway 33, Joint Base Lewis-McChord, Tacoma, Washington, 1553 PDT

The flight of eight helicopters flew in to land on Runway 33. As the lead helicopter, *Outlaw 65*, came in to land, its pilot, Captain Johnny Dixon, looked over at his copilot and asked, "What the hell is all that stuff?"

"I've got no idea," the copilot, Captain Steve Woods, said as he looked at the strange tanks and surface-to-air equipment. "Maybe they're some kind of anti-aircraft display."

"Damn, sir," one of the crew chiefs said, "that stuff to the right looks Chinese. They're the only ones I know that use that dumbass blue camouflage pattern."

The pilot looked to the right side of the field where he saw the missile transporter the crew chief was talking about. Sure enough, the entire vehicle was covered in a digital blue camouflage, similar to some of the U.S. Navy uniforms he had seen. He couldn't remember ever seeing *any* U.S. missile system painted in that color, nor did he remember hearing anything about a visit by a foreign service or other war game that would have brought them into town.

"Damn," the crew chief repeated, "it looks like that anti-aircraft gun to the left is tracking us. What the fuck is up with that? That's just damn creepy."

The pilot looked back to the left and saw several multi-barreled anti-aircraft vehicles. The crew chief was right; it did appear that the guns were tracking the flight of helicopters. They must be doing some training, he thought, using us as targets of opportunity. He wasn't worried about the presence of all of the anti-aircraft defense systems, but he was very, *very* confused about where they had all come from.

Fort Lewis Tower, Tacoma, Washington, 1553 Pacific Daylight Time

 ort *Lewis Tower,* Tigershark 32," the AH-64 Apache called at the same time the Outlaw flight was coming in to land.

"Tigershark 32, *Fort Lewis Tower, go ahead,*" the tower replied.

"*Roger, we're a flight of eight, 15 miles to the southeast, full stop.*"

The Chinese sergeant grabbed the walkie-talkie, swearing in Chinese, as the guns around the field began firing.

Runway 33, Joint Base Lewis-McChord, Tacoma, Washington, 1555 PDT

The pilot of *Outlaw 65,* Captain Dixon, brought his helicopter to a hover at the approach end of the runway. With the rest of his flight lined up behind him, he taxied down the runway a short distance before turning onto the taxiway for the transit back to his squadron's hangar. As he keyed the microphone to talk to ground control for taxi clearance, it seemed like every gun in the world began firing at once at his flight of helicopters. The air was full of tracers as the six anti-aircraft guns began sawing the helicopters apart; their four-barreled 25mm guns spitting cannon shells at the rate of 800 per minute. The gun systems were quickly joined by the machine guns from the tanks and armored fighting vehicles, and tracers criss-crossed all around him, while several surface-to-air missiles leapt from the vehicles to strike the helicopters still airborne, swatting them from the sky.

Captain Dixon knew he was in trouble. The enemy had waited until his helicopter had landed to attack, and he didn't have the airspeed he needed to get away, or any altitude he could turn into airspeed. He lifted off and veered to the right, away from the closest set of tracers, but then had to dodge back to the left to avoid several burning helicopters. He avoided one set of tracers, but the rounds from a second gun slammed into the helicopter, smashing through the cockpit and killing his copilot. He felt the controls go mushy in his hands as the motors died, and the helicopter crashed back to the ground.

Although only five feet up, the helicopter hit hard on the runway, scattering pieces of motor and rotor blades in every direction as it broke apart under the continued hammering of the enemy shells. Hit in the left arm by a piece of the shrapnel, Captain Dixon unfastened his restraining harness and opened the door while bullets and shells continued to batter his helicopter. Having turned nearly 180 degrees as he pulled away from the anti-aircraft gun, he could see all eight helicopters on the ground. While he watched, some of them began spilling soldiers, as each had been loaded with 11 soldiers in addition to their pilots and crew.

Although the troops were just returning from a live-fire exercise, Captain Dixon knew they hadn't expected combat when they returned home, and their rifles weren't loaded. As he exited the helicopter and started running for the cover of the trees, he ran past several soldiers. They had the presence of mind to grab ammunition boxes as they exited their helicopters, but had stopped in the center of the field to load their weapons.

"C'mon," Captain Dixon yelled as he ran by, "you're too exposed here." He looked back over his shoulder to see if they had followed, only to see a titanic explosion as a 125mm shell detonated in their midst, killing all three instantly.

The tree line was only 20 yards away, and hope swelled that he could make it. At 10 yards he was distracted as one of the tanks to the northeast suddenly blew up. He slowed as he turned to look at the source of the gigantic explosion. He neither heard nor felt the 25mm shell that hit him in the head, killing him instantly.

Joint Base Lewis-McChord, Tacoma, Washington, 1601 Pacific Daylight Time

The flight of eight AH-64D Apache helicopters led by *Tigershark 32* saw flames and smoke as they approached the field, and the pilot of *Tigershark 32,* Major Jim Mitchell, was worried that one of the Black Hawks in the flight ahead of his had crashed. Reality was far worse than his fears; he was greeted at his home field by a scene he wouldn't have imagined in his worst nightmares. He looked down to see all eight of the helicopters burning on the ground, with a few of their troops shooting at a variety of tanks and armored vehicles ringing the field.

"What the hell is going on?" he asked his gunner, Captain Ron Heartly.

"Fuck, sir, it looks like we're under attack!" the gunner replied.

Major Mitchell could only see a few soldiers still returning fire, using the crumpled shells of the crashed helicopters as cover. The fire they were taking was coming from a variety of armored vehicles, and their personal weapons were unable to match the much larger shells pouring in on them. Recognizing the futility, most of the soldiers gave up and tried to run for the tree line on the sides of the field. All of them were mowed down within seconds of leaving the cover of the helicopters.

"Light 'em up!" Mitchell yelled to his gunner. Switching to the radio, he transmitted, "*All Tigersharks, Fort Dixon is under attack. Open fire on the armor below!*"

The AH-64D Apache helicopters of the 1st Battalion of the 229th Aviation Regiment (Attack) were also returning from the Yakima Training Center, and the sight of their comrades dying galvanized them into action. The AH-64D Apaches had been using the live fire range at the Training Center and each of the helicopters had flown back to the airfield still armed with whatever ordnance their pilots hadn't been able to expend on the range. Major Mitchell looked over his shoulder; all seven helicopters followed him into battle.

The Apaches were armed with a 30mm chain gun under the aircraft's forward fuselage, and Major Mitchell's gunner put his to use against the Chinese armor. Within seconds, a Type 98 tank exploded under the hammer of his 30mm shells. Mitchell wished he still had some of his AGM-114 Hellfire missiles or Hydra rockets; unfortunately, he had fired all of them the day before, and only the gun had any ammunition...and not much, at that.

Mitchell saw they had surprised the people on the airfield. All of the anti-aircraft guns were shooting at ground targets; however, as he scanned the battlefield he saw the closest one begin swiveling its guns skyward. "Anti-aircraft gun, right, four o'clock," he yelled to his gunner as he yanked the Apache away from the threat. His gunner took it under fire and it exploded.

The eight helicopters hovered over the edge of the field where many of the enemy soldiers in the vehicles below couldn't see them, and most of the enemy force didn't seem to realize they were taking fire from a different direction. During that brief time, the Americans destroyed five tanks and two of the multi-barreled anti-aircraft guns, while only losing two helicopters.

As more and more of the Chinese armored vehicles turned their guns on the newcomers, though, the odds rapidly turned against them; they were tremendously out-gunned. A full load of Hellfire anti-tank missiles might have evened the odds, but they had none. The tanks also began turning to place their well-armored fronts toward the helicopters, and the Apache pilots found it harder to kill them. Meanwhile, they had to dodge an ever-increasing volume of incoming fire, and the Apaches began falling from the sky as surface-to-air missiles were employed against them. Missile contrails filled the sky around the field and, within seconds, there were only two Apaches left. Major Mitchell realized it was time to go.

He keyed his radio to call for a retreat, but an anti-aircraft gun to the left of his helicopter found him first. Before he could flee, the 25mm shells sawed through the aircraft, killing his gunner and wounding him. One shell destroyed his flight controls, and the helicopter crashed into the trees, out of control. Already unconscious, Major Mitchell didn't feel the impact that killed him.

Seeing he was the only one left, the pilot of *Tigershark 47* fled to the east. His aircraft had been hit, and he had to coax it along, smoke pouring from its damaged starboard engine. Unable to grasp what had just happened, the crew of *Tigershark 47* decided to fly to the airfield at McChord, just to the northeast of Fort Lewis. The anti-aircraft guns waiting there could see the smoke trail from *Tigershark 47* while it was still several miles distant; the helicopter and its crew were both destroyed as soon as they came into range.

Gauntlet 501, NAS Fallon, NV, 1615 Pacific Daylight Time

"Are you ready to go?" Commander Fred 'Mighty Mite' Meadows asked the other member of his crew. Mighty Mite, the Commanding Officer of the "Gauntlets" of Electronic Attack Squadron 136 (VAQ-136), sat in his EA-18G aircraft at the end of the runway, itching to go. Based on the F-18 fighter/bomber aircraft, the EA-18G Growler had a crew of two, with the pilot in the front seat and the Electronic Warfare Officer (EWO), who operated the aircraft's electronic systems and jammers, in the back.

"I'm good," Lieutenant Jim 'Basket' Case replied. Basket was an EWO on his second tour. Although he had just arrived at the squadron, Mighty Mite knew he had a good deal of experience with both the aircraft's combat capabilities and the radar parameters of most of their enemy's systems.

"Hey, Skipper," Basket said after a moment, "Did you find out anything else about what's going on at home?"

"No, I didn't," his commanding officer replied, "and it's starting to worry me. I wanted to get up there a lot sooner. We were going to fly up with a couple of the 'Bounty Hunters' of Strike Fighter Squadron 2, but one of their Super Hornets developed a maintenance issue and had to drop out of the flight. CAG wouldn't let us go with just one escort aircraft, so we had to switch out the Bounty Hunters' aircraft with a couple from the Blue Blasters of VFA-34, and then I had to re-brief the entire flight with them. If I sound like I'm frustrated, it's because I am."

"Why's that, Skipper?"

"The problem was, and still is, that the Blasters fly the older F-18C model Hornet, which means fuel is going to be a bit tighter than

I had originally planned. So, not only did I have to re-brief the flight and work out our communications plan, I also had to coordinate getting them to the tanker and making sure they got every last bit of gas they could. It was necessary for the overall success of the mission…but it took time. If there is something happening back home, and it certainly seems like there is, I want to know what's going on *now*, not once whoever it is gets dug in and settled. Nothing else has been heard from the air base since the first few calls, and no one has been allowed on base. We only know that some group appears to be holding the base hostage, the group looks Asian, and they have strange-looking rifles. No one knows who they are, and I don't like it."

"Neither do I," said Basket. "I've got a wife and two children on base. I'm pretty worried about them." He caught movement out of the corner of his eye. "Here come the Blasters."

Basket tried to figure out who was manning the two aircraft as the ground crew began removing the safeties from the two fighters' gun systems, but couldn't. "Who are we flying with, Skipper?" he finally asked.

Mighty Mite looked at his notes. "LT 'Calvin' Hobbs is in 203, and LTJG 'Oscar' Berkman is in 207," he said. "Calvin's a good stick and has been around a while, but Oscar's one of their newbies. I don't know him that well."

Mighty Mite saw the ground crew had finished arming the Blasters, and Calvin gave him a thumb's up, indicating they were ready to go. "The Blasters are ready," he told Basket, who called the Tower for permission to take off. Mighty Mite sighed. They were finally on their way.

Fort Lewis Main Gate, Tacoma, Washington, 1625 Pacific Daylight Time

The convoy of trucks pulled up to the main gate of Fort Lewis on Clark Road, only to find the gates closed and unusual-looking tanks blocking their progress. Two Asian men in strange camouflage uniforms approached the first truck while at least 30 others watched. The two men in the driver's compartment of the truck noticed all the men they could see had their weapons drawn and pointed in their general direction. This didn't resemble any drill they had ever been a part of. Even more ominously, the tanks' main guns seemed to be tracking them, following their every movement.

"Hi," the driver, Sergeant Adams, said as the two men walked up. Sergeant Bill Adams was an experienced driver who had made this trip many times since he had been stationed at the base. He had never had a reception like this, though, especially on a Sunday. He looked around nervously. "We're coming back from a weekend at the Yakima Training Center. We need to get on post so we can drop off the troops and gear."

Both of the camouflaged men shook their heads. "I'm sorry," the closer one said, "but that isn't going to be possible at this time." He pointed at a large plume of black smoke in the direction of the airfield. "As you can see, there was an accident at the airfield, and a couple of large weapons are unsecured. Some gas was also released, so the base has been closed. You can't enter at this time."

"Where are we supposed to go with all of this stuff?" Sergeant Adams asked, nodding with his head toward the back of the truck.

"Do you have weapons and ammunition in the back?" the guard asked.

"Yeah," the sergeant answered, "we've got a whole load of weapons and a bunch of live ammunition."

Both of the guards noticeably tensed. "You're going to have to leave the trucks here then," the second guard said. "We can't let them go out into town."

"So, what are we supposed to do?" Sergeant Adams asked. "Sit here and babysit them or unload them so we can drive the trucks?"

"Actually," the second guard said, "what you're going to do is get out of the trucks and leave. The trucks will stay here, and we'll take care of them for you."

"Excuse me," First Lieutenant Steven Ross said from the passenger seat. "I don't know who you are, and I really don't care a whole lot. What I do know is I signed for this load, and I'm not going to just leave it sitting here. Nor am I just going to go off walking through town. I can't even get a cell phone signal to call my wife to come get me. I understand there's an emergency going on that closed the base. Fine, we'll pull off the road here and wait until it opens again, however long it takes. I, however, am not leaving."

The lieutenant's door was thrown open, and someone reached in, grabbed him and threw him to the ground outside. The lieutenant sputtered something about having the soldier charged with striking an officer, but his voice stopped suddenly when the muzzle of the soldier's rifle was pressed against his nose.

"Hey, now, that's not necessary," said Sergeant Adams, trying to distract the guards and defuse the tension. "We're all on the same team, right? I don't recognize the uniforms, though. Who are you guys, anyway?" As he spoke, he noticed the rifles the guards were carrying weren't M-16s. Not only weren't they M-16s, they didn't look like any American rifle he had ever seen. The configuration was all wrong. His bad feeling got a lot worse; all of a sudden, he wasn't sure he *wanted* to know who they were.

"Get out of the truck!" the guard closest to him commanded. He pointed his gun at Sergeant Adams' face.

Looking down the barrel of one of the strange rifles, Sergeant Adams decided exiting the vehicle made good sense. As he got out, the men who had been standing around sprang into action and surrounded the trucks in the convoy. There must have been additional soldiers who had previously been hidden; within seconds nearly a company of soldiers was pointing rifles at the convoy.

Sergeant Adams watched as the rest of the convoy's soldiers were forced to exit their vehicles and searched for weapons. The unknown soldiers prodded the Americans into a group, and another man came to stand in front of them. By the way he held himself, Sergeant Adams could tell the newcomer was either an officer or a senior enlisted; he was used to command. Getting their attention, he addressed the group. "Who we are is unimportant at this moment, but it will all be made plain to you in good time. In the meantime, it is enough for you to know that the base is closed, and we have orders not to let weapons out into town. Unfortunately, we can't let you stand around here, so you are going to have to go. Where you go isn't important to me; all that's important is that you leave and do not come back. I'm sure your chain of command will be in contact with you shortly. I'm sorry to have to make you walk, but those are my orders. That's also all the information I can give you about the drill that's in progress. All right then, have a nice day."

"Wait a minute," Lieutenant Ross said. "I need a few of my men to stay here and stand guard over our equipment. I'll lose my commission if I just leave it here with someone I don't know, just on your say-so. I need to speak to one of my superiors for authorization."

"You'll lose your commission if you walk off?" the camouflaged leader asked.

The lieutenant nodded.

"If you stay here," the leader said, "you will lose your life!" He drew his pistol. "I am going to count to 10, at which point, I will personally shoot anyone who is still standing in front of me. No questions. Go!" He began to count, and most of the American soldiers started to walk off. Sergeant Adams joined them. The person with the pistol got to 5; looking back, Sergeant Adams saw that the lieutenant still hadn't moved. The leader pointed the pistol at the lieutenant, continuing to count. By the time he got to 8, everyone had stopped, waiting to see what would happen when he got to 10. The man with the pistol had to be bluffing, they all thought.

The leader said, "9." He cocked the pistol for emphasis. The lieutenant didn't flinch, and Sergeant Adams wondered what he was thinking. Sergeant Adams never found out. The leader said, "10," pulled the trigger and fired a round through the lieutenant's forehead. Sergeant Adams ran with the rest of the soldiers.

Conibear Shellhouse, University of Washington, Seattle, WA, 1645 PDT

The boathouse was deserted. It hadn't been easy, but Sara had made it there undetected. Along the way, she had seen additional groups of soldiers herding students in the direction of the Intramural Activities Building. She wondered what the soldiers were doing with the students, and her mind feared the worst for her friend. She didn't think it likely the soldiers had arranged a giant intramural basketball tournament for the weekend and had parachuted onto campus just to set it up. There was something going on, something that involved those big boxes the soldiers had been taking off the helicopters. She didn't know what it was, but she knew it was big. Anything that brought soldiers from another country here had to be extremely serious in nature.

She had no idea what to do. She wanted to help her friend, but she knew there was nothing she could do against armed soldiers. What was she going to do? Sneak up on one of them with a knife, kill him, take his rifle and start a one-woman guerrilla war? Unlikely, since she didn't even know how their rifles worked, much less how to use those grenade launcher things she had seen some of the soldiers carrying.

She needed help. She could go to the police, but she didn't think they would be much help. They were pretty good at crowd control for drunken, unruly students at a concert, but she expected they would be out of their league against armed soldiers who were trained killers. Sure, the police might be able to kill a few of them, but the soldiers were going to win in the end, and they would kill a *lot* more of the police.

She wanted to go home and tell her dad, but she didn't think he was the right person, either. Sure, he was good in the woods and knew how to hunt and fish, but he wasn't trained to fight against soldiers. Not only wouldn't she get Erika back from the soldiers, she was also likely to lose her father. She was rapidly running out of options.

Then it dawned on her; she did know someone who was trained to fight soldiers. Not only someone who *could* fight them, but someone who was an elite soldier, a SEAL, the 'best of the best.' She thought for a minute and could see him at the top of Infinite Bliss; he was tall, handsome, blue-eyed and his name was....Ryan! If she could somehow find him, he would know how to get Erika back. He might even be able to do the sneaking up with a knife thing. Although he hadn't been a SEAL in a couple of years, surely those things were like riding a bike? Once you knew how to kill someone, you wouldn't forget, would you?

Having decided Ryan was her only good option, she moved on to the next problem. How would she find him? How would she find someone who didn't want to be found? If he was living in the national forest, he wouldn't want his house (cabin? tent?) to be found. He would have gone to great lengths to put it where it wouldn't be found, and then he would have camouflaged it to *ensure* it wasn't. Sara knew she had good outdoorsman's skills, but a trained SEAL would have skills on a *whole* different level, right?

She had a second thought. What if he didn't even live in the forest anymore? Then how would she find him? It wasn't as if she could pull out a phone book and look up SEAL to find him. Looking up 'Ryan' was similarly unhelpful. Without his last name, she would never be able to pull his number out of the phone book, even if his apartment *had* a phone. If he didn't live in it much, as she had thought when she met him, would he bother to have a phone? More likely, he would have a cell phone, or even a satellite phone, as far back into the woods as he lived. Her best bet would be to go to Mt. Garfield and try to find him. Perhaps if she got into the general vicinity of where he lived and yelled his name? Advertising his name at the top of her lungs probably wouldn't win her any points with him, but it was the best she could do; it would have to suffice.

Having decided that, she just needed to figure out how she was going to get there. Her first plan to leave the campus was still her best. The soldiers had mostly moved on, and she still had enough time left in the day to take one of the sailboats and make it across the water. From there, she could either try to borrow a phone to call her parents and have them come get her, or she could try hiking to North Bend on her own. However she got to her house, she could borrow one of her parents' cars and drive to Mt. Garfield at first light. Walking around the mountain in the dark was a recipe for disaster. She'd somehow find Ryan and convince him to help. She wasn't sure how she'd do it, but she had a couple hours of sailing time to work it out.

Having reached a decision, she pushed the sailboat into the water and set off. Ryan wasn't getting any closer while she stood there worrying.

Seattle Outskirts, WA, 1700 Pacific Daylight Time

"The lockdown is complete," Lieutenant Colonel Peng Yong said. "I have gotten reports from each of the zones."

"All of our forces were supposed to be in place by now," Colonel Zhang said. "Are they?"

"It appears so," Lieutenant Colonel Peng said. "In the southwest, our blockade is set on I-5, south of the town of Olympia. This blockade is largely symbolic, as automobiles can easily avoid it by using the streets through the city. It does, however, serve to remind the citizens we are there in force, as well as to block any large-scale military convoys that come from that direction. We have two companies of tanks and a battery of anti-aircraft guns; they can defend themselves from anything but a well-organized military assault. There is also a battalion of soldiers deployed in support of the armor. An additional two companies of tanks and another battalion of troops in the area will help ensure United States military forces don't slip through unopposed. There are also four tanks and a platoon of troops stationed at the Olympia airport to ensure it isn't used." Colonel Zhang nodded.

"In the east," Lieutenant Colonel Peng continued, "the blockade is set up at the Olallie State Park, about six miles east of the town of North Bend, Washington. With a major U.S. Air Force base located in Spokane to the east, this blockade is manned by 2,000 troops, reinforced with a battalion of 124 tanks. These tanks are supported by both a PGZ-95 anti-aircraft battery and a HQ-19 surface-to-air missile battery located in North Bend. There are another 500 soldiers and two companies of tanks located 17 miles to the north along Highway 2 to ensure the Americans don't sneak through that way, either."

"Good," Colonel Zhang said, nodding.

"Finally," Lieutenant Colonel Peng finished, "in the north, the last blockade is set up on I-5 four miles south of Mt. Vernon. Two battalions of troops are in the area, as well as a battalion of tanks. There is another force of about 500 troops and two companies of tanks at Lake McMurray four miles to the east to ensure the Americans don't send a force down Highway 9." Lieutenant Colonel Peng paused and looked up from his notes. "I'm sorry, sir, but I still don't see how any of these will stop a full scale assault."

Colonel Zhang smiled. "They are not supposed to. Each of these forces is only supposed to maintain local control of its area; they were never expected to be able to defend against a determined, full-scale American assault. If the U.S. is able to get enough troops into the area, they will be able to break through our forces, if they choose. Our defenses around Seattle are somewhat like an egg. There is a thin shell that surrounds the area, which is strong enough to withstand some attacks; if you hit it hard enough, though, you can crack it quite easily."

"Yes, sir," Lieutenant Colonel Peng said. "That is exactly what I'm saying! How are we supposed to hold Seattle with these forces?"

Colonel Zhang smiled. "The best protection an egg has is that people try to treat it carefully to avoid breaking it. The purpose of our forces is to maintain local control and ensure the majority of the American civilians don't leave the Seattle area. They make better hostages for nuclear blackmail that way."

M.V. Erawan, Pier 91, Seattle, WA, 1745 PDT

Senator Jack Turner jumped up as the door opened. He and his family had been kept in a dark, humid area of the ship for over three hours, and his head hurt from where the soldier had hit him with his rifle. He chilled slightly as three Asian-looking men entered the hold. Two were armed with rifles; the other had a pistol at his side, but kept it in his holster. The way the other two deferred to him, and the aura of dangerous competence he exuded marked the man with the pistol as their leader.

"You are Senator Turner from Oregon, correct?" he asked.

"Yes, I am Senator Turner from Oregon," Jack replied, "and I demand to know what is going on... ugh!" He doubled up in pain as one of the soldiers hit him in the stomach with the butt of his rifle.

"My name is Major Chin Haung," the man with the pistol said, "and I neither take demands nor requests from imperialist dogs like you." He smiled at Mrs. Turner and then turned back to Jack, who was almost standing back upright again. "I do, however, have a request for you."

"I'm not doing anything for you until you let my wife and children go!" Jack said, his voice loud in the confined space.

"Have it your way," the major said, sighing as he opened the door. Eight more soldiers entered the room. They approached the family in twos, grabbing his wife and children and pinning them to the floor. They held the senator against the wall, where he could see what was going on. The major said something to one of his men in Chinese, who nodded sharply and handed over his bayonet to the major.

The major walked over to Janet Turner, idly picking at something under one of his fingernails with the point of the bayonet. Jack could not take his eyes off the long, razor-sharp knife. The major knelt down next to Janet's head and put the point of the knife next to her right eye. She squirmed and struggled to get away from it, but the soldiers were far stronger than she was and didn't allow her to move.

Jack also tried to get away from the soldiers holding him, but they were ready. This time, the butt of the rifle intersected with his crotch, rather than his stomach, and he was again doubled up in pain and nausea. "Wait…" he groaned.

Major Chin looked up at Jack, but kept the knife close to Janet's eye. A drop of blood appeared on her cheek. "No woman should have to see her husband beaten," he said. "Perhaps it is better if I take out both of her eyes so she doesn't have to watch." Both children screamed.

"No," Jack said, still struggling to get his breath back. "Don't do it. I'll do anything you want!"

"Yes," said Major Chin, standing up, "I know you will. My men have been trapped aboard this vessel without entertainment for weeks. I doubt you'd want to see what they could do to your wife and children." He paused, "Especially the little girl…"

"I'll do anything," Jack sobbed. "Anything you want; just leave my family alone."

"Yes," Major Chin said, "I'm sure you will."

August 19
Red Tide Evening

Seattle ARTCC, Seattle, WA, 1815 Pacific Daylight Time

The Chinese soldier controlling the area south of Seattle looked up from his board. "Major!" he exclaimed. "I have three American military aircraft that want to fly over Seattle and land at Whidbey Island."

"Turn them around to Portland," Major Yang Wei replied. "If they ask, tell them that both Whidbey and Seattle have had power failures and are not taking any more aircraft. Tell them you don't know when they will be back open again." He picked up his phone and began dialing. "I will call McChord, in case they refuse."

Gauntlet 501, 30 Miles South of Sea-Tac Airfield, Seattle, Washington, 1815 PDT

"Gauntlet 501, _this is Seattle Center._"

"_Seattle Center, this is_ Gauntlet 501," Basket replied.

"_Roger,_ Gauntlet 501, _I understand you are a flight of three headed to Whidbey Island Naval Air Station, correct?_"

"Gauntlet 501, _that is correct. We're a flight of three, headed to Whidbey._"

207

There was a short pause. *"Roger, 501, be advised that Seattle and Whidbey are both experiencing power outages at this time. All aircraft are being diverted to Portland International. Come right now to a heading of 180, vectors to Portland International."*

"Hey Skipper, they're trying to turn us to the south," Basket said over the intercom system. "The weather is fine—let's go VFR. When we get to Lake Tapps, that big lake down there to the right, we'll head to the northeast and then follow the Cascade Mountains to the north." VFR was short for "Visual Flight Rules," meaning that the aircraft's crew would be responsible for seeing and avoiding all other aircraft; ATC would not provide them any further advisories on approaching traffic. Having flown in the area for many years, all of the aircrew were familiar with a variety of visual references that would help get them home to Whidbey Island.

"Seattle Center, Gauntlet 501," Basket radioed. *"Thanks, but we are going to go VFR from here. We'd like to descend to 15 thousand, 500 feet and proceed visually to the northeast."*

ATC wasn't long in replying. *"I'm sorry, Gauntlet 501, but I can't let you do that. Whidbey and Sea-Tac aren't landing aircraft and won't be for a while. We don't have an estimate on when power will be restored. Come right to 180 now for vectors to Portland."*

Basket wasn't to be denied that easily. *"Center, Gauntlet 501. That's okay, we have enough gas to return to NAS Fallon. We are going to cancel our instrument clearance and proceed visually."*

ATC wasn't going to be denied, either. *"Gauntlet 501, this is Seattle Center,"* a new and sterner voice answered. *"We need to keep this airspace clear! You are to turn south now, or you will receive a flight violation."*

Getting a flight violation would ensure that Mighty Mite would never be the commercial pilot he wanted once his time in the military was over. "Umm…he sounds pretty serious," Mighty Mite said over the intercom. "Maybe we ought to head south, after all."

"Woah! This is weird," Basket said. "I've got what looks like a HQ-9 radar coming from the direction of the Tacoma port." He paused a second and then said, "Never mind; it's not that weird. I forgot the Chinese fleet was in town. I think one of their new destroyers has the naval version of that missile. Maybe one of them was going to Tacoma for some reason or another."

"Yeah, that could be," Mighty Mite replied. "I haven't heard anything about it. Try calling the Center one more time for permission to proceed. If we can't get it, we'll head south. I don't need a violation on my record."

Seattle ARTCC, Seattle, WA, 1817 Pacific Daylight Time

"Gauntlet 501, *this is Seattle Center,*" Major Yang Wei said in his sternest voice. "*We need to keep this airspace clear! You are to turn south now, or you will receive a flight violation.*"

"Sir, they're not buying it. It appears they are trying to get past Seattle to see what is happening at Whidbey," the air traffic controller said, looking at his radar.

"You are right," replied Major Yang. "It appears stronger measures are in order." He picked up his phone again.

Gauntlet 501, 18 Miles South of Sea-Tac Airfield, Seattle, Washington, 1817 PDT

Basket tried one last time, "*Center, 501, how about a practice approach at either Bremerton or Snohomish County Airfield? Are either of those available?*" They were within 20 miles of Sea-Tac Airfield and almost to the lake he had pointed out earlier.

The stern voice replied, even angrier this time, "501, *this is the last time I'm going to tell you. Turn right to 180 now, or I will write up a flight violation for you!*"

"HOLY SHIT SIR!" screamed Basket. "I've got HQ-9 tracking radars coming behind us to the left. They're at McChord Air Force Base! They've locked us up! Chaff! Dive! Get us the hell out of here!"

"*MISSILE LAUNCH!*" screamed one of the Blasters over the Gauntlet's base frequency. "*Missile launch from McChord Air Base! Break right! Chaff!*" All three pilots immediately executed 6-g turns while diving to get as low as possible. As they dove, they dispensed their chaff, little bundles of metal they hoped would confuse a radar-guided missile.

It happened too quickly for the crew of *Gauntlet 501*. Distracted by the communications with Seattle Center, Basket was unable to get his jamming system activated in time. The HQ-9 had a guidance system equal to the U.S. Patriot missile system and missiles that could fly at Mach 4.2 (over four times the speed of sound), or almost 3,200 miles per hour. From launch, it only took nine seconds for the missile to cover the 10 miles to *Gauntlet 501*, and its 400-pound warhead destroyed the aircraft.

The destruction of *Gauntlet 501* helped the two Blasters, as there were now many large pieces of metal falling through the air that functioned even better than chaff. The second missile locked onto one of these, blasting it to smaller fragments. The Blasters continued their high-g maneuvering and made it down to less than 100 feet of altitude, where they hoped to be below the radar horizon of the missile system. As they reached the foothills of Mt. Ranier, with the peak straight in front of them, Calvin made the decision to come back to the northeast. If they could just make it 20 miles further, they'd be able to contact Whidbey Approach and complete their mission. They could then hang a right on I-90 and follow it through the mountains to safety.

"*Oscar,*" he radioed his wingman. "*We're going to go northeast for three minutes and try to call Whidbey. When we get to I-90, we'll follow it to the east and get clear of the SAM trap. Copy?*"

"*Got it,*" said Oscar, sounding shaken.

"*We owe Mighty Mite and Basket, and we're going to complete this mission for them,*" radioed Calvin.

The next two minutes were tense, as the Blasters could see several missile radars looking for them on their threat warning systems. As they came over Tiger Mountain, they were close enough that Calvin thought they ought to be able to reach Whidbey Island. He transmitted several times, but no one answered.

Banking hard to the right over the small town of Snoqualmie, the Blasters turned southeast to follow I-90 through the valley. Looking down as they travelled further southeast, they saw several large truck-mounted SAM canisters moving into positions at a large open area in the town of North Bend. The missiles weren't set up yet, though, and they were unable to stop the Blasters. Calvin couldn't remember what type of missile system it was, but he knew the large canisters were one of the new systems that were extremely dangerous; he did *not* want to come back this way.

The Blasters continued down the valley, lucky to be alive, but their luck soon ran out; although the HQ-19 wouldn't be finished setting up for another 15 minutes, the two anti-aircraft guns at the large truck stop *were* operational, and both of them acquired Oscar's aircraft. Using their optical tracking systems, they didn't give any warning until they opened fire when *Blaster 207* was two miles away. With a combined rate of fire of over 25 rounds a second, the tracers looked like two fire hoses reaching out to embrace Oscar.

"*Break left!*" Calvin yelled over the radio to Oscar. Both aircraft executed hard left turns to follow the middle fork of the Snoqualmie River away from the guns. The maneuver succeeded in making one of the systems miss, but the other stitched a line of holes up Oscar's starboard wing, severing the fuel lines in it and setting the aircraft on fire. The control surface of the wing was also damaged, and Oscar could feel the aircraft wobble slightly. He regained control over the stricken aircraft and breathed a sigh of relief as he was able to level the wings. The relief was short-lived, as a surface-to-air missile slammed into the non-maneuvering aircraft's starboard wing.

The warhead on the missile was small, with only 4 pounds of high-explosive, but with the previous damage was enough to cause the right wing to fail. Calvin watched in horror as Oscar's wing came off, and the plane tumbled through the air, impacting on Granite Mountain a few seconds later. Calvin didn't see an ejection and knew his friend had died on impact.

The loss of Oscar strengthened his resolve to get back to Fallon so that he could return with a fully-armed aircraft. Looking at his gas gauge, he realized he was going to have to climb to a more fuel efficient altitude, and very soon, but knew that he was still too close to the SAM systems, so he continued down the Snoqualmie river valley, using the terrain for cover.

Middle Fork Camp Ground, WA, 1832 Pacific Daylight Time

Ryan O'Leary hid behind a tree. He had evaded the men who had followed him into the hills, and he had made it most of the way up the valley to his cabin. He had just passed the Middle Fork Camp Ground when he heard the sound of a helicopter. Damn, he thought, as he caught a flash of it through the trees. A Chinese attack helicopter. While he didn't know what kind, the big chain gun on the front and the red and yellow star on the side were all he needed to know to identify it as something he didn't want to play around with in the open.

However, Ryan wasn't in the open, he was in a heavy forest, and the helicopter pilot wouldn't know where he was as long as Ryan stayed out of his infra-red sights. The pilot wouldn't expect him to have a surface-to-air missile, either, which would go a long way toward evening the odds between them. Ryan might be able to take out the helicopter if he could get to a spot where he had a decent shot from ambush. If he missed, and the pilot saw where Ryan was, things would go very badly for him, very quickly. It would have to be a shot from behind, he decided, or it wasn't worth the risk.

As the helicopter passed overhead he heard the sounds of gunfire and explosions from down the river valley, and the helicopter stopped its slow search and nestled down into a gap in the trees, unmoving. Ryan knew this was the opportunity he'd been hoping

214 | CHRIS KENNEDY

for, and he ran to get into position. He still had some way to go when he heard the scream of an oncoming jet. Realizing the helicopter's pilot was preparing to ambush the passing aircraft, Ryan knew he had to change his plans.

Ryan ran straight across an open area, breaking cover in his effort to get to a firing position before the helicopter could shoot at the approaching aircraft. He was too late. The jet passed close by, and the helicopter sprang a couple of hundred feet into the air as it passed. The extra altitude gave Ryan a shot at the helicopter, though, and he raced the helicopter pilot to see who could lock up their target and get their missile off first. Ryan readied the missile and, getting an indication the missile had acquired one of the helicopter's engines, fired it at the helo.

As the smoke from his missile launch cleared, Ryan realized the Chinese pilot had fired too; there was a smoke trail leading away from the helicopter toward the F-18 that had just passed by. "Damn it," he said, realizing he hadn't been fast enough.

Both missiles blew up simultaneously.

Blaster 203, Middle Fork Camp Ground, WA, 1832 Pacific Daylight Time

Reaching the junction of the Snoqualmie and Taylor Rivers, Calvin turned right to follow the Snoqualmie River. Having made it out of harm's way, he was starting to feel pretty good about his chances. He had just throttled back to a more fuel-efficient setting when there was an explosion in his left engine, and the fire light came on. He quickly ran through the emergency procedures for shutting down the engine, then realized

RED TIDE | 215

the right engine appeared to be having problems and was losing power, as well. Within seconds, the right motor flamed out. Calvin tried to re-start the motor, but it wouldn't reignite. Low, slow and with a mountain in front of him, he reached up with both hands, grabbed the handles of his ejection seat system and pulled.

The rockets on his seat fired as designed, propelling his seat up and out of the aircraft. Reaching its apogee, the seat kicked away from Calvin, and his parachute deployed. Going through the procedures automatically, he looked up and saw he had a full parachute without any tangled lines. He tried to remember the rest of his parachute training as he realized he was heading for a wooded area.

"Let's see," he said. "I need to come right…I think I pull on the right riser." He pulled on it, and slowly turned to the right. "Sweet!" he thought, now that he was headed for a clear area.

As the ground came up, he realized he was falling a lot faster than he had imagined he would be, and he tried to get himself into the proper landing position. He impacted the ground heavily, rolled awkwardly, and slowly stood up, checking himself for damage. Finding none, and happy to be both on the ground and alive, he unclipped his parachute and began gathering it up.

He jumped in surprise as someone behind him said, "Nice job, dumbass. Can we go, please, before more of the bad guys show up?" Calvin turned to see a big man holding some sort of tube. It looked like he was in tremendous shape, which Calvin guessed was to be expected out here in the boonies.

"What do you mean?" Calvin asked. "That may not have been a perfect landing, but it wasn't bad for my first ejection. And, considering I just had to eject out of my plane and am now 800 miles from

216 | CHRIS KENNEDY

where I need to be, I'm having a pretty bad day. What's up with calling me a dumbass?"

"Well, I'm not the one who just got shot down by a helicopter," the man said. He indicated the tube. "You'll be happy to know that I shot him down so we don't have to worry about him coming back to strafe us." He sighed. "Unfortunately, that was my last SAM, so we'll have to work on acquiring some more if we're going to continue helping the effort."

"Who are you," Calvin asked, "freaking Rambo?"

"Nope," the man replied, "just your friendly neighborhood SEAL who happened to be passing by with a surface-to-air missile. My name's Ryan O'Leary."

"Well, thank you, sir, for taking care of the helo. I never saw it; I just thought I had an engine failure. My name is Shawn Hobbs, but you can call me Calvin."

"I'm no 'sir,'" Ryan said. "You can call me Ryan, or even Senior Chief, if you need to, although I've been out of the Navy for a couple of years now." He shook his head. "Damn sequestration." Calvin could see the mental shrug as he continued, "Well, let's get your chute packed up and get going. We're going to have to hurry to get back to my cabin by dark, and you *don't* want to be walking on the side of a mountain at night. We can talk more on the way."

Wilmington Village Apartments, Tacoma, WA, 2005 Pacific Daylight Time

First Sergeant Aaron 'Top' Smith looked through the binoculars at the gate to Fort Lewis. "Something's definitely wrong there," he said. As the senior enlisted person in the unit, Aaron was known by the honorific 'Top' to the members of the company.

"Dude!" Private First Class Jamal 'Bad Twin' Gordon exclaimed in a distinctly 'surfer dude' accent. "Like, who are those guys? They all look funny, and they've got, like, funny-looking weapons." The Rangers were watching the front gate of the base from the roof of the Gordons' apartment building in the Wilmington Village apartment complex on the other side of I-5. Bad Twin had called everyone in the unit after a friend had stopped by the apartment with a story about how the people at the gate had shot his convoy commander in the head. PFC Gordon didn't know what they'd been smoking on their weekend in Yakima, but obviously the National Guard guys had convinced his friend to do some sort of drugs. He'd better hope there wasn't a surprise urinalysis test this week or he was done for.

"I don't know," Top said. "It's weird; the convoy trucks *are* still parked in front of the gate, just like your friend said."

"Umm, when you say they look 'funny,'" Sergeant Jim 'Shuteye' Chang commented, "I'm sure you mean that in the nicest way, since they look like they're Chinese, like me, right?"

Now that he mentioned it, Top saw that all of the soldiers at the gate did sort of look like Sergeant Chang, whose family had emigrated from the Guangzhou region of southern China when he was a child.

"Dude! Like, he didn't mean anything by it, he's just insensitive that way," PFC Gordon's identical twin brother, Corporal Austin 'Good Twin' Gordon, said. At least that was what Sergeant Chang thought. The two brothers looked so much alike he couldn't tell

218 | CHRIS KENNEDY

them apart, except when they were in uniform and he could see their different rank insignias.

"Regardless of any insensitivity," Top said, looking through the binoculars again, "Shuteye is right; they do look Asian."

"No, Top, not just Asian, but Chinese, like me," Shuteye insisted. "They don't look Japanese or Filipino; they look *Chinese*."

Top looked again. Shuteye was right, they *did* look Chinese. "Okay, I agree," said Top, "they look Chinese. But that doesn't help us figure out what's going on. I don't know of any base security unit that's made up entirely of a single ethnic group. Do any of you?"

Everyone replied with a chorus of "no."

"There's obviously something going on," Top said. "There was a lot of shooting from the direction of the airfield earlier. I have no idea why. There weren't supposed to be any drills or operations this weekend. It doesn't add up." If there was one thing Top had learned in his time in the Army, it was to trust his feelings. When something didn't feel right, it usually wasn't.

As the group watched, they saw a silver Ford drive up to the gate and stop when it was flagged down. One of the guards spoke to the driver, who then turned around and drove off the base. The car came straight across I-5 and pulled into the convenience store next to the apartment complex. "I'm going to go talk to whoever just got turned back by the guards," Top said. "I'll be right back."

Top left the apartment building and jogged over to the convenience store. The silver Ford was still parked out front. As he stood waiting by the car, a woman came out of the store and walked over to the driver's side. She was one of the biggest women Top had ever seen. Not fat, but *big*. She was easily six feet, two inches tall and had broader shoulders than a lot of the men in the company. She also had muscles most of the men would have been proud of. Not weightlifter ugly, but well-toned from a lot of usage. Her long blond hair framed a pretty face; she was very attractive...just in a huge, intimidating sort of way.

"Can I help you?" she asked in a mousy voice that seemed far too high for someone her size. Top was sure it was too high for almost anyone that wasn't a cartoon character.

"Umm, yeah, hi," Top stuttered. He was unprepared for the voice. "I'm First Sergeant Smith," he said holding out his hand. "There's something strange going on, on base, and I wondered if we could ask you a few questions about what the gate guards said when you just tried to get on base."

The woman didn't take his hand; instead, she looked around as if trying to figure out who the 'we' was that Top referred to.

"I'm sorry," she said, "but I generally don't go off with men I don't know, especially ones who are spying on me. Usually I call the police. Sometimes, I just kick the shit out of them. Which is it going to be for you?"

Top was sure that if the voice had been an octave lower, the woman probably would have scared him with the threat. The voice, though, took all of the danger out of the threat. She was big and confident, but he was sure he could take her in a fight; well, he was pretty sure anyway. Happily, he didn't have time to put it to the test.

"No, ma'am," he said. "I'm not trying to do anything other than get some information from you, like I said. I'm going to reach around and get my wallet. Then I can show you I'm who I say I am." He expected her to take a step back to give herself room to run; he found himself a little intimidated when she instead stepped forward into easy grappling range. He was even more intimidated when she took up a stance like *she* was going to be the one to grapple *him*. He pulled out his wallet and removed his military ID. "See, I really am First Sergeant Smith," he said.

"Yes, you are indeed," the woman said, starting to smile.

The smile was even more disconcerting than the threat, Top decided.

"Anyway," he said, "there are a group of us Rangers who have been watching the front gate, trying to figure out what is going on." He pointed to the roof of the nearby apartment building where several of his men could be seen, still looking toward the base. "We'd appreciate it if you'd come tell us what the guards at the front gate said to you when you tried to get on base."

"I'd be happy to do that," the woman said. "It'll be nice to start getting to know some of the men."

"What?" Top asked. "What do you mean, get to know some of the men?"

"I'm Corporal Suzi Taylor," the woman said. "I'm your new rifleman."

NAS Fallon, NV, 2015 Pacific Daylight Time

"Any word from Mighty Mite yet?" Captain Jim 'Muddy' Waters asked.

"No, sir," his deputy, Captain Don 'Bambi' Heron, replied, "and I'll tell you, I'm getting awfully worried. The Hornets should be about out of gas by now, even with what they got from the tanker."

"How about trying Seattle Center?" CAG asked. "Could you give Center a call and see what happened to them?"

"Sure thing, CAG," Bambi said. He went to the phone, looked at a cheat sheet of phone numbers posted by the phone and dialed the one for Seattle Center. Within a couple of rings, it was answered by a pleasant voice that said, "Good evening, Seattle Center, may I help you?"

"Good evening, my name is Captain Heron," Bambi responded, "and I am calling from NAS Fallon. We had three aircraft that flew up your way earlier this evening, and we haven't heard back from them. Do you have any info on the *Gauntlet 501* flight?"

"My goodness," the Center operator said, "I hope you find them. Let me transfer you up to the radar room; they should be able to help you." There was a pause and then a voice said, "Good evening, Assistant Traffic Manager Tom Fuller speaking. May I help you?"

Captain Heron repeated his request for more information on the Gauntlet flight. He was surprised by the response. "Yes, I remember them well, especially since I personally spoke to them," Mr. Fuller said. "They wouldn't do anything we requested of them and almost got flight violated by me for failure to follow directions. Ultimately, they went VFR and proceeded to the northeast, descending until we lost them in the radar clutter. They said they had enough gas to fly under visual flight rules and then return to Fallon. Have they not returned?"

"No they haven't," Bambi said, "and we are starting to get worried about them."

"Well, if you give me your phone number, I'll give you a call if they turn back up," Mr. Fuller replied.

Captain Heron gave him the number, thanked him and signed off. Bambi filled in CAG with what he had learned. "It's odd," he said. "I wonder what was going on that they didn't want to follow

222 | CHRIS KENNEDY

instructions? Mighty Mite must have learned something about whatever is going on at Whidbey that he wanted to pursue, which is why
they went VFR. I have a bad feeling about what they found."

"I do, too," CAG said. "I think we need to come up with a 'Plan
B.'"

"I agree," Bambi said. "I think we need some aircraft with different capabilities up there. Personally, I'd like to send up one of the E-
2s; with their satellite radio, we can stay in touch with them all the
way up."

"I think that would be a good idea," CAG said. "We'll also send a
couple Super Hornet fighters with it." After the first flight had
launched, CAG had asked the air wing maintenance officer to ensure
they had eight F-18s standing by at all times, with four armed for
anti-aircraft operations and four armed as bombers.

"Yes, sir," agreed Bambi. "With the Hawkeye's ability to see a
hostile aircraft a long way out, especially with their new upgrades,
they should be able to identify any threats to the flight long before
they can pose a threat."

"If the Center doesn't know what happened to them, it's time to
send out a group that can find them and bring them home. Launch
'Plan B,'" said CAG.

Joint Base Lewis-McChord, Tacoma, WA, 2017 Pacific Daylight Time

"Dude!" said one of the twins. "You're really,
like, in the Rangers?"

Suzi glared at him. "Really? Do, I look like
a dude to you?" Her gaze returned to the rest of the group. "But, yes,

I'm the first female to complete Ranger School and actually get assigned to the unit. I started out as an intel analyst and have been waiting for the Army to open up the Rangers to women. When I first enlisted, the Army said it would be opening the Rangers to women. It didn't happen as quickly as they said, but I was ready for the opportunity when it finally came."

As the senior enlisted for the company, Top had known she was coming, but hadn't expected her for a couple of weeks. "Didn't your Ranger School class just graduate on Friday?" he asked.

"Sure did," she said. "I jumped on a plane the next day, yesterday, and here I am. I don't have a lot of family, and I wanted to get started. Mostly, I just wanted to put Ranger School behind me."

Most of the men nodded, having all been through it.

"I know," Shuteye said. "Ranger School only lasts 61 days; it just seems like forever."

"Yeah, you got that right," Staff Sergeant Patrick 'The Wall' Dantone added. The Wall was one of the few men in the company that could dwarf Suzi; he had received his call sign after someone said he was 'about as big as a wall.' At 6'4" and nearly 300 pounds, he was a big man. "It's a mental and physical nightmare, especially if you're a big guy that needs to eat." The students were generally awake more than 20 hours a day and eating two or fewer meals a day totaling about 2,200 calories. At the same time, they were also carrying between 65-90 pounds of weapons, equipment and training ammunition. Over the duration of the course, students could expect to carry this load on over 200 miles of patrols. "I lost more than 30 pounds," he continued, "and was a mess for a couple of weeks afterward."

"Did you have any problems?" Top asked. His biggest issue with women in the company wasn't so much that they were females, but

224 | CHRIS KENNEDY

with them carrying their own weight. If Suzi needed special treatment, she would *not* fit into the unit. If she couldn't keep up, he wanted to know as soon as possible.

"I didn't have any problems with the physical or mental stuff," Suzi said. "Sure, it sucked, but I was in better starting shape than most of the guys there. I had worked my ass off for five years by that point; I was *ready*. I can't say the same for the other two women in my class. They expected to get special treatment during the physical stuff; they were both gone by the third day." She paused. "My problem was that I got 'peered out.'"

Top knew that, in addition to getting graded by the instructors, students also had to pass a peer evaluation. Failing to score more than a 60% approval rating from your squad could result in disqualification, though that usually only happened if the student failed peer evaluation twice. Sometimes an individual was singled out by someone else in the squad arbitrarily; because of this, a soldier who was peered out would be moved to another squad to ensure they were given a fair chance to complete the course. If the student got peered out a second time, it was usually assumed the student was either lazy, incompetent, or couldn't keep up; at this point, the student was dropped.

"I'm not saying I'm perfect," Suzi continued, "but there were some people there who didn't want a woman to succeed. No matter what I did, they still made fun of me and voted against me. Generally, about one quarter of the people wanted me to fail, and one quarter wanted me to succeed. The other half didn't give a shit, as long as I pulled my weight and didn't get them captured or killed, which I never did. Still, there were some that were out to get me, and they twisted other students' arms to vote against me." She sighed. "I got peered once, and it was the hardest thing for me to take, because I hadn't done anything wrong, other than be born without a 'Y' chromosome." She shrugged. "I got transferred to another squad, and it was like a breath of fresh air. I completed the rest of the course and was awarded the Robert Spencer Enlisted Leadership Award. Over half of my class dropped out, but I made it through," she said proudly.

Top was impressed; the Spencer Award was the prestigious award given to the student who embodied the highest leadership spirit and ideals; it was not lightly given. The recipient of the Spencer award was hand-selected as *the* best leader. The fact that she got it, in spite of what he expected was some serious backstabbing to ensure she failed, said a lot about her spirit and perseverance. "You're certainly in good shape," he noted. "Most people who go to Ranger School are in the worst shape of their lives when they finish, due to sleep deprivation and the constant work load."

She laughed. "Yeah, that's why I'm just getting here now. I was supposed to be on an early flight out yesterday, but I slept through my alarm and then half the day. I ended up having to catch the red-eye last night." She paused and then laughed. "If it hadn't been for the maid that came in to clean my room, I might still be sleeping. I'm sure she enjoyed cleaning my room; I was so tired I fell asleep completely clothed, without even getting under the covers. There wasn't anything for her to do but stretch the sheets a little tighter."

"How are you doing now?" The Wall asked. He had also been told that Suzi would be coming to his squad, and he took care of his men. And women too, now, he guessed.

"I'm doing better now, although I'd be lying if I said I remembered any of the flights here. Happily, the flight attendants kept waking me up when it was time to get off the plane." She smiled. "I also had to pull over at a rest stop for a few more hours of sleep on the way, but I made it here and am mostly awake now. Mostly."

"We're glad you're here," Top said. "Okay, so now that we've got introductions out of the way, what can you tell us about the gate guards? Did they look Chinese to you? What did they say?"

"Oh, they're Chinese, all right, as are the two Type 98 tanks guarding the gate." She looked out toward the gate. With the better vantage point, she could see a little further. "The tanks hiding back past the gate are Type 99s."

"Are those old tanks?" Top asked. "I know we sometimes buy armored vehicles and take them out onto the test ranges to see how they fare when they're hit with new weapons. Do you know if we bought some of them either to test or blow up?"

"No," Suzi said, "but I really doubt it. The Type 99s are top-of-the-line tanks. They're the best main battle tank the Chinese have and almost as good as our M-1 Abrams."

"Okay," one of the twins said, "so, like, what are they doing sitting on our base?"

"And, like, what are the Chinese doing as our new gate guards?" asked the other twin.

And then they said in unison, "And, dude, *how do we get to drive one of the tanks?*"

Suzi looked at Top in surprise, but Top just shook his head. "Don't worry about them; they were tank drivers before they came over to the Rangers. They still think they can drive tanks and blow things up."

"Dude! We can, like, drive anything you put us in!" one of the twins boasted.

"Dude! We're, like, the best team you have at blowing stuff up, too!" the other added.

"While I'll give you the fact that you're good at blowing things up with the RAWS," Top agreed, "I doubt there is any need for you two idiots to either drive or shoot at any of the tanks sitting at the gate." The twins were one of the weapons platoon's anti-armor sections, equipped with the 84mm Ranger Anti-Tank Weapon System (RAWS).

"The real question," Top continued, "is what to do with this information." He paused, thinking. "I tried to phone the CO earlier, but wasn't able to get him. My cell phone hasn't worked for shit all afternoon, and even the landlines have been out at times. I'd email him, but the internet went out the same time my cell phone died." He paused. The CO was hard to reach anyway; he didn't think the man liked talking to his enlisted soldiers, even his senior enlisted. "I think I'll call the executive officer with the apartment's land line."

Unlike his CO, who was sometimes hard to find, the XO was always available and answered on the first ring. "Hi, sir," Top began, "this is First Sergeant Smith. Have you seen the news today?"

"Hey Top," the XO, First Lieutenant Odysseus Bollinger, answered. "Yeah, there's some weird stuff going on, for sure. I tried to call the CO, but his phone must be out. I was just thinking of running over to his house to see if he had any orders for us, since I hadn't heard from him. My phone's been out most of the afternoon."

"It's not just yours," Top said. "Phones have been out everywhere, and there's some strange shit going on all over the area. I'm standing in the twins' apartment across the street from the main gate of Fort Lewis and, I know this is going to sound unbelievable, but there are Chinese tanks at the front gate."

"C'mon, Top, what's really going on? Is this some sort of test from the CO to see what I'd do if he were ever incapacitated?" the XO asked.

"No sir, the CO didn't put me up to this," Top answered. Although…it did sound like some of the stupid shit the CO would pull. "There really are Chinese tanks at the main gate, as well as a large number of Chinese-looking troops. Of note, the tanks were identified by our new corporal, Corporal Taylor, who used to be an Intel Specialist." He didn't mention that Corporal Taylor was a female. The Chinese at the gate were a big enough surprise.

"Corporal Taylor is already here? Didn't she just graduate two days ago? Shouldn't she still be in bed?" the XO asked. Top sighed. It figured that the XO would know all about her. The XO had his finger on the pulse of the company and was as first-rate an officer as the CO was not. Not much got by him.

"Yes, sir," Top replied. "She's doing pretty well, although I think she's slept the last two days solid."

"I think I slept for three full days after I was done," the XO said. "My wife thought I had died. She was already planning how to spend the insurance money when I woke up." He laughed. "Startled the crap out of her when I said 'hi.' I think she may have wet herself."

Top laughed along with the XO, although he doubted that the XO's wife would have been startled. He had found her to be one of the most methodical people he had ever met. "I doubt that, sir," Top said. "I'm pretty sure she would have checked for a pulse before she started spending the money." He paused. "In any event, sir, I'm calling to see what you'd like us to do. Chinese soldiers appear to be at the gate, and we heard a lot of gunfire and explosions a couple of hours ago from the direction of the airfield. When the group that was at Yakima last week got back from training, the convoy wasn't allowed to enter the base, and the guards confiscated their trucks. I can still see them sitting outside the gate. There was a story that the convoy commander got shot when he wouldn't leave, but I can't confirm that. Corporal Taylor has verified the tanks at the gate are Chinese-made, although I have *no* idea how they got there."

"What's the apartment number there?" the XO asked. "I'll go see if I can find the CO, and then I'll come by and take a look. Why don't you see if you can round up a squad or two of the men, in case we need to do something?"

"Yes, sir, I'll take care of it," Top said. "The apartment number is 206."

"Anything else you can think of that I'm missing, Top?" the XO asked. Unlike the CO, the XO wasn't afraid to take advantage of the first sergeant's many years of experience. With a little bit of molding, the XO would make a fine leader. As long as the CO didn't screw him up.

"No, sir, not at the moment," Top replied. "There's something darn strange going on, but I'm not real sure what to do about it yet."

Near Mt. Garfield, WA, 2020 Pacific Daylight Time

"I don't get it," Calvin said, seated at the table in Ryan's cabin. "What do the Chinese think they have to gain here?" Although Ryan had started out with the intention of making it a one-room structure, he had had enough visitors between his Ranger and aviator friends that he decided to

230 | CHRIS KENNEDY

wall off his bedroom for privacy. The other half of the house was split between a kitchen area and living space. Both men were seated at the kitchen table nursing beers while they discussed their observations of the day. Calvin was tired and sore, having had to walk the several miles back to the house after his ejection, all the while trying to figure out just what the heck was going on. Whidbey Island invaded? Surface-to-air missiles bringing down U.S. aircraft over U.S. soil? Helicopters shooting down planes? Everything that he held as an incontrovertible truth was suddenly found to be a lie. How did it happen? Why?

"Well, I don't know for sure," Ryan replied, "but I called a friend of mine at the Pentagon today about something else. He said the Chinese invaded Taiwan about the same time the power and internet went down today. Kind of a weird coincidence, eh?"

"I guess it isn't a big surprise," Calvin said. "The damn Chinese have been playing around in our cyber stuff for a long time. If they were going to launch something as big as an invasion, they would want to disrupt our communications as much as possible. Even the places with emergency generators would be down for at least a little while, and then trying to regenerate the picture of what was going on would take time. There are probably lots of organizations that don't have emergency generators, either. It would be a giant mess. Half the people wouldn't be able to communicate with anyone else, and no one would have any situational awareness of what's happening. If they disrupted parts of the internet, too, that would make things even more difficult for the civilian leadership and would really screw with our command and control."

"That's what I think happened," Ryan said. "If you think about it, what is the only thing that's stopped the Chinese from invading

Taiwan before? We are," he said, answering his own question. "The only reason China hasn't taken Taiwan before is that we've told them if they try it, we're going to kick their asses. It would be so bloody they haven't wanted to do it and risk starting World War Three. But…" he paused. "What if they had a way to guarantee the United States would *not* respond to an invasion of Taiwan? Do you think they would do it then?"

"Yeah, they might try it…if they thought we wouldn't intervene," Calvin said. He could tell by the look he got that he still wasn't seeing it. "Sorry, I'm having a bad day. Getting shot down does that to you, I suppose. What the hell are you trying to say?"

"Okay, I'll make it a little plainer for you, sir. What do you suppose would happen to Taiwan if the Chinese were able to hold one of our cities hostage to guarantee our good behavior?" Ryan raised his eyebrow inquisitively. "Think they might be a little friskier?"

"Oh, shit," Calvin said, finally understanding a little. "What you're saying is everything going on in Seattle is a giant diversion so they can get away with invading Taiwan?"

"Exactly. What if, say, the Chinese said, 'Let us have Taiwan, and we'll let you have Seattle and all of its inhabitants back unharmed.' What do you think the politicians would do?"

"Shit," Calvin said again. "Who knows? Some would say, 'No negotiating with terrorists,' while others would say, 'Screw the Taiwanese; they don't vote for me.' And then there'd probably be every opinion in between, with lots of running around like a barnyard full of chickens with their heads cut off. Complete hysteria. Who knows? Some of them would probably vote to just go ahead and give Seattle to the Chinese. You *are* talking about the same group of idiots that haven't passed a budget in five years, right?"

232 | CHRIS KENNEDY

"Yeah," Ryan said, "that's pretty much what I think would happen, too. No cohesive planning or decision-making skills among them. I think the Chinese are smart enough to figure that out, as well, which is why I think they've gone and done exactly that. Somehow, they've successfully invaded Seattle and are fortifying it, even as we speak. The anti-aircraft gun that shot down your wingman was one of a group of three I saw at a truck stop on I-90. I had the opportunity to blow one of them up; I was close enough to see they were most definitely Chinese owned and operated. You tell me; why would there be three anti-aircraft guns sitting in a truck stop on I-90 if the Chinese *haven't* taken over Seattle?"

"Shit," Calvin repeated.

"And they say SEALs don't have big vocabularies," Ryan said. "Didn't you have to go to college or something to become an officer? Is 'shit' the best expressive language they could teach you?"

"Yes, I went to college," Calvin replied. "I'm just having a hard time getting my mind to come to grips with the fact that we've been invaded. I don't think this has happened in two hundred years...I'm kinda not used to the idea."

"204 years or so, if my math is correct," Ryan said. "1814 is when the British burned Washington, DC, anyway. That was the last time, if you don't count the Mexicans in Texas. Of course, it wasn't a state yet, so I'm not counting it. And I guess Japan invaded the Aleutian Islands in World War II, but I doubt most people would know about that."

"Okay, see? It's been over two hundred years, and now the foreigners are burning Washington again. Excuse me for having a problem keeping up. Unlike some people, I haven't been blowing up anti-aircraft guns all day."

"You should try it some time," Ryan said. "It's kind of fun. Until they start shooting at you, anyway."

"Yeah, well, I think I've been shot at enough for one day," Calvin said. He paused, thoughtful. "Wait a minute…you blew up one of their anti-aircraft guns, and then a helicopter happens to be here. Was the helicopter that shot me down here because of you?"

"I was wondering when you were going to figure that out," Ryan answered. "Yeah, I'm guessing the helicopter was looking for me. If you'd have had the common sense to wait a couple more minutes before you flew by, I would have shot it down. Well, either that or it would have killed me. One way or another, one of us wouldn't have been here when you happened by. I think the smart money was on me getting the helo, but you never know; I'm optimistic, but I've been wrong before."

"Okay, you're the eternal optimist. So, Mr. Optimist, what exactly are you going to do about what's going on in Seattle?" Calvin asked.

"You mean, what are you going to do about it, flyboy?" Ryan replied. "Only one of us is in the military, and it ain't me. The politicians thought that I wasn't good enough, or something, and sent me home. What are *you* going to do?"

"Well, my specialty is blowing things up from the air," Calvin said, "but I'm fresh out of airplanes, and the closest replacement jet is over 800 miles away. I'm open to suggestions."

"I don't have a plan yet, but I'm for going to bed early, getting up early and going into town to see what's going on. Once we know, we can make a plan. While we're there, maybe we can get you some new clothes so that you don't look quite so much like an out-of-place aviator. Maybe we can even find some trouble to get into along the way. How about that?"

"Some of my best friends got killed today," Calvin said. "I'm definitely up for some payback."

Ryan smiled. "I hoped you'd say that."

"By, the way," Calvin asked, "do you have a phone I can use? I probably ought to call the squadron and let them know I'm okay."

Joint Base Elmendorf-Richardson, AK, 2045 Alaska Daylight Time (2145 PDT)

"What in the *bloody hell* is going on?" Lieutenant General Tom Simpson asked. General Simpson wore many hats, including Commander of Alaskan Command and Commander of the 11th Air Force; more importantly, he was also the Commander of the Alaskan NORAD Region (ANR). "As the ANR Commander, I am responsible for directing all the air operations in Alaska to defend against hostile threats. How am I supposed to do that if we don't know who the enemy is?"

Lieutenant General Simpson had called his staff together in his conference room at Joint Base Elmendorf-Richardson in Anchorage, Alaska, to figure out what was going on and to put together a plan for the next 24-48 hours. Elmendorf functioned as the headquarters for the ANR, one of the United States Air Force's Sector Operations Control Centers. Equipped with the best technology money could buy, the mission of the control centers was to function as the primary command and control center for its North American Air Defense Command (NORAD) region during crisis or attack as long as it was able. Six E-3C airborne early warning and control aircraft were also assigned; command and control could be transitioned to them for survivability if the tactical situation warranted. Information was also passed to the NORAD Combat Operations Center at Colorado Springs, Colorado.

"All I really want to know is if we are at war with China or not," Lieutenant General Simpson said. "Has Congress declared war?" he asked. General Simpson was a tall, rail thin man who was always full of energy. He also had 33 years of service in the Air Force and was used to getting answers when he asked.

"No word yet, sir," his chief of staff, Colonel Devyn Walker, replied. "Congress is meeting in DC right now, but they haven't been able to come to a decision. So far, all we have is the state of alert we were put on this afternoon when the ambassador from China said it was conducting military operations in Taiwan. China never actually declared war, which has hampered some of the decision makers. If they had just said, 'We declare war,' everything would have been simple. We would have invoked all our defense treaties and started defending Taiwan."

"I suspect that is what the Chinese wanted," the general said, "an America paralyzed by indecision."

"Probably so," Colonel Heather Vincent, his operations officer, agreed. An excellent planner, Colonel Vincent had a wide variety of options prepared for defending Alaska...but they were only good if she was given the authorization to put them into effect. "By only declaring a 200 mile exclusion zone around Taiwan, they are limiting where we can apply force to get them to back down. At the moment, we don't even have permission to turn back the passenger airliners that are still flying from China to the United States. All we can do is just watch them fly by."

The general looked to his intelligence officer, Colonel Amanda Ware. "Well, if we are unable to do anything here, can you at least tell me what is going on in Taiwan?" he asked. "How is the battle going?"

Colonel Ware, a short, heavyset woman with thick-rimmed glasses, looked the part of an introspective intelligence officer. She sighed prior to giving her assessment. It's never good when she starts that way, the general thought. "Well, sir," Colonel Ware began, "the Chinese appear to have invaded Taiwan quite effectively. We have been watching one of their recent drills for the last week; apparently, it wasn't a drill, it was the real thing. On the good side, we have a fairly accurate idea of their order of battle; however, that list of forces is pretty long, and almost all of it seems to have gone straight into Taiwan. The Taiwanese forces appear to be in full retreat from the southern portion of the island. We are unable to confirm any of this, though, as all of our reconnaissance satellites in the area are non-responsive."

The general looked confused. "What do you mean, 'non-responsive'?"

"We lost communications with them," Colonel Ware said. "We believe they have been shot down by Chinese anti-satellite (ASAT) missiles. We've seen them testing some kind of new exo-atmospheric kinetic kill vehicle for use with their HQ-19 surface-to-air missile system. We weren't sure if it was for ballistic missile defense or to be used as an ASAT system, but it appears to work very well in the ASAT role."

"We lost *all* of our satellites?" the general asked.

"Yes sir, all of them," Colonel Ware confirmed. "Our global positioning satellites and our communications satellites are also gone.

Any operations we undertake in the area are going to be severely degraded."

"So, we really don't have much of a clue about what's going on there, do we?"

She shook her head. "We *just* got in touch with Okinawa and our other bases in the area. Even though Okinawa is outside the 200 mile exclusion area, it appears to have been pasted by Chinese ballistic and cruise missiles. The airbase was particularly hard hit."

She paused, shaking her head again. "I just got word that the Chinese Ambassador delivered a note of apology to the president for the, quote, missile that went off target and struck Okinawa, unquote. There's no way the attack was an off-target missile, unless it had about 30 warheads that happened to fall off and hit individual targets. Not only that, but they would have been hard-pressed to analyze the data, agree on a response, write it and deliver it to the president in the limited amount of time since the strikes. The note of apology is nothing more than a clever public relations ploy to put us off balance and score points with the media," she concluded. "I'm sure Okinawa was the planned target for those strikes."

"Do we have any intel on Chinese operations in our area of responsibility?" the general asked.

"No, sir," Colonel Ware responded. "All we've been told is to 'watch out for anything out of the ordinary, especially things going on in northwest Washington State.' Sorry, sir, I know that's not much help. I have all of my staff in here working at the moment, but the loss of power and then the internet for so long has hampered our collection and analysis efforts. I *am* able to tell you the country-wide blackout that occurred simultaneously with the invasion of Taiwan has definitely been attributed to Chinese hackers, even though the

Chinese are saying they had nothing to do with it. It doesn't take a genius to figure out it was intended to disrupt communications and command and control at the time senior commanders needed to confer about what was to be done about Taiwan."

"Do we know what we are supposed to be watching for in northwest Washington State?" the chief of staff asked.

"No sir," Colonel Ware replied. "We weren't told what was going on there, and I don't think anyone knows exactly, but there have been some strange events and communications have been disrupted in the area. Apparently, all the cell phone towers are out in the Seattle area, but no one has been able to figure out why. This disruption seemed to start at the same time as the power outage, but it seems like it's more than that; power and communications haven't been restored there yet, unlike in other areas, and some landline calls to people in the area reported an exercise in progress at NAS Whidbey Island, although no one knew there was one planned. The lack of communications has the senior leadership at both NORAD and the Pentagon worried; if the folks in Whidbey and Kitsap don't hurry up and break radio silence, there are already whispers about which officers are going to lose their jobs. It's a mess sir, and no one is sure why. Of note, we also haven't heard anything from the Western Air Defense Sector Operations Control Center, located at McChord Field in Tacoma. They appear to be operational, but are not putting any tracks into the air defense system."

"General, we did notice one thing earlier about that region," Colonel Vincent said. "The operations center said there seemed to be an unusually high number of passenger aircraft flights from China to Seattle today. They asked one of the passing airliners why there were so many flights, and the airline pilot answered that they were a charter flight bringing automobile industry people to a conference being held there. We looked it up on the internet, which had come back up at that point and confirmed there was indeed a major trade show going on in Seattle. Still, it seems like there is more traffic than could be expected. If we were told to watch for something out of the ordinary, that's it."

"All right," the general said, "that's at least something we can work on. I want every single airliner coming from China intercepted by a section of F-22s. If there is anything even the slightest bit out of the ordinary with any of them, I want it diverted here to Elmendorf for customs check-out. Every airliner gets intercepted, but I want the interceptors to join on the airliners from behind and stay out of sight for the time being. There's no sense having them run to the press as soon as they get on the deck, complaining that they were intercepted for no reason. Let's see if we can find out what these guys are up to."

Near Mt. Garfield, WA, 2110 Pacific Daylight Time

"Okay," Calvin said; "I'll let you know what we find out." He turned off the phone.

"So, they didn't believe you?" Ryan asked.

"In a word," Calvin said; "no." He paused. "You saw how long it took me to believe what's going on here, and I lived through it. Hell, I got shot down and still didn't believe it. My air wing commander is 800 miles away, so he's having an even harder time believing. The Chinese have taken Seattle? It's crazy, especially since he called Seattle Center, and they say everything's fine. It's far easier for him to believe you were somehow mistaken about what you saw at the truck stop, and I had an engine failure or something. After all, you are 'some sort of hermit living in the woods with delusions of being a SEAL.' Obviously, you're going to take every opportunity to make yourself sound brave and heroic to the naval aviator who just landed in your midst."

"What did he blame the disappearance of the other two planes in your formation on, spontaneous combustion?" Ryan asked.

"Those, he's not so sure about. They must have flown into each other and blown up, causing my airplane to also be damaged, thus the explosion I saw. He's willing to believe there might be a terrorist action taking place in the area; certainly, something strange is going on at Whidbey. A full-scale invasion, though, isn't something he's ready to believe." Mimicking the CAG's voice, he continued, "Well, son, ejection is a very traumatic occurrence and, in all likelihood you've sustained a concussion. I know it may seem like the world is against you at this moment, but I think that in the morning you'll see things as they really are, once you have a clear head again. Please have someone take you to the nearest hospital, and we'll send a helicopter up for you in the morning."

"He really said that? You're imagining things because you have a concussion?" he paused. "How does your concussion make me imagine what I saw?"

"You probably were telling me about a truck with a gun rack in the back window, and I dreamed it into an anti-aircraft artillery piece," Calvin said. "My feverish imagination is playing tricks on me and is distorting everything you say to me. He sounded so sure of himself at one point, I almost had to pinch myself to make sure *I* still believed me." His eyes narrowed as he looked at Ryan. "I'm not concussed and being paranoid and imagining all of this, right? Actually, please tell me I am. This would surely be a great dream to wake up from."

"Sorry," Ryan said. "I wish we were both paranoid delusionals. Unfortunately, this is real life, no matter how unbelievable it may seem. While you may have had to eject, you still seem pretty clear-headed to me, especially for an aviator."

"You know what's worse?" Calvin asked, ignoring the jibe.

"What could be worse than not believing in a war you're already losing?" Ryan asked.

"They already put together a flight to come look for us," Calvin said, "and CAG is still going to send it up here to see if they can find any survivors from my flight. They're going to be armed in case there is 'some act of terrorism' going on," Calvin used his fingers for air quotes, "but he doesn't plan to tell them about my 'delusional ramblings.' He shook his head, remembering the surface-to-air missile site he saw being set up. "I can't help but feel they're screwed. I don't have many friends in the Kestrels, but they're still on our side; I hope they'll be okay. I don't know how they did it, but the Chinese have brought in an awful lot of bad shit. In addition to the anti-aircraft systems that got my wingman, I *know* I saw what was either a Russian S-300 or S-400 system, or whatever they call it in China. They're both big, truck mounted missiles that are very distinctive. The S-300 system is as good as a Patriot; the S-400 is better. If the next group comes in high, either one of those systems could swat them like flies. Vaya con dios, my brothers, vaya con dios."

"All right," Ryan said, trying to change the mood, "I've got something I probably ought to show you before we go to bed."

"What's that?" Calvin asked.

He watched as Ryan lifted up a large carpet in the middle of the floor, revealing a locked trap door. "This is something that might make our lives a little easier," he said as he removed the lock and lifted the door. He paused, then said with a Spanish accent, "Say hello to my little friends." Ryan walked down the steps into the darkness and turned on a light. In the basement of his cabin, Calvin saw an armory that most survival nuts would have killed for.

Calvin whistled lowly as he took it all in. "Damn..." The space was a 20' x 20' square concrete room with racks of weapons on three sides. Shelves brimming with ammunition graced the fourth side. There was a large table in the center of the room with stations for cleaning weapons and reloading ammunition on top of it and supplies for cleaning and reloading underneath. There was even a little dehumidifier running quietly in one of the corners.

Calvin began to wonder whether Ryan did have all of his marbles, or if he had indeed turned into some kind of survivalist nut-job, like his air wing commander had suggested. Looking at the room full of weapons, 'nut-job' no longer seemed so far-fetched. Although there weren't *quite* enough weapons for a full-scale army battle, there were certainly enough for several major skirmishes. "Damn! This is...incredible. This far into the woods, how were you able to do all this? The concrete work alone would have been pretty challenging, much less getting all these racks and ordnance."

"Well, the best part about being a SEAL is you're a member of a team, and all of those guys have a variety of skills. You're also pretty close with the guys who are going to insert you into enemy territory, and even closer with the guys who are going to get you back out again. I know quite a few people who can fly helicopters, and lifting this stuff in by helo was a LOT easier than humping it up the mountain on my back. Of course, it cost me some good whiskey, but hey, it was worth it."

"Um…your friends used military helicopters to bring all this stuff up here?" Calvin asked. "How did you arrange *that?*"

Ryan looked a little sheepish. "Well, they *usually* used civilian helicopters, because using military helicopters would *obviously* be a misuse of taxpayer funds, wouldn't it?" He smiled. "Sometimes, though, special forces need to practice backcountry operations, and troops have to be dropped off in unprepared territory. Well, my mountain is about as unprepared as it comes, so it is a perfect place for them to get some training. The fact that they left some things here when they hiked back out doesn't mean they left it for me, just that they didn't need it at the time and will probably come back some time to get it. It's *prepositioned*," he said. Ryan thought for a second and then asked, "How do you suppose I got the generator out back to power the lights or chill your beer? It would have sucked to try to get *that* up the mountain."

It was Calvin's turn to look sheepish. "I never thought about it, I guess. I'm concussed, remember? I'm just making it up as I go."

"Honestly," Ryan said, "the hardest part was getting the hole dug out. As you may have guessed, I'm not adverse to hard work, and I've had plenty of time on my hands. I just asked for help moving some of the heavy stuff when I needed it. I know a couple of guys in the 160th SOAR at Fort Lewis in Tacoma, and they were able to work it into their normal operations or rent a helicopter at the local airport if they needed."

"Besides flying like an eagle," Calvin asked, "what is a sore?"

"The SOAR is the United States Army's 160th Special Operations Aviation Regiment, also known as the 'Night Stalkers.' It's a helicop-

244 | CHRIS KENNEDY

ter squadron that provides support for the Army's special operations forces, as well as the special operations troops from other services when needed. The 160th is headquartered at Fort Campbell, Kentucky, but has battalions scattered throughout the country; the 4th Battalion is located here in Tacoma at Joint Base Lewis-McChord. Because of the missions they fly, the aviators in the 160th SOAR are the best-qualified in the Army; getting into the fields around here is a snap for them." Ryan paused and then indicated the racks of weapons. "In any event," he said, "how this got here is less important than the fact that it *is* here and available for our use now that we need it. Now…knowing that you're a flyboy and not a *real* combat troop, how experienced are you with rifles, shotguns, pistols and grenades?"

"I'm pretty good with everything except the grenades," Calvin said. "My dad was a big hunter growing up, so I'm comfortable with rifles and shotguns. I also made myself proficient on the range with my combat pistol, a Browning Hi-Power 9mm, just in case I ever got shot down behind enemy lines. Grenades, not so much." Looking around, he noticed some gray blocks of putty on one of the sets of shelves and the stacks of metal objects next to it. Stunned, he asked, "Is that C4? Claymores, too? How many wars are you planning on fighting in the Washington woods?

"Well, it never hurts to be prepared," said Ryan with a shrug, "and I think current events are proving me correct on that point. Besides, most of this is just stuff I collected over my time in the Navy." He held up a Russian-made AK-47. "This rifle, for example. Its owner didn't need it anymore, so I brought it home to take care of it. I was just doing my part for the environment and recycling it." He set it down and picked up another rifle from the rack. "This is what I think will work best for you. It's an M-16 with an M203 grenade launcher attached." He paused, trying to look serious. "Before we go any further, I think it's important to make you aware that it is illegal for civilians to possess grenades, so of course I don't own any or have any in my possession." Looking at a set of shelves in the corner, he laughed. "But, what do we have here? The top shelf has some grenades that look like they just might fit a M203 grenade launcher. I wonder how they got there?" He turned back to Calvin and asked, "Have you ever used the M203 grenade launcher?"

"I've played all the Modern Warfare video games," Calvin said, "so I know what it is and generally how it works. I've never shot one in real life, though."

"That's at least a start, I guess," Ryan said, as he lapsed into his best weapons instructor voice. "As a novice, you should know that the M203 is a 40mm grenade launcher, and it's classified as a 'Destructive Device' under the National Firearms Act because it is a non-sporting firearm with a bore greater than one-half inch in diameter." He laughed. "That being said, you can actually buy a M203 launcher on eBay. They're kind of pricey at about $2,000 apiece, plus a $200 transfer tax, but you can get them. You can also buy training ammunition for them for about $15 per cartridge, although actual high explosive 40mm grenades are a whole lot more expensive. *If* you can find them, you're going to pay about $500 per cartridge, but they're very rare. Each grenade also constitutes a destructive device on its own and must be registered, which requires an additional $200 transfer tax payment *for each round*. Finally, once you've got them, you have to comply with the governmental high explosives storage requirements. All of that is a pain in the ass, which is why I'm glad

246 | CHRIS KENNEDY

someone left some on this shelf here, so we don't have to go shopping for them."

He pretended to look a little closer. "Well, what do we have here? Looks like we've got a couple types of high explosive rounds, some illumination rounds and some CS gas rounds. Hmm..." He pointed at the olive drab rounds as if just seeing them for the first time. "Let's see. These olive green ones are high explosive. The ones with the gold markings are general purpose high explosive that will kill everything within about 5 meters and cause casualties to anyone within about 130 meters. That means, don't shoot one close to you, as you are likely to get hit too. If you can't fire it a little way down range, don't shoot it at all. The ones with the white markings are dual purpose. They explode like the ones with the yellow markings and with the same kill radius, but they can also penetrate about 2 inches of steel armor. Good stuff. These illumination rounds are for making light at night, but you can also use them to signal. We probably won't need any of these tomorrow. The last ones with the gray aluminum body and black markings are a form of tear gas which is very effective for riot control or urban operations. While *most* people agree that the CS gas inside this grenade is non-lethal, let me tell you, you do *not* want to get it in your eyes."

"Got it," Calvin said. "What does "CS" stand for?"

"Nothing I know of," Ryan answered. "What you need to know is that it's nasty stuff. The chemical reacts with the moisture on your skin and in your eyes, causing a burning sensation and the immediate uncontrollable shutting of your eyes. It will feel like your eyes, nose and throat are on fire, with massive amounts of tears, coughing, and mucus discharge from your nose, as well as disorientation, dizziness and restricted breathing. It will also burn your skin if you are sweaty and/or sunburned. Most of these effects will wear off within an hour, but your life will absolutely *suck* for that hour, making you wish you were dead, and the burning feeling may persist for much longer than that. Any clothes you get it on will have to be washed several times to get it out; it's easier just to throw them away."

He thought a bit. "Oh, yeah, one other thing. I don't know if the Chinese will have dogs, but the CS gas is less effective against them because their tear ducts are less developed, and they are protected by fur. Hit them with high explosive, instead." Ryan picked up a blue grenade and showed Calvin how to load the grenades into the launcher and watched him practice a few times. "With just the two of us, you need to know how to shoot these, in case I need covering fire to get out of something stupid I've gotten myself into."

"I think I've got it," Calvin said, "although I'd love to practice fire a couple of these before I need them in combat."

"No problem," Ryan replied. "These blue ones are practice rounds; you can shoot a few of them on our way to town tomorrow." He looked at the lower shelves. "Hey, look at this! Here are some no-kidding hand grenades, too." He looked at Calvin. "These things are definitely illegal for civilians to possess—good thing you're in the military! You'll have to carry all of them, since I'm not allowed to." Calvin frowned at him. At just under a half pound each, a load of them would be heavy, especially with all the other gear he saw he wanted to take. "Maybe I can help carry some," said Ryan, "but remember, they're yours; I'm just helping you carry them. You said you've never used a grenade before, correct?"

"No, I haven't," Calvin said, "but I know generally how they operate. Hold it in your throwing hand with your thumb on the safety lever. Pull the pin and throw the grenade toward the enemy. Once you throw it, duck so you don't frag yourself when it blows up."

"That's right," agreed Ryan. "When using a grenade, the object is to have the grenade explode with the target in its effective range and you outside it. The grenade you're holding has an effective kill zone of about five meters, and it will cause serious casualties out to about 15 meters. You do want to stay down, as fragments can fly as far as 230 meters, which is a lot farther than you or I can throw it. Like the saying goes, close counts with hand grenades; most people within 15 meters of one going off are injured enough to render them effectively out of the battle."

"Aren't you supposed to release the arming lever and count to three prior to throwing them?" Calvin asked.

"No," Ryan said. "That's called 'cooking off,' where you intentionally hold onto an armed grenade and allow its fuse to burn partially, thereby shortening the time to detonation after throwing. Doing this *can* keep an enemy from taking cover or throwing it back, but it is very dangerous, as fuse times can vary from grenade to grenade, and you *don't* want to be holding it when it goes off. Just pull the pin and give it a hard throw to where it needs to go and get down; leave the rest of that macho shit to the pros."

"Okay," Calvin agreed.

"One thing I *would* like," Ryan said, "is a call when you throw it if I'm nearby. Give me a yell of 'frag out' or 'fire in the hole' or something, so I know to get down. I've got enough metal in my body; I don't want to collect anymore."

"No problem," Calvin said.

"All right, big boy," Ryan continued, loading Calvin up with gear, "let's see how much you can carry."

Runway 31, NAS Fallon, NV, 2130 Pacific Daylight Time

"*Fallon Tower,* Eagle 602 *checking in for takeoff,*" Commander Anthony Sutton called. The Black Eagles' commanding officer was also the mission commander for the flight.

"Eagle 602, *Fallon Tower, winds are 315 at 8 knots. You are cleared for takeoff, Runway 31,*" replied the tower.

"Okay, guys and gals," Commander Sutton said, "We're cleared for takeoff. Let's put our game faces on. CAG expects us to find out where the other flight went, and we're going to do just that." *Eagle 602* pulled onto the runway and took off.

"Hey, Skipper," one of the Hawkeye's pilots, Lieutenant Kristen Reynolds, said, "aren't the Kestrels flying up with us?"

"Yeah, the two Super Hornets from VFA-137 will be taking off in about ten minutes," Commander Sutton replied. "Since they fly about twice as fast as we do, we'd just slow them down on the way up. This way, they can fly a more fuel-efficient profile and save some gas until we get a little closer."

"How are they going to be armed?" Lieutenant Charles Sileno asked. Sileno was one of the air control officers in the back of the aircraft who would be responsible for guiding their escorts to investigate any unknown aircraft.

"They'll have plenty of air-to-air ordnance," replied Commander Sutton. "They're each going to have two AIM-120 AMRAAMs, two AIM-9 Sidewinders and a full load of ammunition for their 20mm guns."

"That's cool," said Lieutenant Sileno. "I just hope they don't need it."

Joint Base Lewis-McChord, Tacoma, WA, 2245 Pacific Daylight Time

"Hi, sir," Shuteye said, opening the door. "Welcome to the party, Lieutenant." The company's XO, First Lieutenant Odysseus Bollinger, walked into the crowded apartment and nodded to the assembled group. In addition to Top, Shuteye and Corporal Taylor, he saw The Wall, the twins, and the sniper team of Private First Class Steve 'Tiny' Johnson and his spotter, Private First Class Mike 'BTO' Bachmann. PFC Johnson was black and an absolute mountain of a man; at 6'5" and well over 300 pounds, he was the only person to make The Wall look normal-sized. Johnson was the company's .50 caliber sniper. In his giant paws, the oversized sniper rifle that was a heavy load for anyone else looked like a kid's toy gun. His spotter, BTO, was his exact opposite. BTO was as white as Johnson was black, barely five feet tall and 140 pounds, and as fiery in personality as Tiny was withdrawn and reticent. Compared to Tiny, BTO looked like a little Chihuahua running around a Great Dane.

He smiled at Corporal Taylor. "Welcome to the company," he said in greeting. "Sorry our meeting couldn't be under better circumstances." Looking over at the twins, he continued, "I should have known you two would be here. Whenever there's trouble, the Gordon brothers can't be far away." His vision moved to Top. "And let me guess, the twins are already trying to figure out how to steal one of the tanks and shoot its gun, right?"

Top laughed. "How'd you know, sir? That's exactly what they wanted. Either that, or to blow one up."

"They're very predictable," said the XO. He looked at one of them and continued, "isn't that right, Jamal?" The twins just laughed.

The XO got serious and looked at Top. "Okay, what do we know?" he asked.

"Not very much," answered Top. He directed the XO over to the kitchen table where some maps had been set up.

As they walked off, The Wall asked the twin identified as Jamal, "Was he right?" Jamal nodded. "How does he *do* that?" The Wall asked. Jamal just shrugged, unknowing. The Wall was amazed; the XO *never* got the twins wrong. Even with a 50/50 shot, The Wall got them wrong about 90% of the time.

"Okay," Top said, "here's what I've got so far. If we go down the road past the State Farm Ops Center, we can cut across I-5 and be at a wooded part of the base. We can either go over the fence, try to dig under the fence, or cut the fence; your choice, XO. Personally, I'd rather not vandalize the base. It kind of goes against everything I've ever stood for."

"I think we'll go over it," the XO said. "The fence doesn't have razor wire; we can climb over it and not have to explain to the base CO why we destroyed his fence. We will be a little more obvious while we're going over it, but it's less to explain if we're wrong."

"After that," Top said, "we can stick to the trees until we get to the airfield. We'll have to cross a block of buildings to get to the air-field, or go way out of our way; we'll just have to wait until we get there to decide which we want to do. We'll get a good look at the field and anything else we can see along the way, and then we'll come back. We'll be going in unarmed, so we will avoid all contact with anyone not known to be American."

"All right, we'll just have to see what there is to see, and then we'll meet back here to decide." The XO paused and looked up at Top. "Who do you recommend for this little walk in the dark?"

"No offense sir, but I'd like to lead it. I've got the most experience in stealth ops. I'll take Shuteye, who is pretty agile and looks like the folks we saw at the gate, so he might be able to fit in if needed. I'd also like to take Corporal Taylor, if she's up to it. She's the most up-to-date, having just completed the Ranger School, and she's the best person we've got to identify anything we might see of foreign manufacture." He looked at the newest member of the company. "What do you think, Suzi? Are you able?"

"Rangers lead the way!" she exclaimed. "Yeah, Top, I'm good," Suzi confirmed. "Let's go before I fall asleep again."

Top loved her spirit. "Out of curiosity, do you have a call sign we can use, if needed?"

"Yeah," she said, looking embarrassed. "They call me 'Deadeye.'"

"Like, why's that, dude?" asked one of the twins from behind her.

Suzi spun around on him and unleashed a withering glare at him, staring him down for a full five seconds. She ground out in a low voice, unlike anything they had heard her say previously, pausing between every word, "I...said...I...am...not...a...dude." After a short pause, he seemed to crumble a little and looked down; a very un-surfer-like "sorry" coming from him. The twins would later alternately characterize the gaze as 'scary' and 'creepy.'

She turned back to Top and sighed. "Sorry," she apologized, "I'm still a little out of sorts from Ranger School. They started calling me 'Deadeye' because I'm a pretty good shot."

"A pretty good shot?" Top asked.

Suzi shrugged. "Yeah, I don't miss much."

The Wall looked quizzical. "You don't miss much when?" he asked.

"I don't miss…just about ever," she answered.

35,000' Above Elmendorf, AK, 2145 Alaska Daylight Time (2245 PDT)

"Diceman 131, Focus 105," the E-3C Sentry AWACS operator called the flight of two F-22s from the 90th Fighter Squadron.

"105, Diceman 131, *go ahead*," Captain Sally 'Sassy' Pinione, the pilot of the lead aircraft, answered.

"131, *your target is at 75 miles, bearing 180 degrees, angels 350*," the AWACS operator said. "*The aircraft is on a Beijing-to-Seattle flight plan and is the fourth aircraft in four hours that said they were taking businessmen to a conference in Seattle. The ops center wants you to go take a look.*"

"131 *has the target, 179 degrees and 74 miles*," Sassy said, as her radar found the target and locked onto it, focusing down to its narrow tracking beam of 2° azimuth and elevation.

"*That's your bogey*," the AWACS operator said. "*Your target is supposed to be a commercial airliner, so approach from its 6:00 position so you don't scare its passengers.*"

"*Roger, that*," Sassy said, as she turned her $150 million aircraft to the south. "*We'll go take a look.*"

As the Diceman section went in search of their target, the E-3C was controlling another F-22 section on a different airborne command and control frequency.

"Bulldog 214, Focus 105," called the E-3C Sentry to the second section of F-22 Raptors from the 525th Fighter Squadron. "*Your target is 210 degrees for 95 miles, angels 370 and is a commercial airliner headed from Shanghai to Seattle.*"

"Bulldog 214 *has the bogey at 208 degrees and 93 miles,*" said Major Jim 'Lizzie' Borden, the lead fighter in the section.

"*That's your bogey,*" confirmed the AWACS. "*You are to approach from its 6:00 position so you don't scare its passengers.*"

"*Roger,*" said Lizzie. "*They'll never see us coming.*"

Onboard Diceman 131, 2155 Alaska Daylight Time (2255 Pacific Daylight Time)

"Focus 105, *this is* Diceman 131," Sassy Pinione radioed, "*We are behind the bogey, and it looks like some sort of tanker aircraft.*"

"*Say again,* 131," the AWACS operator replied. "*It's a tanker?*"

"*That is correct. It is a tanker. It looks like a Russian IL-78 Midas tanker aircraft, complete with two hoses streaming behind it, one from each wing.*"

"*Roger that,* 131," the AWACS operator replied. "*Remain in position at its six o'clock while we request further instructions for you.*"

"*Wilco,*" Sassy said. She was bringing her aircraft a little further to the left to ease in behind the giant tanker aircraft when her wingman's aircraft suddenly blew up, with two obvious explosions in the area of its engine exhaust.

"Holy shit!" she screamed. Keying her radio to transmit, she got out, "Focus 105, Diceman 131; *my wingman just blew…*" at which point her aircraft was hit by the third and fourth Chinese PL-9 missiles. It blew up, as well.

Focus 105 tried to call *Diceman 131* three times; all three calls went unanswered.

Onboard Bulldog 214, 2200 Alaska Daylight Time (2300 Pacific Daylight Time)

"Focus 105, *this is* Bulldog 214," 'Lizzie' Borden radioed as the section pulled in behind the big AWACS aircraft. "*Pretty funny. We're at your six o'clock.*"

"*Bulldog 214, I don't understand. What do you mean, you're at my six?*" the AWACS operator answered.

"Focus 105, Bulldog 214," the F-22 lead responded. "*We have joined on the bogey, and it's the AWACS. How'd we do sneaking up on you?*"

"Bulldog 214, Focus *is currently 80 miles north of your position. Whatever you just joined on is* not *us, over.*"

"*Okay* Focus, *if it's not you, it's some other AWACS plane. I can see the giant dome above the aircraft.*" He paused. "*Wait a minute, the shape of the airframe is all wrong. The aircraft we just joined on looks like a Russian A-50 AWACS!*"

"Bulldog 214; *be advised that there is also an unknown tanker aircraft approximately 30 miles east of your position. Between the tanker and the AWACS, there may very well be enemy fighters in your vicinity. Please advise if you see anything visually or on your radar.*"

There was no response from the Bulldog flight, nor would there be, as the F-22s had been destroyed by the second section of J-20 aircraft. The J-20 stealth aircraft were fifth-generation fighters, whose design and manufacture were in a large part based on technology stolen from the United States' F-22 and F-35 projects. They were very stealthy until their doors opened to fire their missiles, but by then they were behind the U.S. fighters where the Americans couldn't see them. In just over ten minutes' time, the U.S. lost four aircraft valued at over half a *billion* dollars. It was one of the costliest battles in American history, and the Americans were unaware it had even happened.

KIRO-TV, Channel 7, Seattle, WA, 2300 Pacific Daylight Time

A squad of soldiers broke into the control room of KI-RO-TV, Channel 7. "Hey, guys, easy," Dalton Marshall, the director for the 11:00 News, said. "What's going on?"

The leader of the troops approached him holding a DVD. "You will play this at the start of your 2300 news show," the soldier said.

"Well," the director said, "at the start of the show we normally go straight to the anchor who talks about what happened today. I can't play something that I haven't seen, anyway. It's against station policy."

"Yes, you can," the soldier said, "or I will find someone that will."

"Like who?" the director asked. "No one will do it for you. It's against station policy, and they'll lose their job if they do."

The soldier aimed his weapon and fired once. The director fell backwards, shot through the forehead. "They'll lose their *lives* if they don't," the soldier said. He turned to the station's floor director, who was also in the control room. "I would like you to play this DVD at the start of the 2300 news show," said the soldier. "I would also like you to make sure the network has a feed and knows it is coming. You may tell them there are soldiers here forcing you to do it; whatever it takes to make it happen is all right with me."

"I believe that can be arranged," the new director said, looking at the body of his predecessor. "No problem."

Precisely at 2300, the address ran on KIRO-TV, Channel 7, and every other TV station in the Seattle area. "Good Evening, people of Seattle and Tacoma, and the rest of the United States," said a uniform-clad man. "I know you were expecting your local news, but I have a more important announcement. My name is Colonel Zhang Wei of the People's Liberation Army of China, and I come to you today to urge everyone to remain calm while you listen to what I have to say."

"As you may be aware, we reclaimed the island of Taiwan today, as has long been our right. As the People's Republic of China (PRC) has always held, the Republic of China (ROC) ceased to be the legitimate government of China when it fled mainland China in 1949. At that time, the PRC succeeded the ROC as the sole legitimate government of China, with the right to rule all of China, including Taiwan. This was confirmed by the U.N. General Assembly, which noted in its Resolution 2758, "the representatives of the Government of the People's Republic of China are the only lawful representatives of China;" thereby recognizing the PRC's sovereignty over all of China, including Taiwan. Other precedents for Taiwan being part of China include the Cairo Declaration, the Potsdam Proclamation and the Japanese Instrument of Surrender in World War II. Since Taiwan has always been a part of China, any question of its secession should be agreed upon by all one billion Chinese citizens, not just the 23 million who live on the island. The PRC believes we have the legal right to extend our jurisdiction to Taiwan and have done so today. There is only one China, of which Taiwan is an inalienable part. The people of China are united today in celebrating the reunification of our country, just as the German people were united in celebration nearly 30 years ago with the reunification of their country, which had also been unjustly divided by outsiders."

"Unfortunately, the United States politicians have long disagreed with our position and have used military threats to keep us from reunifying our country, as was our right under international law. We did not believe they would allow us to reunify our country without conflict and bloodshed, so today we have taken measures to ensure this does not happen. At this time, the People's Republic of China is currently in control of the greater Seattle area, from Whidbey Island in the northern part of Washington State to the outskirts of Olympia in the south. Any military aircraft approaching within 200 nautical miles of Seattle will be destroyed. Any ship underway within 200 nautical miles of Seattle will be destroyed. We do not want, nor do we intend, to hold this area long-term. We have, however, taken the opportunity to hold it at this time as a guarantee that America will refrain from participating in what is solely a matter of Chinese sovereignty. It also serves as an assurance of American good behavior. We regret there has been some loss of life in the Seattle area due to the aggressive actions of certain American citizens, but we are happy to say this loss has been minimal. We would like to keep it that way, but this will be determined by what actions the United States' military takes. *Any* combat in such a highly-developed urban area is bound to result in a *significant* loss of civilian life."

"We would like the civilian populace of Seattle to resume their normal lives and conduct business as usual. You may not believe me, so I have several people here I hope you *will* believe. With me this evening are Representative Matt Bennett, the U.S. Representative from Seattle, Senator Jack Turner, the U.S. Senator from Oregon, and someone everyone should recognize, Governor George Shelby from the State of Washington. I believe Governor Shelby has something he'd like to say." The camera panned to another podium behind which three men stood, Representative Bennett, Senator Turner, and Governor Shelby. All three looked scared, as could be expected of men who had rifles pointed at them from off camera. The pistols pointed at the heads of their loved ones off camera also served to help guarantee their cooperation. Senator Turner looked worse for the wear with a big bruise on his temple.

Governor Shelby moved forward, took the podium and said with a wan smile, "My fellow Seattleites, I come before you tonight to ask you to remain calm and continue to go about your normal daily routines." He continued, reading from a teleprompter, "The benevolent Chinese do not want to hurt anyone. They only want to ensure our country negotiates a fair and impartial settlement to the Taiwan question. Please do not try to flee the area; doing so will only put you in contact with Chinese soldiers enforcing the borders, who will send you back. It is better to remain in your homes and resume your normal routines. In particular, schools will be open tomorrow to promote a sense of normalcy." He looked serious as he continued, "By all means, do NOT try to do anything foolish or cause a disturbance.

Many of the soldiers here are special forces, who will deal with any problems both swiftly and harshly. It is in your own best interest to remain calm and do nothing that will cause yourself or others to be harmed. My friends here assure me they will leave as soon as they are able, and that will happen quickest if everyone does their part. Thank you for your support in this most trying of times." He stepped back from the podium and looked at Colonel Zhang.

The camera followed his look and focused on Colonel Zhang, who nodded and continued, "The city is under martial law at this time, and anyone caught breaking the law will be severely punished. There will be a midnight curfew; everyone should be off the streets from midnight until 6:00 a.m. We ask for everyone to remain calm while we allow the diplomats to work out a peaceful resolution to this unfortunate disagreement. We wish for nothing more than a peaceful resolution; however, do not doubt our resolve. Your military forces need to know, as they have already found out, that we will use all means at our extensive disposal to repulse any attack into the Seattle area. Any forces within the 200 mile exclusion area have until midnight tonight to leave the area. After that time, anyone who is found armed will be shot on sight, with no questions asked. Similarly, any military aircraft, ship, or vehicle in the area will be destroyed."

"Please stay tuned to your local radio and television stations, as more information about procedures to be followed will be announced shortly. Remain calm, follow these instructions, and everything will be fine." He smiled. "Disobey these instructions and there *will* be consequences. Thank you."

White House Situation Room, Washington, DC, 0230 EDT

(2330 PDT)

"Y ou have absolutely got to be freaking kidding me," the president swore after watching a replay of Colonel Zhang Wei's address to Seattle and the rest of the nation. Wearing a t-shirt and sweat pants he had thrown on to come watch the video, he could already see his place in history cemented as 'The President who Let China Invade the U.S.' So much for his legacy. He would be an absolute pariah. "The unmitigated gall of that man and that country!"

The president tried to get control of himself. Looking at his Secretary of State, Isabel Maggiano, he said, "Well, if nothing else, I would say that makes it official. We have been invaded. Please advise NATO we are invoking whatever article it is in the Charter."

"Yes, sir," the Secretary of State said. "I believe it is Article 5 that states an armed attack against one shall be considered an attack on all." She shook her head. "Who would have ever guessed the United States would be the only nation to invoke Article 5, much less that we would do it twice? The other nations may not have agreed Article 5 applied after the World Trade Center bombings, but it should be pretty damn apparent this time that an armed attack has occurred."

"You can let the other nations know I expect them to honor their pledge," the president said. "This is one of those times when we will remember who our friends were."

"I will talk with the ambassador to NATO and have him invoke Article 5 with the North Atlantic Council," Isabel replied. "With the admission of guilt we just saw on TV, I would have to imagine the NATO nations will be in favor of some sort of unified response. Even France is going to have a hard time weaseling its way out of this one."

She continued, "I have also held discussions with the Prime Minister of Canada, and he has assured me of their support. They have already begun moving some of their forces to the Vancouver area to support us in whatever action we decide is necessary."

"Good," the president said. "Keep working the phones. The Europeans should be at work shortly; let's see what support they can provide, both here and in Asia. I want the biggest possible coalition of the willing to stop Chinese aggression in both Taiwan and the United States. Don't leave any diplomatic stone unturned, no matter how small. If the Government of Malawi has a tug boat to contribute, *I want it!*"

Onboard *Diceman 125*, South of Elmendorf, AK, 2245 ADT (2345 PDT)

"Focus 105, *this is* Diceman 125," the division leader, Lieutenant Colonel Dave 'Smoke' Sanchez, radioed. "*We're checking in with a flight of four.*" Launched in an effort to chase down the unknown AWACS aircraft, the four pilots of Diceman flight had been told after they launched that it appeared the Chinese were in possession of at least a part of Seattle, Washington. With the AWACS heading toward Seattle, it was obvious the aircraft was Chinese and that there were also other fighter aircraft, probably stealth, in the vicinity of it. They didn't care. The pilots had one overriding objective they all agreed on: they were going to chase down and kill the Chinese aviators who had killed their friends and squadron-mates. All of them.

The first four aircraft had been unprepared for their confrontation with the Chinese; this time would be different.

"Diceman 125, Focus 105," the AWACS replied. *"You're going to be hard-pressed to catch them, even at your current rate of speed."*

"Diceman 125 *understands*," Smoke replied. *"We can give you a little bit more speed. Do you know if we've been cleared to land in Comox?"* The Raptors were currently in supercruise, going about one and a half times the speed of sound. They were able to go faster by using afterburner, which dumped raw fuel into the engines' exhausts to achieve extra thrust, but it meant using their fuel reserves at a prodigious rate. If they used afterburner, they would not have enough fuel to return to base. The Canadians had a base in Comox, British Columbia, which was located about 150 miles northwest of Seattle. If they had permission to land there, they could use afterburner and still have enough fuel to make it to the airfield. Smoke realized landing anywhere in the Seattle area now was probably a 'bad thing.'

"That's affirmative, Diceman" came the reply from the AWACS. *"You are cleared to land at Canadian Forces Base Comox, British Columbia. They are expecting you and are trying to get an AWACS of their own to Comox, but it probably won't be airborne until tomorrow morning."*

"Roger, we are cleared to recover at Comox," repeated Smoke. He switched to the squadron's tactical frequency to talk to his wingmen. *"Let's boogie,"* he said, as he advanced his throttles into afterburner. The two Pratt and Whitney F-119 turbofans replied with an extra kick of acceleration, boosting the speed of the division beyond double the speed of sound. They were over water, so they didn't have to worry about damage from the sonic booms they were making. They wouldn't have cared anyway.

Eagle 602, **100 Nautical Miles SSE of Seattle, 2355 Pacific**

Daylight Time

"Eagle 602, *this is Seattle Center on Guard. If you hear this transmission, switch to frequency 134.95 and ident.*" The control facility had been calling the E-2D for 15 minutes. After about 5 minutes of no response on its primary frequency, the ARTCC had switched to the emergency distress frequency ("Guard") that all aircraft were required to monitor. By telling the E-2D to "ident," the Center was telling him to push a button on his Identification, Friend or Foe (IFF) system that would let the Center personnel know the E-2D crew could at least hear them, even though they weren't able to reply.

"Continue to ignore them," Commander Anthony Sutton said over the E-2's intercom system. Commander Sutton had told his crew not to respond to the Center when it had called them 15 minutes earlier. "We have no intention of turning back, so there isn't any reason to talk to them," he said. "They will just have to assume our radio is broken and clear out the traffic in front of us."

"What about the Hornets?" asked Lieutenant Kristen Reynolds, one of the Hawkeye's pilots.

"They don't have their IFFs on, so Center will have a hard time seeing them," said Commander Sutton. "I had the Hornets file a separate flight plan, too; hopefully, no one will even be aware of their presence."

"Eagle 602, *this is Seattle Center on Guard. You are entering restricted airspace. Turn back to the south now or risk being fired upon!*"

"Who do they think they're kidding?" asked Lieutenant Charles Sileno, one of the air control officers. "Since when does Center have a surface-to-air missile capability they can use? The only way they could shoot us down would be to scramble some fighters…and no fighter is going to shoot us down without visually identifying us first…and no fighter is going to mis-identify an E-2 or the two Super Hornets that are flying racetrack patterns around us. That's just stupid!" He laughed.

"Continue to the north," said Commander Sutton. Looking at his watch, he asked, "How close are we to Seattle?"

"We're about 200 miles out," said Lieutenant Sileno.

"Eagle 602, Falcon 300," said one of the Hornets on the Black Eagles' squadron frequency. Falcon 300 was flown by Commander Brandon Read, the commanding officer of the Kestrels. He was known as a 'by the book' kind of leader. There wasn't a lot of grey area with him. "*I'm getting kind of uncomfortable not talking to the Center.*"

"Falcon, Eagle," replied Commander Sutton. "*Don't worry about it. We'll call him when we get to about 100 miles out. By then we'll have an idea of what's going on in Whidbey.*" The Hornets could leave if they didn't like it, thought Commander Sutton. He'd been given a mission to find out what had happened to the earlier flight and, by God, he was going to do so.

"Eagle 602, *this is Seattle Center on Guard. This is your last chance to turn south now and contact me on 134.95, or you will be destroyed.*"

"Hah," said Lieutenant Sileno. "Good luck with that!" The rest of the air control officers laughed at what was obviously a hollow threat.

"Eagle 602, *this is Liberty,*" called CAG Waters on the satellite radio. "*Where are you at the moment?*"

"*Liberty, this is* Eagle 602," replied Commander Sutton. "*We are about 180 miles south of Seattle.*"

"*TURN SOUTH NOW! THE CHINESE HAVE CONTROL OF SEATTLE!*"

The clock struck 0000. It was too late.

"Missile launch!" cried Lieutenant Reynolds from the cockpit. The launch of the giant surface-to-air missile could be seen 200 miles away. It looked like the launch of a space rocket. "Multiple launches!"

"*Missile launch!*" Commander Read radioed. "*Lots of missiles inbound. Break right! Dive! Chaff!*"

The aircraft maneuvered wildly, but they couldn't escape the high performance missiles. *Eagle 602* and *Falcon 303* were destroyed. With a range of 240 miles, the 175 mile shot was easily within the performance envelope of the missile, and the initial barrage of six missiles, two at each aircraft, was able to destroy two of the three aircraft.

Falcon 300, flown by the Kestrels' commanding officer, saw the missiles as they launched and dove for the deck, releasing all his chaff as he went. As the missiles closed, he executed an 8-g turn away from the direction of the missiles' approach, and he succeeded in breaking the radar lock of the missiles aimed at him. They missed. He continued down and behind Mount St. Helens, using the bulk of the mountain to protect him from the radars searching for him.

The flight back to NAS Fallon was long and lonely.

Terminal 46, Port of Seattle, Seattle, WA, 0005 Pacific Daylight Time

Captain Ma Gang, the company commander for Company A, 2nd of the 489th, watched as the container was offloaded from the *M.V. Hanjin Kingston*. Unlike the other containers that had been offloaded during the afternoon, this one was being unloaded *very* carefully. It could have been the talk

Captain Ma had with the crane operator prior to the operation, in which he promised a wide variety of punishments if anything happened to the container. It might also have been due to the large 'Danger' sign painted in red on every side of the container that had his attention. The captain didn't care, just so long as the crane operator got the container to the pier safely.

The process was slower than when the earlier containers had been offloaded, but there was no longer the same sense of urgency. A slow, careful offload was far more preferable with this container in any event.

The container reached the pier and the two ZBD-08 infantry fighting vehicles waiting there. Captain Ma took a quick look around the pier to ensure there wasn't anyone around who shouldn't have been. The pier was quiet, although the ship continued to unload the last few containers of supplies it had brought to America.

Reaching into his pocket, he pulled out the key to unlock the container. He was the only person who had the key; no one else in his chain of command even knew what his mission was. Captain Ma had been given the key personally by Vice Premier Han Yong, who was his uncle and knew he could be trusted with the mission. Ma opened the doors of the container and looked inside at the five-foot-long wooden box strapped to the floor. It was hard to imagine one little box could do so much damage.

Moving out of the way, he had his men unstrap the box and load it into the waiting vehicle. With it safely inside, the captain and his men got into the other vehicle, and the two IFVs drove off for the short trip back to Safeco Field.

Joint Base Lewis-McChord, Tacoma, WA, 0025 Pacific Daylight Time

Top and the rest of the infiltrators let themselves into the twins' apartment where they were welcomed back by the same group of soldiers who had been there earlier. Suzi's right sleeve had a huge gash covered in blood. "Are you all right?" the XO asked.

"Yes, sir," Suzi replied. "Sorry, lack of sleep made me a little uncoordinated. I lost my grip going over the fence and caught my sleeve, and the fence shredded it. It was a new shirt, too, damn it."

"She did that on the way back," Top said. "We didn't have any problems on the way in. We made it across I-5 and over the fence without anyone noticing us. Our biggest problem was just keeping our bearings in the forest. We had to stay close to the road so we could see where we were going. It was a risk someone would see us, but we were able to make it to the field without incident." He paused.

"And, what did you see?" the XO prodded.

Top shrugged. "Well sir, it ain't good. The Chinese have taken the base. I don't know how they did it; I don't know how they got here. I only know two things; the Chinese *are* here, and they are here *in force*. There are tanks on the airfield, as well as anti-aircraft guns and surface-to-air missiles."

"Good ones, too," Suzi added. "I couldn't get close enough to see if they were the Russian S-300 or S-400 series of missiles, but I can tell you that they're bad news for anyone who tries to come here through the air."

"Yeah, they're bad news; it's also bad news for us getting any sort of weapons from the armory," Top added. "We went by the armory, and the Chinese have it locked up tight with patrols and klieg lights so no one can sneak up on the facility. Whatever we decide to do, we're going to have to do it with whatever civilian weapons we can scrape together."

"Okay, that sucks, but isn't too unexpected based on what's going on at the front gate," the XO commented. "I think we'll have to call it a night, and I'll go brief the CO and see if we can get in touch with anyone above us in the chain of command. Why don't all of you bunk here tonight so I can reach you if needed. If you hear from anyone else, grab them if possible."

With that, the XO left.

"Hey, Top," one of the twins said. "I know someone who has weapons we can use. What about that buddy of yours who lives up in the mountains? Didn't he have a pretty big armory? Suppose he'd share with us?"

"Yeah, I'm sure he would," Top said. "He hates commies even more than he hates authority. I'm sure he'll want to know about what's happening. I'll give him a call."

Onboard *Diceman 125*, 100 miles Northwest of Seattle, WA, 0030 PDT

"*It looks like we're going to get a shot at either the tanker or the AWACS before it lands at Sea-Tac airfield,*" said Lieutenant Colonel Dave 'Smoke' Sanchez. Before they had lost contact with *Focus 105* the AWACS had given them a vector to the Chinese aircraft, and they had been able to lock up one of the planes at a distance of about 175 miles. Smoke figured it must be one of the bigger aircraft to get a good lock at that distance.

"*Have you heard anything else from* Focus?" Major Charles 'Tractor' Massey asked. "*A little more info would be nice.*"

"*No I haven't,*" Smoke said, "*and I doubt we will. We're going about 700 miles an hour faster than they are so they aren't going to catch us. We're on our own. At least this time we know we're at war; the Chinese aren't going to get us as easily as they did Sassy and Skeeter.*"

"*How close do you want to get before we shoot at them?*" Tractor asked. "*They're getting pretty close to Sea-Tac.*"

"*Well, I haven't had any indications that we're being tracked by any of the Chinese SAM systems yet,*" Smoke said, "*although there are some located a long way away to the south. The only search radar I see is a SPY-1D radar, off one of the Navy's* Arleigh Burke-*class destroyers. We're at 100 miles now; I was planning on about a 95 mile shot.*"

"*Roger, that, sir,*" Tractor said.

The distance to the Chinese AWACS clicked down to 95 nautical miles. As the target was slow and non-maneuvering, Smoke judged it was in range and prepared to fire. Before he could, he was distracted by a burst of flame, slightly to the left of the nose of the aircraft. It almost looked like a rocket launch, he thought, and it was rapidly followed by a second, a third, and a fourth. He immediately realized missiles were being launched, and as they turned to point in the Raptors' direction, that they had been launched at *him*. It didn't make any sense—the only radar on that line of bearing was the SPY-1 radar. Was the U.S. Navy shooting at him?

He didn't have time to think about it. "Missile launch, left of the nose!" he screamed into the radio. "Separate and scram north!" Gone were any thoughts about shooting down the Chinese AWACS;

the only thing important now was getting his division's aircraft out of harm's way.

USS *Shoup* (DDG-86), Everett Naval Station, WA, 0035 Pacific Daylight Time

"Fire!" ordered Commander Gao Qiang. The executive officer of the PLAN destroyer *Kunming*, Commander Gao had been promoted to be the new commanding officer of the *Shoup*.

He projected an air of confidence as the master chief pushed the button to launch the missiles.

"It was nice of them to leave their IFF on," said Master Chief Hu Yan from the weapons station. "It made tracking them very easy."

"Yes," agreed Commander Gao, "it also identified them for us. As they were stealth fighters, they would have been hard to see without the IFF identification." He didn't know how many there were, as only one had left its IFF on, but he guessed there were either two or four of them, based on their normal operating parameters.

"What do you think, Ashley?" he asked Petty Officer Ashley Lafont, who had helped set up the shots. "Will we hit them?"

Petty Officer Lafont said nothing; she just stood next to the wall with tears streaming down her face.

"Cheer up," said Commander Gao. "You didn't shoot at them yourself, and they have a fighting chance to avoid the missiles. See, look," he said, pointing at the radar. "The aircraft is maneuvering. It has obviously seen that we shot at him." He paused, watching. "Isn't this fascinating, Master Chief Hu? It is a contest between their stealth

272 | CHRIS KENNEDY

technology and their best radar. Five American dollars, Master Chief. Who do you think will win?"

"I don't know, sir," said Master Chief Hu. "We did kind of cheat by using their IFF for targeting. I'm going to guess that the missile wins."

Onboard *Diceman 125*, 100 miles Northwest of Seattle, WA, 0030 PDT

Most of the pilots were lucky and their planes' inherent stealth characteristics, combined with their evasive maneuvers, helped them defeat the missiles. The pilot of the fourth aircraft in the formation, First Lieutenant John 'Nugget' Simmons, was new to the squadron and still adjusting to life in Alaska, as well as the new aircraft. He was also unprepared for combat. He hadn't remembered to turn off his IFF when he ran through his 'Pre-Combat' checklist. Not only was the *Shoup* able to track the formation because of him, it was also able to track him once the missiles were launched, and to pass on additional tracking data to the missiles in a mid-course update. With a good targeting solution on his aircraft, all four missiles tracked in on him.

His aircraft's stealth defeated two of the missiles; they never saw the aircraft and flew overhead past him. Two missiles acquired his aircraft and guided on it. He saw the third missile coming, and he punched out some chaff while maneuvering and was able to break the missile's lock. He never saw the fourth missile while he was evading the third, and it guided on his aircraft and exploded next to it. The blast blew the aircraft from the sky.

USS *Shoup* (DDG-86), Everett Naval Station, WA, 0035

Pacific Daylight Time

"I hate losing," Commander Gao Qiang said as he handed the American five-dollar bill to Master Chief Hu. He looked at Petty Officer Ashley Lafont, who was now sobbing, and the soldier holding her at bayonet-point. "I think I will need some comforting for my loss. Please escort Petty Officer Lafont to my state room."

Commander Gao looked back at the Master Chief as he started to follow them out. "I guess sometimes losing isn't so bad, after all."

Near Mt. Garfield, WA, 0037 Pacific Daylight Time

"Hello," Ryan mumbled into the phone. He'd been sleeping.

"Are the baby SEALs going to bed early now?" Top asked. "The party's just getting started down here."

"Big day, today," Ryan replied. "I got to blow some stuff up, got shot at, shot down a helicopter; fun stuff. Just trying to get a little sleep so that I can get up and do it all over again in the morning. It looks like it's going to be a big day."

"Oh, so the word about what's going on has even reached you at your mountain hideaway?" Top inquired.

"Yeah, the Chinese invaded the mountains and are killing people," Ryan answered.

"They're down here, too," Top said. "They've taken over Fort Lewis and have a variety of tanks, troops and SAMs here; more than I've ever seen."

"It's worse than we thought. Well, we were already coming down the mountain tomorrow. I'll give you a call in the morning, and we can get together and decide what we need to do."

"Sounds good," Top agreed, signing off. "I'll talk to you tomorrow."

Interlude Six

"China Invades Taiwan"

Preceded by a ballistic missile and aircraft bombardment, China invaded Taiwan today. Although the Taiwanese government maintains it still has control over the island nation, the government also admits it will not last long if its allies do not come to its aid.

Although confirmed information is difficult to obtain due to the chaos resulting from the attacks, sources are reporting China began a devastating missile and aircraft bombardment this morning at 5:00 a.m. local time. The bombardment was not confined to the island of Taiwan, as the American airfield at Okinawa was targeted as well.

The invasion also coincided with a power and internet outage that appears to have been nearly world-wide in nature. Authorities have been unable to determine why Taiwan's power and internet grids failed at the moment the attack was launched, but the loss of both of these systems severely degraded Taiwanese and Allied command and control, resulting in a tremendous loss of coordination among the forces defending Taiwan.

In addition to the aerial attacks that have rocked Taiwan, there have been numerous reports of ground-based attacks and sabotage at defensive installations. These attacks have been attributed to Chinese

276 | CHRIS KENNEDY

Army and special forces troops that are believed to have been insert-
ed into the country in the preceding weeks.

Defense sources are estimating that the majority of the attacks in the
initial barrage were conducted by Chinese DF-15, DF-21 and DF-31
ballistic missiles, with follow-on attacks conducted by Chinese H-6
'Badger' aircraft employing a variety of bombs, rockets and cruise
missiles. Defense sources are reporting at least four of the Badger
aircraft have been shot down, although they also admit to having lost
a number of their own aircraft that were caught unprepared on the
ground.

Although details are sketchy at this time, it appears a number of Chinese merchant vessels and civilian aircraft were in fact transporting
soldiers who were used in the initial assault to capture key installations. The Taiwanese soldiers are defending their country with every
means available, but they are rapidly being overwhelmed as China
reinforces its troops by both land and sea. Without assistance from
the United States and its allies, it does not appear they will be able to
hold out very long.

- *World News Online*. Posted August 20 by Susan Clements

Epilogue

White House Situation Room, Washington, D.C.,
August 20, 0620 EDT

"Sir, I'm afraid to say it, but Taiwan's screwed," the Chairman of the Joint Chiefs of Staff said. "Their entire defense plan is for their armed forces to do nothing but hold on until we can get there. Every single 'Defense of Taiwan' exercise we've ever run has assumed the United States would lead the defense, as well as throw in the overwhelming majority of the forces. The Taiwanese have some high-quality equipment, but they are completely overwhelmed. Without us, I repeat, they're screwed."

"What about other countries, our allies?" the president asked. "Can we expect some of them to come to the aid of Taiwan until we can get there?"

"Not freakin' likely," the Chairman of the JCS answered. "We signed a joint declaration on security with Japan in 1996, but without us, it's unlikely Japan will do anything. They've got some excellent ships and planes, but they'd be overwhelmed, too. At this moment, I'm betting the Japanese Premier is defining 'the area surrounding Japan' clause in the treaty to mean 'we'll defend everything north of Okinawa; Taiwan is right out.' Our allies in the ANZUS Treaty, Australia and New Zealand, are further away and really don't have the equipment to be a viable threat. Besides, the loss of economic ties with China would probably prevent Australia from doing anything on their own; their economy couldn't withstand the trauma if hostilities went longer than about a week."

"In the past, we've exercised with a lot of countries in our 'Defense of Taiwan' RIMPAC exercises, including the United Kingdom, Canada, Japan, South Korea, Australia, Chile and Peru. The UK would help, but they don't have any appreciable forces in the area. They'd need time, which Taiwan doesn't have. Canada would help, but I think they're unlikely to go wandering across the Pacific with the Chinese sitting 100 miles from Vancouver. South Korea would help if we were there, but without us, they don't have enough equipment to be able to move anything into the area without uncovering themselves and giving the North Koreans easy access into Seoul. They're unable to help. That leaves Chile and Peru; too little, too far away, and not very likely to want to piss China off without the United States there as their big brother to back them up. That only leaves the Russians, who could, I guess, attack mainland China if we could somehow convince them it was in their best interests…and if we wanted to start World War III. Failing that, Mr. President, the Taiwanese are screwed."

He paused and then said, "For that matter, Mr. President, we're not a whole lot better off ourselves. We have an entrenched foe in our cities, holding our citizens hostage. We don't have a lot of options to get out of this cleanly. Maybe we should just give them Taiwan if they'll agree to go back to China peacefully."

"It's worse than you know," the Secretary of State said, running into the room. "The Chinese ambassador just told us that their forces busted into our nuclear arsenal in Bangor and have brought some of our nuclear weapons into Seattle. They warned us that any attack into Seattle has the possibility of 'accidentally setting them off.' They said they are 'high yield,' but we have no idea what exactly that means."

A look of horror filled the faces of everyone in the room.

"We're screwed, too," the Chairman of the JCS said.

Silence filled the room.

Finally, one voice spoke, "Maybe not," the Chief of Naval Operations said, "I've got an idea."

* * * * *

The Americans

Civilians:

Matt Bennett	U.S. Representative from Seattle
Sam Burton	Man with No Cell Phone Service
Erika Gardner	University of Washington Student
Tom Green	Mayor of Seattle
Adrienne Griffin	Daughter of the USS *Shoup's* XO
Stacy Hough	Delta Ticketing Agent
Bill Jacobs	President of the United States
Isabel Maggiano	United States Secretary of State
Juan Mendez	Sea-Tac Police Officer
Barbara Morgan	Air Traffic Manager, Seattle ARTCC
Ryan O'Leary	Former SEAL Senior Chief Petty Officer
George Shelby	Washington State Governor
Sara Sommers	University of Washington Student
John Thomas	Seattle ARTCC Operator
Jack Turner	U.S. Senator from Oregon
Janet Turner	Senator Turner's Wife
Joey Turner	Senator Turner's Son

Military:

Sergeant Bill Adams	Fort Lewis Convoy Driver
Ensign Patrick Allen	Softball Hero
PFC Mike "BTO" Bachmann	Ranger Spotter
Rear Admiral Dan Barnaby	CDR, Navy Region Northwest
LTJG Steve "Torch/Oscar" Berkman	VFA-34 F-18 Pilot
First Lieutenant Odysseus Bollinger	Ranger Company XO
Major Jim "Lizzie" Borden	525th Fighter Squadron Pilot
Petty Officer Ed Brown	ATC, NAS Whidbey Island
LT Jim "Basket" Case	VAQ-136 Naval Flight Officer
Sergeant Jim "Shuteye" Chang	Ranger Fire Team Leader
SSGT Patrick "The Wall" Dantone	Ranger Squad Leader
Petty Officer Brad Davis	USS *Shoup's* Softball Team
Captain Johnny Dixon	*Outlaw 65* Pilot
LT Raul Espinosa	USS *Shoup's* Softball Team
Captain John Galloway	Navy Region Northwest Ops
LT John "Constant" Gardner	VFA-34 F-18 Pilot
Cpl Austin "Good Twin" Gordon	Ranger RAWS Gunner

PFC Jamal "Bad Twin" Gordon	Ranger RAWS Loader
LCDR Ernie Griffin	XO of the USS *Shoup*
Chief Dan Hamilton	ATC, NAS Fallon, NV
Captain Ron Heartly	*Tigershark 32* Copilot/Gunner
Captain Don "Bambi" Heron	DCAG, Carrier Air Wing 2
LT Shawn "Calvin" Hobbs	VFA-34 F-18 Pilot
Private First Class Steve "Tiny" Johnson	Ranger Sniper
Petty Officer Ashley Lafont	USS *Shoup* Weapons Operator
Commander Steve MacGuinness	CO, USS *Ford*
Petty Officer Mathis	Petty Officer of the Watch
Commander Fred "Mighty Mite" Meadows	CO, VAQ-131
Major Jim Mitchell	*Tigershark 32* Pilot
LT John Musselman	USS *Ford* Duty Officer
Captain Sally "Sassy" Pinione	90th Fighter Squadron Pilot
Petty Officer Esteban Ramirez	USS *Ford* PO of the Watch
Commander Brandon Read	CO, VFA-137
Lieutenant Kristen Reynolds	VAW-113 Pilot
1LT Steven Ross	Fort Lewis Convoy CDR
Lt. Col. Dave "Smoke" Sanchez	90th Fighter Squadron Pilot
Lieutenant Charles Sileno	VAW-113 NFO
1LT John "New Guy" Simmons	90th Fighter Squadron Pilot
Lieutenant General Tom Simpson	ANR Commander
First Sergeant Aaron "Top" Smith	Ranger "Top" Sergeant
Petty Officer First Class Tim Smith	Admiral Barnaby's Driver
Captain Jim Spence	Navy Region Northwest Intel
Chief Bill Stevens	ATC, NAS Whidbey Island
Commander Anthony Sutton	CO, VAW-113
Corporal Suzi "Deadeye" Taylor	Ranger Rifleman
Colonel Heather Vincent	ANR Operations Officer
LTJG Tim Wallace	USS *Shoup* Duty Officer
Colonel Devyn Walker	ANR Chief of Staff
Colonel Amanda Ware	ANR Intelligence Officer
Captain Jim "Muddy" Waters	CAG, Carrier Air Wing 2
LT Bill Weathersby	Admiral's Protocol Officer
Commander Jane Wiggins	CO, USS *Shoup*
Captain Steve Woods	*Outlaw 65* Copilot

The Chinese

Civilians:

Fung Qiang	Ambassador to the United States
Jiang Jiabao	President
John Huang	Chinese Sleeper Agent
Han Min	President Jiang's Aide
Han Yong	Vice Premier
Li Min	Vice Premier
Peng Jun Jie	Seattle Mariners Baseball Player
Rong Xiannian	Premier
Sun Juan	Vice Premier
Zhu Jie	Vice Premier

Military:

Senior Sergeant Cheng Yong	Special Forces Trooper
Major Chin Haung	Special Forces CDR
Captain Chou Min	Special Forces Company CDR
Captain Du Jun	Special Forces Company CDR
Commander Gao Qiang	Executive Officer, *Kunming*
Lieutenant He Fang	Operations Officer, *Changsha*
Captain Hon Ming	Commanding Officer, *Henna*
Master Chief Hu Yan	Master Chief, *Kunming*
Lieutenant Colonel Huang Mong	Chinese Hacker
Private Lau Jie	Special Forces Trooper
Lieutenant Commander Lin Gang	Air Operations Officer, *Long*
Captain Liu Fang	Special Forces Company CDR
Captain Ma Gang	Company A CDR, 2nd of 489th
Major Pan Yan	Special Forces Battalion CDR
Lieutenant Colonel Peng Yong	Special Forces Regimental XO
Lieutenant Sun Xiuying	Weapons Officer, *Kunming*
Captain Tang Ping	CO, *Kunming*
LCDR Wong Chao	Operations Officer, *Kunming*
Major Yang Wei	Special Forces Battalion CDR
Colonel Zhang Wei	Special Forces Regiment CDR
Admiral Zhao Na	Chinese Fleet Commander
Captain Zhu Jing	Type 99 Tank Commander

#####

The following is an excerpt from:

Occupied Seattle

Chris Kennedy

2nd Edition Available Now from Chris Kennedy Publishing

eBook, Paperback, and Audio

Excerpt from "Occupied Seattle:"

"No kidding," Captain George 'Pasta' Macari, the copilot of the RC-135 Rivet Joint aircraft, responded. "We haven't been this far west since we got here. Do you suppose the tanker guys know about the exclusion zone? Should we call them and say something?"

"I don't want to transmit while we're refueling," Taco replied, "and we're almost full. As soon as we are, we'll unplug and go back to where we're supposed to be orbiting."

"Hey, umm, do you guys realize we're within the exclusion zone?" the evaluator, Major Jim 'Pokey' Bryant, asked from the back of the aircraft. "I show us at 198 miles."

"Yeah," Taco answered, "we were just talking about that. We're getting a little uncomfortable up here. We're almost full. As soon as we are, we're going to detach and head straight east away from the exclusion zone. Really, do you think they can see the difference between 200 and 198 miles? We haven't done anything aggressive or provocative all morning. I doubt they'll be worried about us…"

About the Author

A bestselling Science Fiction/Fantasy author, speaker, and publisher, Chris Kennedy is a former naval aviator and elementary school principal. Chris' stories include the "Theogony" and "Codex Regius" science fiction trilogies and stories in the "Four Horsemen" military scifi series. Get his free book, "Shattered Crucible," at his website, http://chriskennedypublishing.com.

Chris is the author of the award-winning #1 bestseller, "Self-Publishing for Profit: How to Get Your Book Out of Your Head and Into the Stores." Called "fantastic" and "a great speaker," he has coached hundreds of beginning authors and budding novelists on how to self-publish their stories at a variety of conferences, conventions, and writing guild presentations, and he is publishing fifteen authors under various imprints of his Chris Kennedy Publishing small press.

Chris lives in Virginia Beach, Virginia, and is the holder of a doctorate in educational leadership and master's degrees in both business and public administration.

Titles by Chris Kennedy

"Red Tide: The Chinese Invasion of Seattle"

"Occupied Seattle"

"Janissaries: Book One of The Theogony"

"When the Gods Aren't Gods: Book Two of The Theogony"

"Terra Stands Alone: Book Three of The Theogony"

"The Search for Gram: Book One of the Codex Regius"

"Beyond the Shroud of the Universe: Book Two of the Codex Regius"

"The Dark Star War: Book Three of the Codex Regius"

"Asbaran Solutions: Book Two of The Revelations Cycle"

"The Golden Horde: Book Four of The Revelations Cycle"

"Can't Look Back: Book One of the War for Dominance"

"Self-Publishing for Profit"

"Leadership from the Darkside"

* * * * *

Connect with Chris Kennedy Online

Website: http://chriskennedypublishing.com/

Facebook: https://www.facebook.com/chriskennedypublishing.biz

* * * * *

Made in the USA
Las Vegas, NV
22 October 2022

57977296R00164